The Gift is a peek into an Iowa farm family. It pieces the present day and past into a quilt filled with details about World War 2. Through the eyes of Gracie, the main character, readers see how past trauma and life choices impact family relationships for generations to come. Those who enjoy books about family, quilting, and the 1940s will find this one to be a comfortable read.

~Jolene Philo, Author of:
Does My Child Have PTSD?

Quilt lovers will flock to this novel which offers mystery, love, betrayal, and family reconciliation played out in two connecting eras."

~Barbara Lounsberry
Emerita Professor of English, University of Northern Iowa
Author of, Virginia Woolf diaries trilogy

Sometimes we need to be taken back in time. Life's stresses may seem insurmountable, so it's good to be reminded that those living in other eras endured extreme pressures also. Cherie Dargan's debut novel, *The Gift*, reminds us that "simpler times" may not have been so simple after all, and have much to offer our contemporary society. As the heroine, Gracie, unravels long-kept family secrets through the cassette tapes her grandmother left for her, she learns how our foundations help us through disturbing situations and difficult decisions. This story embraces the past to offer a heartwarming read in the present.

~Gail Kittleson, author of:
With Each New Dawn
Land that I Love
Until Then

Cherie Dargan's debut novel, *The Gift,* is just that—a gift. The book weaves themes of love, family secrets, broken hearts, as well as gifts of family, friendship, sacrifice, and community that bind us. *The Gift* offers a panoramic view of life during and after World War II and how it shaped the lives of those who fought and those who supported our troops at home. Dargan's breakout novel is an excellent choice for those who love to read true-to-life stories about history, romance, redemption, and resilience—or who simply love a good book drawn from the pages of real life.

~Shelly Beach
Co-Founder, Cedar Falls Christian Writers Workshop
Award-winning author of:
Hallie's Heart
Morningsong: A Novel

I love this story! Cherie Dargan can sure paint a beautiful word picture! She spins a gorgeous adventure in the first installment of her *Grandmother's Treasures* series where she treats us to an up-close look at one of her personal family stories in *The Gift.* I, for one, am grateful. It's a colorful, lush and adventurous story, infused with grit, determination, and gutsy, likable characters (especially the females!). Her descriptive style had me craving corn muffins and chili as well as traveling and travailing with her on her journey of discovery. I would highly recommend this book and I can't wait for the next in the series!

~Wanda Sanchez
Executive Producer for Salem Radio Network
Award-winning author of:
Love Letters from the Edge

the gift

jubilee junction, iowa
town map

MAP LEGEND

1. Jubilee Junction Depot
2. Retirement Home
3. Community College
4. Jubilee Junction Café
5. Courthouse
6. Museum
7. Newspaper
8. Ruby's Restaurant
9. Vern's Farm
10. Violet's Farm
11. Rich's Farm
12. Cemetary
13. Vera's Farm
14. Library
15. Quilt Shop
16. School

NORTH
W E
S

GRANDMOTHER'S TREASURES
Book 1

For John
Happy reading!
Welcome to Jubilee
Junction

the gift

a dual time-line novel

Cherie Dargan

CHERIE DARGAN

WordCrafts Press

The Gift is a work of fiction. The author has endeavored to be as accurate as possible with regard to the times in which the events of this novel is set. Still, this is a novel, and all references to persons, places, and events are fictitious or are used fictitiously.

Published by WordCrafts Press
Cody, Wyoming 82414
www.wordcrafts.net

For the Lewis sisters
Reva, Charlotte, and Jeanne
who taught me to treasure family

gracie's family tree

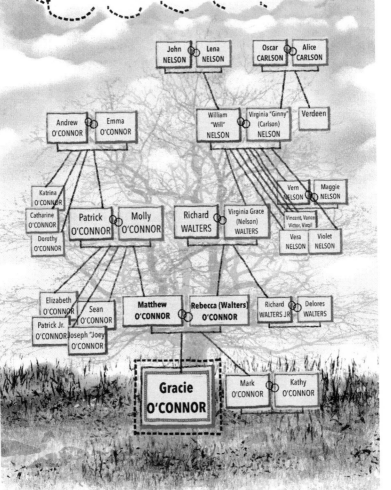

One

Gracie's Gift

"The best way of keeping a secret is to pretend there isn't one."
~Margaret Atwood

August 2012—Jubilee Junction, Iowa

As I headed south of Jubilee Junction towards my family's farms, the beauty of the rolling hills and fertile fields struck me again. My ancestors, some of the earliest settlers in this part of central Iowa, worked hard to clear timber to build houses and fences, put in crops, and raise cattle, hogs, chickens, and horses. Grandma Grace once told me it took the first four generations to clear all our land, about a thousand acres of prime soil, near the Jubilee River.

Turning onto the county blacktop, I drove past the Founders Cemetery, where so many of our pioneers were buried. The cemetery dates to the 1850s, and every Memorial Day, as we decorate our family graves, someone tells another story.

Several minutes later, I passed Uncle Vern's farm with its rows of green corn stalks with golden tassels and arrived at Aunt Violet's farmhouse. I drove down the long driveway, gravel crunching under my tires, and admired the neatly painted outbuildings, large farmhouses, and mature trees, shrubs, and flowers. They planted the field next to her house with soybeans, and the cows mooed in my uncle's pasture across the road.

It was a Monday afternoon in late August. The new semester had started last week. My 'To Do' list was full, but my family was gathering for supper at Aunt Violet's house. Next to Grandma's house—where my Uncle Rich and Aunt Delores now lived, not far away—Aunt Violet's farmhouse ranked as one of my all-time favorite places. I'd spent time here since childhood and could hardly believe this place would sit empty in a week.

My father's dusty Tahoe and my brother Mark's older F-150 were parked beside my uncle's F-350, full of furniture neatly tied down. Drawn by the aroma of Mom's chili and her chocolate chip cookies, I walked to the door and knocked.

"C'mon in." Her cheery tone made me feel right at home.

The mudroom wall with half a dozen hooks and a long bench below reminded me of childhood visits and seeing Uncle Bob's barn coat—redolent with barn smells—hanging there, next to Aunt Violet's outdoor jacket. She and Dr. Bob raised their four children in this house, retired here, and he died peacefully in his sleep seven years ago.

Mom arranged her freshly baked cookies on one of Aunt Violet's china plates. Her deep brown eyes welcomed me. "Hi Gracie, thanks for coming."

"Need help?" I set my purse on a chair.

"No, we're all set. There's chili in the crock pot. We have corn muffins and salad on the sideboard. I made lemonade and Aunt Violet made her sun tea. Dish up—we're just starting."

Upstairs, a faint thumping came from Aunt Violet, walking around with her cane.

I inhaled the chili's pungent spices of chili, turmeric, and cumin as I filled a bowl and poured myself some sun tea. "Aunt Violet's not moving because she's sick, is she?"

"She's fine, but Uncle Bob's been gone for seven years now." Mom pushed her blond bobbed hair back. "This house is too big for one person. I also worry about all the stairs. Violet's going to have her own place, and help if she needs it, at the Prairie View Senior Center. She has something for you, a gift from Grandma Grace."

"Grandma died two years ago, so why am I getting her gift now?"

Mom sighed. "Aunt Violet found it and kept it safe. Let's go into the dining room, shall we?"

I followed her into the dining room where Mark, Dad, and my sister-in-law Kathy sat at the table eating. We'd shared many meals in this long, sunny room filled with Grandma Ginny's china hutch and her sideboard along one wall next to her oversized table.

I'd only taken time for a granola bar at lunch, so I welcomed the sight of butter, strawberry preserves, honey, and bowls of shredded cheese, crackers, and sour cream arranged in the center.

Four more place settings waited for Aunt Violet, Uncle Vern, his wife Maggie, and me.

"Gracie!" Kathy's hazel eyes sparkled. She had long, brown hair tied back in a ponytail.

I set down my food and tea. Dad stood up to hug me, resting his chin on top of my head for a moment, and Kathy squeezed my shoulder.

Mark threw a muffin my way, which I caught, feeling smug. He shared Dad's height and was tanned and muscular from farming with Uncle Vern. He and I shared Grandma Grace's bright blue eyes and dark blonde hair, his cut short military-style, and mine curly and shoulder length.

Mark and Kathy were three years older than me. She taught high school speech and had become a close friend.

Mom set a bowl of tossed salad at my place, and Kathy handed me the Dorothy Lynch dressing.

"Shouldn't we wait to eat?" I asked.

Kathy shook her head. "Aunt Violet told us to start, and she would be down shortly. Maggie is helping her sort a few more things to give away. Vern's up there with them."

Aunt Violet and Aunt Maggie were Mom's aunts, so, my great-aunts, but Grandma Grace suggested they keep names simple when I mistakenly called her sister "Grape Ant Biolet." In my defense, I may have been three or four. Only two of Aunt Violet's children lived in Iowa—both out of town—and Aunt Maggie's four children had scattered around the state. Since Grandma Grace's death, Mom had stepped into the role of surrogate daughter to both aunts and stayed connected with their children, who appreciated having someone nearby.

We all dived into our meals and chatted.

A few minutes later, Uncle Vern called for Mark from the landing. "I need help with this gift for your sister."

Dad and Mark shoved back their chairs. "Coming, Uncle Vern," Mark called.

Soon the two of them appeared on the landing, carrying a strange object with handles at each end, the contents covered in several oversized black garbage bags. Uncle Vern followed.

A strange thought came into my head as they got closer—*whatever is in there is going to change my life.* Butterflies fluttered in my stomach, and I put down the spoon.

Mark asked Mom where she wanted it.

"Just put it beside the couch."

They brought the load into the living room and then returned to the table.

Mom brought Uncle Vern a bowl of chili, and then some salad. Mark passed him the basket of muffins.

Uncle Vern helped himself to some sour cream, crackers, and cheese and tasted his chili.

"Delicious! Becky, you got your mama's recipe just right." He buttered a corn muffin and glanced at me. "Sweet's been keeping this treasure hidden away for you since your Grandma Grace died." He used his childhood nickname for Violet.

"Sour threatened to burn it more than once." His nickname for Violet's twin, Vera. "She would love to get her greedy old hands on this, but we ain't gonna let her anywhere near it, are we?"

The baby of the family, Uncle Vern appeared younger than his mid-eighties, with silvery hair and mischievous blue eyes. "Vera's coming to get the last of her stuff out of storage tomorrow. But your grandma's gift will be safe at your house by then."

I nodded and played with the last fragment of my muffin. Just thinking about Aunt Vera made me reconsider eating anything at all. Sour described Vera perfectly, who seemed the opposite of her twin, Violet. Violet embodied generosity, humor, and kindness. Vera was bitter, sharp-tongued, and someone most of us avoided. She lived in Mankato, Minnesota, with her daughter, Donna, who must be a saint.

Noises came from upstairs, so Mark and I walked up to investigate and carried down several boxes. Aunts Maggie and Violet followed us and entered the dining room. Mom brought them their food.

Uncle Vern patted the empty chair beside him. "I saved you a place, Maggie."

"Thanks, dear." Aunt Maggie sat. "I'm famished!"

Aunt Maggie was barely five feet tall, with lovely green eyes, red hair turned silver cut short, and had kept her British accent. She and Vern met in England during World War II. Wearing jeans and a green button-up shirt, she looked ready to work.

Aunt Violet, in her late eighties, had bright blue eyes and fine features and silver curls cut short. She loved vibrant colors like the turquoise pantsuit she wore today, and her sense of style extended to her cane, which one of her great-granddaughters decorated with her favorite colors of purple, turquoise, and pink duct tape.

"Oh Becky, you didn't need to do this, but I'm so glad you did." Aunt Violet added cheese and sour cream and ate her chili. Mom made sure they both had food before she sat back down and finished her meal. The women in my family took care of each other.

At the end of the meal, Mom passed around her fabulous chocolate chip cookies. I'd watched her make them dozens of times, but when I tried her recipe, my cookies turned out a little overdone. Her cookies came out soft in the middle and crispy on the edges, and the chocolate melted in your mouth.

Aunt Violet took the last bite of her cookie and sipped her sun tea. "Gracie, your grandma made me promise to save this treasure for you. I'm so glad you could get it today." She walked over to her comfortable recliner with the help of her cane, and Mom and Aunt Maggie moved to the couch. Kathy and I followed, kneeling beside my mystery gift as the butterflies did a tap dance in my stomach.

Kathy helped me remove the garbage bags to reveal a vintage wicker basket with wooden handles. Inside, several shoe boxes sat on top of a quilt with two aprons, a photo album, an old *Life* magazine, and a large scrapbook underneath.

"What a beautiful treasure from the past. And what a lovely old quilt. Who made it?" Kathy asked.

Mom leaned over and tapped Aunt Violet's wrist. "Is this the quilt you made with your mother and aunts after the war?"

Aunt Violet nodded. "Yes, it's the California quilt. Go ahead, Gracie."

I opened the first shoebox, full of old-fashioned cassette tapes, neatly labeled. The second shoebox held a silver cassette player, an album with several dozen black and white photos, a handful of postcards, and several folded-up letters. I sat quietly, thinking about Grandma putting all these things together for me. But why didn't she show them to me herself?

In the silence, Aunt Maggie told me, "I loved Grace. She and Violet welcomed me to the United States, and your family, and became my sisters and loyal friends. I wish she were here. But I imagine Violet will tell you about the things in the basket." Aunt Maggie turned to her sister-in-law, and Aunt Violet nodded.

"Yes, come see me after I get moved in—how about next Wednesday, after work? We'll listen to the tapes and talk."

"I'll be there."

Mom admired the aprons. "Grandma Ginny wore the gingham one to gather eggs, didn't she, Uncle Vern? She put the eggs right into the big pocket."

"How did she do that and not break any eggs?" He shook his head and glanced at his watch. "Mark and I should get this load to the storage unit. Vi, what do you want to do with the furniture you don't need?"

Violet asked, "Mark, do you need anything? I have two bedrooms full of beds and dressers I don't need. Gracie?"

Mark nodded. "Sure, let's look."

I thought of the dressing table and bench in the back bedroom. "Could I have that little dressing table and bench?" I asked her.

Aunt Violet nodded. "They belonged to your grandma Grace, so it's yours."

Then she walked upstairs with Mark and Kathy to pick out what they wanted. Mom followed. She'd put out the word to the family and our pastor.

Uncle Vern and Dad drank coffee and chatted quietly.

Aunt Maggie sat on the couch with a thoughtful look on her face. "I miss her too, Gracie."

I lingered a minute longer, running my hands over the faded quilt. What was that scent—lavender? I lifted the quilt, and found four sachets, one at each corner of the basket. I picked one up and sniffed. Yes, lavender. Grandma Grace thought of everything. But what can an old quilt and some cassette tapes tell me about my family? What happened between the twins—Vera and Violet—and why doesn't anyone talk about it? Teary-eyed, I tried to sort out my emotions.

Mom came back downstairs, and Aunt Maggie got up to help her clear the table. She gave me a gentle pat as she walked by. I joined them, loading the dishwasher, washing some pieces, and putting things away.

Afterward, Dad and I collected all of Aunt Violet's pictures from the walls on the first floor, wrapped them in the newspaper, and placed them in big tubs. He and Mom promised to scan them at *The Jubilee Times,* our family's newspaper, and share the pictures.

Knowing how little I liked to cook, especially for one, Mom sent some leftovers with me.

"We'll meet back here Friday evening," Mom reminded me. Dad, Mark, and our cousins planned to pack up another load Wednesday to clear the house, and Violet would stay with Vern and Maggie until Saturday.

Mark carried the basket out to the car. "I'll help Dad get your table and bench wrapped up and drop them off this week."

"Thanks, Mark." I put the bag with food and my purse in the front passenger's seat and popped the Subaru's rear hatch. "Lots of memories here, huh?" I closed the passenger door.

Just as Mark slid the basket into the back of my car, a truck turned down the drive, coming toward us. I shaded my eyes, trying to identify the driver. When the truck pulled up beside us, I recognized cousin Donna behind the wheel, and in the seat beside her sat Aunt Vera.

Two

Aunt Vera's Demands

"You want to believe that there's one relationship in life that's beyond betrayal. A relationship that's beyond that kind of hurt. And there isn't."

~Caleb Carr

*D*onna had scarcely parked the truck when Aunt Vera lurched out, waving her cane, using the side of the truck for support. "Do you have the California Quilt there?"

Mark pushed me toward the driver's side of my car. "You'd better go."

I climbed inside while he hit the button to close the lid.

"I know you have the quilt," Aunt Vera shouted. "You can't hide it from me!"

Donna got out of the car, sounding exasperated. "Mother, calm down. You promised to behave."

"Sorry! Thanks," I waved to Mark, backed out, and headed down the driveway.

I didn't look back or stop until I reached the Jubilee airport, two miles away. I pulled over, tried to slow down my breathing, and called Mom.

"Gracie? Did you forget something?"

"Mark and I stood talking by my car when Donna and Aunt Vera drove up, and she started yelling about the California quilt. Mark told me to go, but I feel like I messed up. I'm so sorry."

"For goodness's sake, you didn't mess up. You didn't know Donna and Vera would arrive early. They told me they would be here tomorrow."

"I feel so bad about leaving Mark. Should I come back?"

"Mark's a veteran of the Iraq war. He can manage her, and we're all here, too. Oh, I hear her yelling now, so I'll get Vern and Maggie."

I drove home, upset I'd been such a coward. All my life, I tried to avoid Aunt Vera because she was obnoxious and rude. But I had another reason. When I'd been about five, I'd been playing outside with Mark and some older cousins. Dr. Bob got an emergency call. He and Aunt Violet left to go to the hospital.

I'd needed a drink of water, so I opened the kitchen door and into Great-Grandma Ginny's kitchen when I heard Vera call her sister 'Saint Violet' in her nasty voice. I walked into the living room, past my surprised parents, and planted myself in front of Aunt Vera.

Hands-on my hips, I chided her, "You said a bad word. Mommy says we don't say the 's' word." Somehow, I thought "saint" might be the 's' word Mark whispered about with our cousins.

Vera sneered, "You think you can tell me what to say? You're just a child."

I burst into tears and ran to Mom.

Grandpa Richard stood up and glared at Vera. "Don't you ever talk to my granddaughter in that rude way again."

Mom scooped me up into her arms and carried me to the kitchen with Aunt Maggie for a cup of tea and cookie. Dad followed.

Great-Grandma Ginny said, "Vera, hush up!" as she left the room to check on me.

Grandma Grace stood up. "Why are you so cruel? Gracie's a smart little girl. She hears right through you, sister." Then she came out to the kitchen to comfort me.

Much later, I overheard Grandpa Richard tell Mom that Vern had looked at Vera sadly. "Why do you make it so difficult to love you, big sister?"

Everyone else looked angry and was ready to defend me.

Vera grabbed her purse and stomped out the front door, slamming it.

I'd avoided her for twenty years for a reason. Finally, I realized why.

Reliving that humiliating childhood memory distracted me from enjoying the drive home past fragrant flower beds, bean and

9

cornfields almost ready for harvest, and a family of horses cavorting in a large corral at my cousin's farm. A drive in the country usually relaxed me. Not today. Hearing Aunt Vera's voice made me feel five years old again.

I made a trip to get the food, my messenger bag, and purse inside my house, then carefully carried Grandma Grace's basket to the guest bedroom and put it on the double bed, covered with a quilt done in Grandmother's Garden with pinks, blues, and purple.

I thought of pulling down the window shades as if Aunt Vera might snoop, hiding in the rose bushes outside, and then shook my head at my imagination as I shut the door.

Agatha, my calico kitty, pushed against my leg as I bent down to pet her. "Hey Agatha, did you miss me?"

A farm kitty, one of four orphans Mark found earlier this summer, Agatha provided companionship and entertainment.

I filled her food and water bowls and settled on the couch. A few minutes later, Agatha purred as she jumped up and stretched out.

I slipped my laptop out of the messenger bag and checked my phone. My boyfriend, Steve, had sent several text messages earlier, so I called him.

"Hey Steve, it's me. I had supper with the family at Aunt Violet's and left my purse on a kitchen chair, so I just now saw your messages. Sorry."

"No problem. I wanted to check on our weekend plans. You're coming Saturday?"

"Yes. We're moving Aunt Violet to town that morning, remember?"

"Did you see the message about the job opening in Des Moines, Gracie? The job's a perfect fit for you."

"I saw the ad." I braced myself for another round of our semi-annual fight.

"Jubilee Junction is a nice little town. But you're never going to get a full-time job with benefits like this one. With your MA in journalism, you can move to Des Moines and get a proper job. You can make good money and we can think about getting married."

"I have a proper job—several of them. I enjoy teaching writing and literature, and I love creating exhibits at the museum. I also enjoy helping my parents at *The Jubilee Times*—it's been in our family for 150 years, remember?"

His voice turned harsher. "I'm tired of only seeing you twice a month. This long-distance relationship isn't working. I want you here, in Des Moines. I love you. Didn't we just talk about this?"

"You talked, Steve. You asked me to think about moving in together, but you didn't listen to me. I love you, but you're making me crazy right now. I don't want to live in Des Moines."

"My work is here. You need to move to be with me. We could live in Ames, I suppose."

"We shouldn't argue about this right now. I'll see you this weekend. We can talk more then."

He exhaled. "Sure. When are you coming?"

"I'll head down Saturday afternoon. I told Stephanie."

"K. Love you."

"Love you."

Afterward, I realized I hadn't told him about the gift from Grandma Grace. Add that to the things we'd talk about this weekend.

My parents dropped off the mirrored table and bench on Thursday, and Dad helped me move them into my bedroom. I moved makeup into the drawers and put my jewelry box on the table. Lightly touching the wood, I remembered all the times I sat here back in Grandma Grace's house, and she let me put on a necklace or use lipstick. Now, I sat on the bench and looked in the mirror. For a moment, Grandma's face smiled back at me. I blinked and saw my face reflected, of course.

Friday, we attacked what remained in the farmhouse, boxing things up for donations, and then sweeping and dusting. Saturday afternoon, I headed down to Des Moines to stay with Steve's younger sister, Stephanie, for part of Labor Day weekend. I took a few country roads past corn and soybean fields, an apple orchard, people's vegetable and flower gardens, families out in their yard tossing balls around, mowing, getting grills out of the garage, and children playing. I drove past several abandoned farmhouses as corporate farms bought up more land.

Stephanie and I got along well. She was two years younger and worked for one of the large insurance companies as a secretary. On Saturday night, Steve and I attended an outdoor concert with her and some of her friends.

We visited the Art Center and met some of his work friends for lunch the next day.

On Sunday evening, we attended a cookout for Steve's boss, the state senator. With so little time alone, we didn't talk about the job or our relationship, so I enjoyed the visit.

On Tuesday morning, I headed to *The Jubilee Times* to work on a couple of articles. Mom stepped out of her office as I admired the plants from Aunt Violet's house. She could only take three or four to the new place and gave the rest to Mom, who arranged the plants along the wall past the reception desk, where a row of six large windows overlooked our historic downtown.

Three of the smaller plants occupied tall pot stands with the other three pots on the floor. One enormous ZZ plant filled the corner—ZZ was short for Zamioculcas Zamiifolia—and it featured glossy, green leaves. The plant was seven years old, a gift after Uncle Bob died, but it was too big for her new apartment.

"What do you think?" Mom asked.

"Looks great. This space looked sort of empty before."

Then, Mom brought up Grandma's gift. "I've seen that basket tucked away in your grandma's upstairs linen closet all my life. Once, she told me it made Aunt Violet sad, so she hid it away."

"I don't think of Aunt Violet as a sad person."

"Me either. I peeked inside the basket once, but I didn't feel comfortable looking at anything."

"What happened in California? Why would Aunt Vera want to destroy a quilt? And what makes this a *California quilt*? I have a million questions, Mom."

Mom nodded. "Me, too. Mom didn't talk about the basket or California very much, at least around us kids. I heard a few things at family gatherings, mostly that Vera had hurt her sisters. The great-aunts told us Grace and Violet were blessed to have each other. All I know is my mother wanted you to have her vintage basket and everything inside. Now, hopefully, those tapes—and Aunt Violet—will explain what it all means."

Three

Story of an Hour

"Is solace anywhere more comforting than in the arms of a sister?"

~Alice Walker

*T*he next day, as I walked up the steps of Nelson Hall, the early morning sunshine flooded the foyer of the second-floor hallway through its floor-to-ceiling glass windows. The fall semester was my favorite time of year that I always associated with buying notebooks and pens, starting new classes, and watching the changing of the seasons with football games, the harvest, and the holidays.

They'd propped some classroom doors half-open on the back hallway, and the voices of several teachers giving lectures in 8 AM classes spilled out. I headed for the Adjunct's office halfway down the main hallway.

As I entered, Shelly sat marking papers with a red pen. She glanced up. "Morning, Gracie!"

"Good morning, Shelly." I placed my messenger bag and purse on the floor and set my travel cup of iced tea on the desk. My Intro to Literature class started in 40 minutes. I got out my laptop, logged onto the college Wi-Fi, and started skimming through my presentation.

I tried to focus on the lesson plan but kept thinking about the basket in my guest bedroom. Today, Aunt Violet and I would listen to the first cassette tape.

Shelly, my best friend, tidied a stack of papers and turned to her computer, but stopped. "Frances gave notice she's resigning. You should apply for her job—it's full-time with benefits. Unfortunately, you'd have to step in halfway through the semester, because she's leaving at the end of September."

Tiara, one of the other teachers, stopped by my desk. "You two girls are twins again."

Shelly and I glanced down at our denim skirts and light blue, button-up shirts. She added a colorful scarf, and I wore turquoise jewelry and a belt. Otherwise, we'd dressed in the same outfit again. Shelly controlled her long red hair with colorful headbands, while I kept my blonde curls in a messy short bob.

"We've been best friends since middle school," Shelly explained. "We have the same style."

I nodded.

"Did you mention Frances' position? Are you applying, Gracie?" Tiara asked.

"I haven't seen the ad, but I don't know if I can do it *and* juggle the museum."

Tiara looked skeptical. "Really? You would give up a full-time job with benefits to hang out at the county museum?" She stood beside my desk, her eyebrows raised. A proud Black feminist with long natural curls and big brown eyes, she was someone I respected—and sometimes feared just a little.

"Don't forget, I'm also writing articles for *The Jubilee Times*. I'm never bored, and I don't spend every minute grading essays like my friends who teach writing full time," I defended myself.

Tiara smiled. "Girl, you're young. The ink on your degree is still wet. There's plenty of time to score the perfect job. But don't wait too long, okay?" She settled at her desk, putting her purse and messenger bag down.

In her mid-forties, Tiara loved both her radio gig and teaching. Shelly, Tiara, and I had become close friends over the past four years, and Shelly and I considered Tiara our mentor and cheerleader. She was six feet tall with the heeled boots she loved to wear, and she was a community activist. Tiara loved bright colors and favored suits, dresses, and long skirts, always looking the polished professional.

I told them about Grandma's gift—and about going to visit Aunt Violet and listening to the first tape today.

"You should get some answers," Shelly suggested.

Tiara nodded. "Can't wait to hear all about it."

I checked the time. "Thanks for the therapy, you two. Better get to class." I grabbed my things.

Shelly looked up and grabbed her bag, too.

As I turned the corner, I nearly collided with a stranger headed in the opposite direction. His messenger bag bumped me, so my clipboard, textbook, and three-ring notebook came dangerously close to sliding onto the floor, and my purse and shoulder bag slipped down.

"I'm so sorry! Let me help." He deftly slipped the shoulder bag and purse up on my shoulder and straightened the book on top. Our eyes met briefly, and he smiled—gorgeous brown eyes flecked with gold.

"Hi, I'm David MacNeill. I'm supposed to be teaching in room 210. I must have gotten turned around. Sorry for bumping into you."

"Hi, David. Welcome to JJCC. You're almost there—just two doors down. I'm Gracie O'Connor, and this is my classroom. Nice to meet you."

"Thanks. See you around, Gracie."

Reluctantly, I entered the classroom and put my things down on my desk. Was I blushing? My cheeks seemed a little warm, and I hoped my students wouldn't notice. Thankfully, several of them rushed in after me.

Today we planned to discuss one of my favorite stories, "Story of an Hour," by Kate Chopin, told in just two pages. A family friend sees a telegram about a terrible train accident with his friend listed as dead, so he rushes to tell the man's wife. She has a heart condition, so he breaks the news as gently as possible. Fortunately, her sister is there to help. The woman goes up to her room to process the news. She thinks about how different her life will be without her husband.

There would be no one to live for during those coming years; she would live for herself. There would be no powerful will bending hers in that blind persistence with which men and women believe they have a right to impose a private will upon a fellow-creature. A kind intention or a cruel intention made the act seem no less a crime as she looked upon it in that brief moment of illumination. And yet she had loved him—sometimes. Often she had not. What did it matter? What could love, the unsolved mystery, count for in the face of this possession of self-assertion which she suddenly recognized as the strongest impulse of her being!

"Free! Body and soul free!" she kept whispering."

Later, she walks down the stairs with her sister, having accepted the news, when in walks her husband—very much alive. She collapses and dies, and the story ends with a cryptic line. "When the doctors came, they said she had died of heart disease—of the joy that kills."

After a brief look at my presentation, putting the story into context, we broke into small groups. I walked around the classroom and listened to the small groups talk about the story.

Later I asked, "What about the role of the train wreck in this story? Notice the family friend double-checks the telegram, listing the casualties before he delivers the sad news."

I showed them a picture of Jubilee Junction's Train Depot from the turn of the century, and a faded telegram as part of the slideshow.

"Man, the telegram looks sort of like a tweet," one student observed.

"Can you imagine having to pay for each word in a tweet? Telegrams were one of the earliest ways to communicate over distance and often gave sad news, especially during times of war, and yes—you paid by the word," I explained.

Several students looked skeptical. "Pay for each word? You messing with us?" muttered Jimmy.

I glanced at him and smiled, then shifted back to the story. "What happens in the space of just a few paragraphs in this story? Has anyone taken an Intro to Psychology class where they talked about the grieving process?"

Hands went up, and a few people nodded their heads.

Sarah, sitting in front, spoke up. "This lady gets stressed out when her husband's friend comes to tell her about the train wreck, and her husband is dead, and she goes to her room to be alone, so she's grieving, right?"

Jacob, one of her small group partners, jumped in. "She's thinking about how good her life will be without having to deal with him. That's cold. Was her husband a jerk or something?"

Samantha pointed out, "I keep looking at this sentence about people trying to change other people—I don't think it's such an old-fashioned story, after all."

I brought up the Wikipedia article with Elizabeth Kubler Ross's five stages of grief and asked, "Do you notice how the main character experiences all these stages in a two-page story? First denial, then anger, bargaining, depression, and acceptance."

"Remember the context of this story. Why would she suddenly feel free to live for herself if her husband died? What choices did women have in 1894? We listed them on the marker board: housewife, schoolteacher, nurse, nanny, factory worker, cook, seamstress, shopkeeper, office worker, switchboard operator, and domestic servant.

As students made comments, I thought about our family history. In 1897, Grandma Grace's mother, Virginia (Ginny) Carlson, was born to a busy working mother of six sons and two daughters. Her father owned a carriage business, a livery for boarding horses, and farmed with his brother outside Jubilee Junction—which was the county seat and a growing community back then. Everyone worked hard with little time for reflection or literature.

Finally, we examined the sentences at the beginning of the story and at the end, both mentioning the main character's heart condition, and discussed briefly why she died. The students made lots of comments as the small groups figured out the plot, theme, characters, and other terms applying to the story. We also talked about the story's feminist theme and the author, Kate Chopin, who seemed to have been born 100 years too early.

As class ended, students were still chatting as they turned in their small group notes for participation points. I left the classroom with a smile on my face. With students willing to speak up, it was going to be a wonderful semester. This class full of students excited to learn is why I loved teaching. I hurried off to the office to switch bags for my next class—trying not to look for David, telling myself, *I have a boyfriend.*

Four

A Proper Introduction

"Denial ain't just a river in Egypt."

~Mark Twain

After my second class, I packed up my bags, stopped to grab a chef salad from Aunt Shirley's Café, and headed over to the county museum, where I had spent my afternoons for the past two years.

When Carl hired me as the Special Exhibits coordinator, he told me, "This is a wonderful museum, but let's face it. We mostly appeal to men with our displays about farm equipment and comparisons of horses vs. tractors. That's ignoring half of our citizens. I want you to find creative ways to appeal to women with our displays, and I'd like to incorporate more technology. I also need your help to organize things."

Carl definitely needed my help. I spent the first six months doing an inventory of all the exhibit materials—sorting, organizing, and sometimes tossing a few things damaged beyond repair, such as some old uniforms with extensive moth damage. For a long time, Carl had been the only full-time, paid employee—dependent on volunteers and his board. He'd found funding for two part-time positions and hired me and a secretary.

I discovered we had lots of great volunteers, but they didn't put things away after exhibits ended, and they filled the basement up with cardboard boxes and tubs, but we didn't know what we had or where to find it. I needed to find better storage solutions and a way to track inventory. Then I began labeling items and creating an online spreadsheet.

We featured some of the stranger objects we found in my first exhibit, Found at the Museum. First, we numbered the items, including a lot of old household objects, tools, and kitchen appliances. We then asked visitors to identify each object from a list of three choices. After they selected their guess, they would find out the answer, along with a brief paragraph about the object. People with smartphones could use the QR code on each item. Those without could read the question on the front of the laminated cards then flip them over for the answer.

We did a second exhibit about women's work on the farm in the 1900s. We described all the chores typically done by women by the days of the week and displayed some tools women would have used. Monday—washing. Tuesday—ironing. Wednesday—mending. Thursday—market. Friday—baking. Saturday—cleaning. Sunday—Day of Rest.

Then, last spring, we moved some old display units and discovered a closet. Inside we found a trunk with several antique quilts long ago donated and then forgotten. The first one I dug out was a colorful old Crazy quilt dating back to the turn of the century, and the other one was a Star quilt in pastels. Both quilts were wrapped up in old sheets, and they were in remarkably good condition.

They were a little musty, but I had several techniques for dealing with those smells. Fortunately, we had a washer and dryer at the museum down in the basement close to my office. I gently placed the quilts one at a time into the dryer, along with several dryer sheets. Those two quilts gave me the idea for my third exhibit—Quilts Made in Jubilee County.

Grandma Grace had a saying—*every quilt has a story*. So, I'd spent months gathering more quilts and doing research to find their stories. I tried to date each quilt and identify its pattern. Quilts had fascinated me since childhood when I went with Aunt Violet, Aunt Maggie, and Grandma Grace to their quilting club, where they sat at a big quilting frame with an enormous quilt spread out and worked and talked.

Today, I needed to sketch the layout for the display and recheck my list of quilts and patterns. I walked upstairs with my clipboard and tape measure to measure the exhibit space. We planned to place ten netbooks throughout the display for a slideshow and needed small tables near outlets. I measured the space, noting the location of outlets on the clipboard.

Carl worked nearby, answering a volunteer's question. Then, a man I didn't know walked up to Carl, and they shook hands. Close to six feet tall with curly brown hair, he dressed casually in khaki slacks, a shirt, and a sweater vest but carried himself like a professional. He turned around, and I noticed his brown eyes and glasses. I recognized him as David, the man who had bumped into me earlier. Carl and David walked towards me. When they came closer, David smiled warmly and held out a hand. "Hello, again, Gracie."

I shook his hand, almost unable to tear myself away from his lovely brown eyes. I reminded myself again, *I have a boyfriend.*

Carl introduced us. "This is Dr. David MacNeill, the new history teacher at JJCC. You've met Gracie O'Connor, our special exhibits coordinator. She's an adjunct at the college and helps at *The Jubilee Times,* where her father's the editor. You two have a lot in common. You both love history, doing research, teaching at JJCC, exploring and writing about the Midwest, and eating at Aunt Shirley's. David moved here from the Chicago area and could use a friend to show him around town. I met him earlier this summer when he interviewed."

"I told Carl about nearly knocking you down earlier and thought we needed a proper introduction," David grinned.

I blushed, remembering his hand on my shoulder, adjusting my purse and messenger bag. I scolded myself, *What are you, fifteen? What would Shelly think?* Out loud, I joked, "Those hallways can get brutal between classes. I should have put my books in my bag."

Carl explained, "I told David you might have some suggestions about the town for a newcomer. After all, you grew up here." He looked at me and waggled his eyebrows.

Carl and I had a running, inside joke. Born in Marshall County, he moved to Jubilee Junction when he got the assistant director job at the museum twenty years ago and married a local girl. Now Carl was the director, and his children attended Jubilee High School, but a few of the older people still considered him a *newcomer*.

David thanked him and then turned to me. "I think I've seen you at the Jubilee Cafe, Gracie. So, you must have good taste."

"Yes, but I call it Aunt Shirley's because she's Mom's cousin." I thought for a moment. "Have you been to the library? My friend Charlotte is the librarian, and they have a small but respectable Special Collection. We have several parks, walking trails, and there's the old train depot visitor's center. The airport is kind of cool, and there are several historical buildings you might like to tour downtown."

David smiled. "The library is on my list. I drove past some parks. Maybe you could give me a tour sometime?"

I nodded, mesmerized by his eyes, agreeing to the tour—*Because I'm a polite person, right?*

He looked at his watch. "I need to get back to campus for my afternoon class. Thanks for the book, Carl. Gracie, see you around. I promise to watch for you in the hallways from now on. I'm also looking forward to your quilt exhibit, which Carl says will be wonderful."

David left, and I went back to measuring the exhibit area, aware of my flushed cheeks. I'd sensed something special when David held my hand. A volunteer raised her hand, and Carl left, so I didn't have to face my boss looking flustered.

After work, I stopped by my house to grab the shoe box with the tape recorder and cassette tapes and headed for Aunt Violet's apartment, part of a senior living complex in town. I opened my car door and inhaled the scent of the lilac bushes and roses. Over the past twenty years, the apartment complex expanded with three buildings now, a raised bed community garden, housekeeping, and nursing services, and meal delivery services.

Aunt Violet greeted me at the front door. "Gracie, you're here!"

We walked down the hall. "I never want to move again, but my family did the hard work. I've made two new friends. And speaking of friends, look at the sweet gift Vern and Maggie dropped off earlier."

We arrived in the kitchen, and I saw a small gray and white tabby lapping delicately out of a water bowl. The kitten looked up and meowed. Aunt Violet scooped her up into her arms. "This is Beatrix."

I reached out to pet her. She sniffed my hand and then meowed. "Oh, she's friendly."

"Maggie thought I needed a new cat. I've missed Snowball." Snowball died two years ago, at eighteen. For as long as I could remember, Aunt Violet always owned a cat.

She set the kitty on the floor and washed her hands. "I made sun tea, and your mama dropped off some of her oatmeal chocolate chip cookies, so we shouldn't let them get stale. They're on the counter. Can you get them?"

I washed my hands and got a heady whiff of oats and chocolate while opening the plastic container of cookies. I placed several on a plate and carried it back to the table. Meanwhile, she poured glasses of her delicious sun tea. I plugged the tape recorder into a nearby outlet and inserted the first tape.

"So, how did your visit go with your sister Vera last weekend? I suppose you heard she arrived while we loaded the basket into my car. Mark told me to leave."

"Yes, Donna apologized for her mother yelling at you. Her work schedule changed, so they came earlier. She'd sent your mom an email, but your mom hadn't seen it yet. Maggie and Vern calmed Vera down. Mark and the boys out at my old farmhouse loaded up Donna's big truck in no time, and then she and Vera drove to Vern's house to rest. We met for supper at Perkins and visited at Vern and Maggie's house."

She took a sip of tea. "Donna and Vera spent the night with them and left the next morning. Your parents joined us as well. She never asked me about the California quilt." Aunt Violet grinned at me.

"So, what's this about, Aunt Violet? Why does Vera want the stuff Grandma Grace set aside for me, and why didn't Grandma Grace ever say anything to me about her gift?" I tried to ignore the butterflies in my stomach I got every time someone mentioned Aunt Vera.

"There has always been something wrong with my relationship

with my twin sister. For years I tried to ignore it. When we were younger, I just gave in. If she wanted something, I let her have it." She paused.

"Mama dressed us alike but used different colored ribbons in our hair. If Vera liked my ribbon better, she would whine until I switched with her. Mama had little patience for such nonsense, not with eight children and a farm. Our relationship changed years ago, when I finally stood up to her, and Vera still hasn't gotten over it." Aunt Violet sighed. "Let's listen to the first tape."

I pressed play, and we both sat back to listen.

Tape #1, Family History
Grandma Grace's voice sounded warm and reflective.

Gracie, I've been thinking it's time for the younger people to hear our family stories. I love my cassette recorder and decided I would rather *tell* you the story than write it down. Today is June 1, 1998, and it's been fifty years since most of this happened.

Are you wondering why I gave you the wicker basket and the California quilt, Gracie? Think of them as visual aids. You've just turned twelve, and when I look at you, I see your mother at your age, with those lovely, wise eyes. I don't think you're old enough for me to tell you these stories yet, but I'm tired of keeping Vera's secrets. As long as our parents were alive, our family found it too painful to discuss what happened in California during World War II. If we did, there would be tears, angry shouting, slamming doors, and then silence.

Let's start with some family history. Three families founded Jubilee Junction. Great-Grandfather Peter Nelson was an *herb doctor*. His friend Michael O'Connor was a lawyer, and a third man, Great-Grandfather Charles Carlson, farmed. They settled in the area five years before the railroad came in 1860 and became friends. Along the way, we saw several Nelson/O'Connor unions—including your parents, and Carlson/Nelson unions—as with my parents.

My parents, Virginia "Ginny" Carlson and William "Will" Nelson, met in a country school. Ginny and Will married as teenagers and worked hard for his grandpa Nelson, and by the time the three girls came along, Daddy managed the livestock and tended to the sick animals. They outgrew that first little house with the four boys. So, they moved into a bigger farmhouse and raised a big family—with three girls and five boys.

Violet, Vera, and I were young women like you back in the early 1940s. We grew up on our farm next to Grandpa Nelson, with our other Grandpa Carlson's farm not far away. We attended the Methodist church by the cemetery and went to school in a one-room country schoolhouse through eighth grade, and then we attended high school in Jubilee Junction, just a little country town back then—

A knock-on Aunt Violet's front door interrupted us. She looked apologetic. I shrugged and stopped the tape. She answered the door, and Uncle Vern and Aunt Maggie came in bearing gifts.

"We don't want to interrupt," Uncle Vern apologized. "But Maggie wouldn't let me drive home until we dropped off cat food, litter, and treats."

They brought the bags into the kitchen and hugged me.

"So sorry, girls. We thought we'd beat Gracie here, but we stopped for tea and chatted up a few people," Aunt Maggie confessed.

Uncle Vern eyed the plate of cookies, so I handed him one and then gave one to Aunt Maggie.

"Always room for a cookie." Uncle Vern grinned, and Aunt Maggie nodded.

Aunt Violet held Beatrix in her arms. "Thank you again. I love her."

They left, waving goodbye.

Five

Come to California

"A woman is like a teabag—only in hot water do you realize how strong she is."

~Nancy Reagan

*W*e settled ourselves at the table again, and I clicked the tape to resume.

∽

Our parents were wonderful, and we had four big brothers: Vincent, Victor, Virgil, and Vance, and a baby brother Vern. Yes, my mother loved names starting with V—her parents named her Virginia, remember? She named me Virginia Grace, as the oldest daughter, but everyone called me Grace.

We had lots of extended family in the area, and it seemed like we always had a wedding or baby shower to attend, clothes to mend, clothes to wash and hang up on the lines, animals to feed, crops to plant or harvest, quilts to stitch, bread to bake, dishes to wash, and gardens to weed, and babies and children needing tending.

The beginning of what would become World War II—when Germany invaded Poland on September 1, 1939—shocked us. We felt like we were watching the funnel cloud of a tornado on the horizon and wondering if it would come our way. But the war seemed far away across the sea with us safe in America.

We saw ourselves as grown up, with our lives spread out before us like a beautiful quilt, with only a few of the pieces stitched in place. But everything changed when the Japanese bombed Pearl Harbor on December 7, 1941. The war altered our lives, our community, and our family forever. Can you imagine the entire world at war?

I graduated from Jubilee Junction High School in May 1940. I helped Daddy, driving tractors and fixing them when they broke down. He called me his tomboy, and I loved the nickname. I asked my younger brother Vern for two pairs of his dungarees and two work shirts, and Mama bought me a pair of heavy overalls, heavy gloves, and good, sturdy, Red Wing boots. I loved the speed laces! We owned several John Deere tractors called *two-bangers*. I had learned to work on the engines with Daddy from the time I turned eleven or twelve.

He taught me how to set the engine timing, change plugs, service the air cleaner, change the oil, clean the radiator, check the air in the tires, start the engine on eighty-seven octane fuels for warm-up, and then switch to the cheaper distillate. He also taught me to listen to the engine and how to adjust. Later, Vern and I helped him upgrade from steel wheels to rubber.

Vera hated to get dirty, so she begged out of working in the fields. She helped Mama with the garden, did chores in the house, and helped my grandfather with the books for the farms. Violet loved animals and didn't mind some dirt, but she cared little for working on machinery. When the big boys were out working in the fields or helping one of our relatives and something broke down, Daddy, Vern, and I would fix the problem together.

Daddy told me I was real mechanical for a girl, but Mama thought I would be a wonderful schoolteacher, so I attended the Iowa State Teachers College in Cedar Falls in the fall of 1940. I earned my Normal Teaching License by attending an expedited session. The following spring, the Superintendent hired me to teach for the fall of 1941 at the Prairie Valley School, just up the hill from my Grandpa Carlson's farm.

I taught at the Prairie Valley School for two years and each summer I spent several weeks cleaning and organizing the classroom beforehand. The superintendent gave me a new set of *McGuffey Readers*, but when school started that first year, I noticed my students didn't read well. I created some study guides for them—workbooks I typed for each student at home on my new Smith Corona typewriter, which I bought with money I received as graduation gifts. The workbooks proved to be a fine teaching tool and helped the students remember key dates, vocabulary, important people, and events. They made reviewing the material much easier, and within a few months my students' reading scores had improved.

The twins graduated in May 1941. Vera wanted to go to Chicago to work in an office. She took secretarial courses and found a job at the Jubilee County courthouse. Violet started taking nursing classes in the fall of 1941.

Our youngest brother, Vern, graduated in May 1942. Two months later he left for the U.S. Army Air Forces.

One of our older brothers, Vance, had fallen from the big windmill as a teenager and hurt his hip and knee. He never healed up right and used a crutch to walk. But Vance could get up on the tractor and used the hand clutch—which is great for people with bad legs—and found other ways to be helpful.

With only Vance at home, our father and uncles were working even harder. My grandpa Nelson and Papa John Carlson supervised our hired help, and several of my great-uncles helped as well.

The summer of 1942 brought improvements to our town and county as electricity changed our routines. President Franklin D. Roosevelt created the REA, or Rural Electrification Administration, with an executive order in 1935. However, electricity took time to reach rural areas of Iowa, since it required the formation of co-ops. Think of everything you do that uses electrical power. Can you believe we survived for so long without electricity?

The electrician needed a helper, and my father suggested I apply since school had let out for the summer. Mr. Shellenberger hired me, so I put on my dungarees, work shirt, gloves, and boots, and learned about how to work with electricity.

First, we wired up the schoolhouse in early June. I watched him carefully, handing him tools, asking questions, and running out to his truck for more supplies. I was proud I knew which tool to hand him, and he liked I knew how to use them, too. Then he came down to our farm and changed our lives. Once we turned on those lights, we couldn't imagine going back to the dim, smoky kerosene lamps. Dad liked not having to pump water by hand when the wind didn't blow. Mom liked not having to crank the cream separator by hand.

Mr. Shellenberger taught me how to wire up the receptacles and light switches and to screw on the cover plates in the barn and house. I found the work a wonderful challenge, and I worked with a vengeance to prove myself. I was mighty proud of my work when I finished. We wired up several outbuildings and workshops, then we wired up both of my grandparents' farms and moved to my Uncle Jim's place.

By now, it was early July, and I needed to get ready for the new school year, typing up the worksheets and study booklets. So, my career as an electrician's helper ended, but Mr. Shellenberger told me if I ever gave up teaching, I could work with him.

Father seemed proud of my skills with tools, but Mother seemed horrified at the thought of me doing something so unlady-like.

She told me, "We're happy you could help him wire up the farms. You saved us a lot of money, Virginia Grace, and you did an excellent job. I'm happy you're not giving up your teaching job though, after all your hard work at college."

Father winked at me. "I think Grace would make a wonderful electrician, and imagine all the work she could do in Jubilee Junction! But she's a fine schoolteacher, too."

I kept busy between preparing for the fall classes and helping my Uncle Robert get ready for rationing. He owned the Jubilee General Store. We had a town meeting at the schoolhouse to tell people how the rationing system would work. Women were especially worried about rationing sugar, so we wanted to help them understand the point system.

Each person got twenty-eight ounces of meat and four ounces of cheese a week. A pound of sirloin cost nine points, while a can of pineapple required twenty-four points. We received fifty points per household member each month. Each person might get the following for one week: one egg, four ounces of margarine, four strips of bacon, two ounces of butter, two ounces of tea (about twenty-five tea bags), one ounce of cheese, and eight ounces of sugar.

Every week, Mama took our combined ration cards to shop. Later, rationing was something we remembered most about our daily routines during the war.

We made up the difference from the limited points with vegetables and fruits we grew ourselves, so we grew lots of vegetables—some of them more appealing than others. Daddy always joked, *put salt on it,* when rutabagas got on the menu. We kept fresh vegetables in our root cellar, and we smoked meat, and we canned vegetables by the quart. Our great-grandparents had planted apple trees, cherry trees, rhubarb, and all kinds of berries, so we made lots of applesauce, jellies, jams, and canned fruit. We also grew sorghum to make molasses, so mama could make her famous molasses cookies.

We were lucky to live on the farm, with chickens and eggs, beef, dairy products, as well as pork, and turkeys. Mama made a lot of stews, soups, and casseroles to stretch our meat as much as possible.

I found an old ration card, and a flier aimed at farmers. It's in my little trunk, Gracie.

"You also serve—you who stand behind the plow pledged to feed the Soldier, the Worker, the Ally, and, with God's help, all the hungry victims of this war! You also serve—you who farm, you who pray and sacrifice. You'll feed the World even if it means plowing by lantern light, and harvesting by hand—even children's hands—even if it means putting up the trucks and going back to covered wagons once again...

The U.S. Department of Agriculture Urges you to:
See your County USDA War Board
Meet your 1943 farm goals
Keep tractors working
Take good care of your machinery

Conserve your trucks
Turn in your scrap
Buy War Bonds
Farmers must win the Battle of the Land
with the machinery they already have."

No one had to tell our family to work with what they had, because there were five big family farms when I was growing up: ours, our two grandfathers, Uncle Jim, and Uncle Robert. We worked together to plant and harvest. We hired workers together, and we took good care of our equipment.

Then, a letter arrived from our cousin Ed in the spring of 1943, which changed all our plans. By now, Violet worked for our town's doctor as a nurse, and Vera managed the office at the courthouse. I intended to sign my teaching contract for Fall 1943, already seeing myself as an old maid country schoolteacher.

"Come to California," Ed wrote. "We need you. With the men away to war, they're hiring women to build ships and airplanes, drive Generals around, and work as secretaries and nurses. You three girls can help us win this war!"

He added that although he'd registered for the draft a year and a half ago, he decided to go ahead and sign up. So we could be there for his wife, Mary, and their little boy, Eddie, while he is deployed. He's said he would leave for training in about eight weeks.

That's enough for now.

Six

The Sisters Pack

"We all grow up with the weight of history on us. Our ancestors dwell in the attics of our brains as they do in the spiraling chains of knowledge hidden in every cell of our bodies."

~*Shirley Abbott*

Aunt Violet patted my hand. "Our family has had its share of hard times, but I cherish my memories. Our faith in God and each other kept us going."

"I remember Mom saying that Grandma taught in a country school, but not anything else."

"She knew how to troubleshoot engines and a lot more." She closed her eyes, swept back in time.

I didn't ask. I took out the first tape and put in the second one.

Tape #2, Persuasion and Preparation
Grandma Grace's voice sounded cheerful.

Ed grew up on a nearby farm. His father—my uncle Jim—and my father were close. Ed graduated three years before me. In 1940, Ed packed up his old car and headed for California with Mary, his bride of two years. Mary's aunt and uncle had moved to the Chula Vista area several years earlier when they inherited a boarding house.

Ed and Mary stayed with them until they found an apartment and jobs at Bartlett Aircraft Factory. They promoted Ed at Bartlett's, while Mary quit when she got pregnant and stayed home with Eddie.

Of course, we needed to persuade our parents to let us go to California. The twins would turn twenty in two months, and I was only twenty-one. However both Ed and Mary were twenty-four, and they had lived in the San Diego area for two years and were building a nice life for themselves. He told us he could serve his country by building planes until he got called up.

After he wrote to us, he sent a letter to our parents, promising to look after us. Ed told them Mary's aunt Mae would have two rooms vacant in two weeks. Confident he could help us get jobs at one of the aircraft factories or on the nearby Navy base, he urged us to come. Finally, our parents agreed we could go.

I wrote a letter to my school board, explaining I wouldn't be available to teach next fall because I was going to California to build bombers. On my last day of school, the children performed in a recital, and we invited the parents. We served cookies and lemonade. My superintendent and two of the school board members attended.

Mr. Lewis, the superintendent, shook my hand warmly after the program. "We're going to miss you, Miss Nelson. You've been an excellent teacher, and your students have done well. Contact me when you get back from California, and we'll find you a new school."

Several of my children shyly brought me homemade cards, and their parents came up to shake my hand. I received several compliments. James, my scholar, came up and shook my hand. "I'll never forget you, Miss Nelson. Thank you for getting me the extra science books." I knew James would make a wonderful doctor and was happy to have helped him.

I realized I would miss the children, but I looked forward to our adventure. My superintendent gave me a letter highlighting my two years as a teacher and commending me for my hard work. I placed his letter in a portfolio to take with us, along with a note by Mr. Shellenberger, complimenting my work as an electrician's helper. My father also wrote a brief note documenting my work on the farm with tractors' engines.

Violet and Vera gave their workplaces their notice as well. Vera proudly showed us the letter of reference her supervisor gave her.

The doctor also gave Violet a letter of reference and a small first aid kit for the trip.

The Saturday after our parents gave in, our paternal grandparents showed up with gifts. Grandpa and Grandma Nelson brought us large suitcases and messenger bags. Grandma Nelson held each of us close for a moment and whispered to check the inside of the messenger bags. Later, we found $100 tucked away in an envelope inside the messenger bags. Grandma also gave each one of us a money belt to wear under our clothes.

"Watch each other's things. Don't put all your money in your purse in case it gets stolen. Use the money belt on the train trip. My brother worked for the railroad and always used his. Open a bank account out there. Ed will help. He's a good boy." Grandma's eyes filled, as did mine and Violet's.

Grandpa Nelson gently embraced us and told us to be his good girls. "Have fun in California, but don't forget to come home." Then he found his handkerchief and blew his nose loudly.

The next day, we ate Sunday lunch at our Carlson grandparents' home. Afterward, we sat down in their large living room to visit.

Grandpa Carlson smiled. "We understand you girls are taking the train west to have an adventure. We want to help." He gave each one of us an envelope with $200, a large amount of money in those days. "I checked, and a ticket to California will cost you $50, and you'll need cash for the boarding house." His eyes twinkled.

Grandma Carlson clasped each of us to her chest for a moment. "Take care of each other." She tucked a new handkerchief in our hands.

With our new suitcases, we began packing. We took two dresses, two skirts and blouses, pajamas, and all the rest. I tucked my portfolio with stationery, envelopes, pens, and pencils into the front pocket. I added a couple of small writing tablets and a couple of my favorite novels. Mama stopped me as I was about to wrap my boots.

She fretted, "Leave those dirty old boots here! You'll need to buy work clothes and shoes out there. Ed and Mary should be able to help you find the right stores."

Just two weeks after getting Ed's first letter, we'd purchased our tickets and packed our suitcases. Our aunts helped Mama make a new dress for each girl for the trip. I wore a short-sleeved brown floral dress with a full skirt, comfortable and cool. The twins also dressed nicely for the trip, with Violet in a bluish-purple floral dress and Vera in a red and white floral dress.

That's all for now, Gracie.

Seven

Sharing the Tapes

"Distance doesn't ruin relationships but silence does."
~Farid F. Ibrahim

Aunt Violet smiled, with a few tears in her eyes as she grabbed a Kleenex.

"I'm sorry, this must be emotional for you, listening to these tapes and reliving those days." Aunt Violet seemed far away in her thoughts.

"Yes, but your Grandma Grace is right. It's time for your generation to hear our stories. Your mother knows bits and pieces." Aunt Violet paused, blew her nose. "None of us would be the same. My parents couldn't fix things between me and Vera, and we couldn't be in the same room without fireworks when came back. Your grandma Grace and I were always close, but we got closer in California. Now, enough of that. Tell me about your progress with the quilt exhibit."

"I've collected about two dozen quilts so far. Things are coming along getting all of their details documented, so we're on track."

I wanted to ask, *What happened in California?* But I stopped because of the look on her face.

"How is Steve doing in Des Moines?" Aunt Violet asked.

I sighed. "He likes his job and loves living in Des Moines. He keeps asking me to come down for the weekend. I stay with his sister Stephanie, and she's become a friend. Steve and I get along until he pressures me to get a job and move to Des Moines. He doesn't want to be a lawyer anymore. He wants to go into politics and run for state office, but I can't see myself living in Des Moines and being married to a politician."

"Have you two talked about this?"

"We've argued about it. He thinks I should leave Jubilee Junction, but I'm happy here. This is my hometown—my family is here."

Aunt Violet looked at me. "I don't think Steve is the only one who has changed. You used to talk about working for *The Des Moines Register*, didn't you?"

"Yes, I got excited when I landed the reporter's job in Ames, but then Dad had a heart attack. I needed to be here."

Aunt Violet patted my arm and smiled. "Eventually, you'll figure out what you want the most. Are you enjoying hearing your grandma's voice again?"

"Yes. I miss her. I didn't know you three girls were out in California during the war. Suddenly, World War Two doesn't seem so long ago."

I popped out the cassette tape and placed it back into its case.

"Bring the photo album next time." She sent me off with a few of Mom's cookies and a hug. Her kitten followed us, meowing, so Aunt Violet picked her up. "Goodbye, Gracie."

"Goodbye, Aunt Violet—and Beatrix. See you next Wednesday." Then, juggling my bag of cookies with the shoebox and my purse, I headed back to my house to work on a column, prep for class, and do some planning.

I fixed a grilled cheese sandwich and ate it with some iced tea and two leftover cookies, my mind still focused on Grandma's voice on the tape.

Agatha jumped up on the table and set her little butt on my clipboard to remind me she needed more water and a treat. Afterward, she curled up nearby for a nap while I looked at my planner, reviewed assignments for next week, and made notes for the column.

I stood up to make "a cuppa tea." Then I sat back down at the kitchen table, sipping my tea and thinking about Grandma's story so far—I compared her stories to what I'd studied about World War II in high school when it seemed like ancient history. Listening to her story, I realized just two generations separated me from those who fought in World War II—and those who helped on the home front. Uncle Vern had fought in World War II and Aunts Maggie and Violet had taken care of injured soldiers. I'd experienced having one brother go to war in Iraq—how would I have dealt with three older brothers going to war, and then my baby brother, too?

Checking the clock, I called Mom.

"Hi Mom, got a minute to talk? We listened to the first two tapes. Grandma Grace talked about the three big families settling here, her parent's meeting, the three sisters in high school, graduating, and getting jobs. Then, Cousin Ed sent a letter inviting them to come to California in 1943."

Mom exhaled. "I've never known about the letter taking them to California. I've heard a few bits and pieces, but I'm so happy she's put the story together. I'd like to hear those tapes, too." Mom sounded wistful.

"Sure. Do you have a cassette tape player?"

"Yes, I have one with two places for cassette tapes at the office, so I can play tapes or make copies of them. It's my old boombox from the 1990s."

"Great. I'll bring them to the newspaper office tomorrow. Grandma's such a wonderful storyteller. I could imagine her as a teenager and then a young woman."

"Yes, my mother was a wonderful storyteller."

A few days later, I told Mark and Dad the story of Grandma Grace helping to wire the farm when electricity came to their rural county.

"She knew her way around tools. I remember hanging out at the N&W office and helping her work on a plane in my teens. But I can't imagine working on the farm without electricity." Mark smiled, remembering. "I can see her wiring up the farm."

Dad looked thoughtful. "Your grandma was very handy. If I ever needed a tool, I knew where to go. Between Grace and Vern, who needed a hardware store? She knew how to use tools—and how to take care of them, too."

The next time Steve called, I told him about the family stories on the tapes. "I always liked your grandma, and I think she liked me.

Your Aunt Violet is a sweet lady too, and I'm glad you're spending time with her to listen to those tapes. So, are you coming to Des Moines again? You could always stay with me."

I hesitated. "I'm busy with the exhibit."

We agreed to compare schedules and plan a visit. After our goodbyes, I thought of all I needed to do and fought off a sense of panic. I needed to put together the exhibit, as well as teach classes, grade papers, and write weekly columns. How would I get everything done and still keep Steve happy?

Eight

Every Quilt Has A Story

"Don't waste your time in anger, regrets, worries, and grudges.
Life is too short to be unhappy."

~Roy T. Bennett

*G*randma Grace used to say, "Every quilt has a story." I'd spent the summer searching for the stories of my quilts at the museum. I asked those who donated the quilt to tell me what they knew about the quilt and share memories about the quilt. I added information about the pattern, the fabric, or other features that might tell us its story.

As word spread that I needed quilts for the exhibit, families across the county dug into attics, trunks, closets, and basements. My extended family donated half a dozen more quilts over the summer. Now, I was almost ready to complete the layout of the exhibit, create signage, and put together a virtual tour for our website.

I parked my Subaru, grabbed my purse, salad, and museum messenger bag, and entered the side door where my boss, Carl, greeted me. "I signed for two packages yesterday, so you probably have more quilts. They're on your worktable downstairs."

"Thanks," I told him. "Your contact at the Grout in Waterloo gave me a lot of information. I hope to have my layout to show you by tomorrow. Can't wait to unpack those new pieces." I headed for my workroom downstairs.

"Talk later, Gracie." Carl turned towards his office.

I walked down the steps to the basement and opened the first door to my workroom, filled with cabinets, counters, and several long tables, as well as my desk. Two dozen quilts lay on the long back counter. Carl had placed the packages on a worktable by my desk. I put my things down. While I ate my lunch, I looked over my notes about the history of the quilts. I would tackle the two packages only after I washed my hands.

A half-hour later, I donned a pair of thin cotton gloves and unwrapped two quilts. The first was perfect for a baby. Intricately stitched together, with tiny individual squares done in pastels, it was a classic Grandmother's Garden pattern and two feet by three feet. A note tucked into the tissue paper wrapped around the quilt gave information about it and permission to display it. The quilt dated back to 1910. I grabbed my digital camera to take some photographs.

The second quilt, a deep pink, done in the Double Wedding Ring pattern, would fit a full-size or queen bed. An envelope tucked inside had documentation about it as well. The next three hours passed all too quickly as I made more notes and took pictures of the newest quilts, added them to my sketch of the exhibit's layout, and looked at my photos.

We'd gathered an impressive group. One red and white Drunkard's Path, a blue and white Drunkard's Path, four Wedding Ring, four Grandmother's Garden, four Crazy Quilts, three Jacob's Ladder, two Tulip Circle, three Red Schoolhouse, three Log Cabin, three Sunbonnet Babies, two Bear's Paw, two Nine Patch, and three Schoolhouse.

After downloading the latest photos to the computer, I updated the exhibit list and descriptions in the spreadsheet, and carefully folded the new quilts on the back counter with protective wrapping around each one. I was going to need to expand my sketch of the display.

Removing the gloves, I saved the document, thinking about another quilt. With so much to do for the exhibit, the wicker basket sat on my guest room bed, the California quilt still folded inside. I'd stared at the part of the quilt I could see, wondering what was its story?

Shelly glanced up from her desk as I entered the adjunct office. "Morning, Gracie!"

"Good morning, Shelly." I placed my bags beside the desk and set down my travel cup. I claimed the desk in the back right-hand corner my first semester here, four years ago. About a dozen adjuncts in the Communications Department shared the office.

"OK, tell us about those tapes, "Tiara demanded as she walked into the office and sat down at her desk.

So I did, summarizing what we'd learned.

"Girl, your Grandma Grace was one badass woman. A little country schoolteacher who worked on tractor engines with her daddy, helped bring electricity to her family's farms, and flew planes? I wish I'd have known her." Tiara smiled at us.

Shelly nodded. "I agree. Your grandma was an amazing lady."

We all dug into our bags and retrieved papers to grade or materials to prep. Ten minutes later, Shelly looked up from her papers. "It's interesting your grandma used cassette tapes instead of writing the stories down. It's low tech, but personal."

I nodded. "Yes, hearing her voice makes all the stories seem more real."

"Don't get me started, girls. So much of history is told by men— and usually white men," Tiara remarked. "All too often women's voices and their stories get ignored or silenced. I hope someone is archiving or digitizing these tapes of yours because they're precious."

I assured her my dad was working on it, but all afternoon I thought about her comment.

Steve either called or emailed Mom, because when I stopped by *The Jubilee Times*, she stepped out of her office to talk.

"We appreciate you helping us out, Gracie, but are you sure you can juggle three jobs? I haven't done ads, but I bet I could figure them out."

Mom was the business manager for the paper and handled obituaries and some of the brief news articles. My brother wrote stories about Ag topics, and Dad did the hard news, editorial page, and layout. Aunt Delores worked twenty hours a week at the front desk, answering the phone, running errands, and taking money for subscriptions and ads. I helped by writing columns about the museum and college and picking up whatever needed to be done.

"Mom, I'm doing fine. Did Steve call you?" I wasn't sure if I was more angry or embarrassed.

"He's worried, dear. He thinks we're holding you back from the big city. Maybe we are." She paused, looking around the room. "*The Jubilee Time's* been in your father's family for over 150 years, and he loves the newspaper. I love the *Times* too, but our revenues are down. Grandma Grace's investment helped us upgrade and bought us some time, but the money will be gone by the end of next year. We need to generate more revenue."

I looked over at Dad who was talking on the phone and scribbling on a notepad. I turned on the computer and got to work. Mom walked back into her office and sat down.

Brad, the advertising guy, recently deployed to Iraq with the Iowa National Guard. I majored in journalism and worked on the college newspapers at Jubilee Junction Community College and Iowa State, so I figured I could manage ad sales.

I grew up spending time at the newspaper office, with the smell of paper and ink, and the excitement of Friday afternoons when the paper got printed. Now computers and modern presses had replaced the typewriters and old-fashioned printing presses which once filled the basement. The second floor held our archives, with more file cabinets, several long tables, and some comfy chairs. The third floor housed an apartment from the days when my parents lived over the offices, right after they married.

Dad complained the small-town weekly newspaper offered the lowest paying job he'd ever held when he looked at the number of hours he worked per week, but he also derived more satisfaction from journalism than any other work. Of course, he grew up in a newspaper family.

He told me once, "The weekly newspaper is a grab bag of sometimes tedious chores, including taking and processing your own photos, covering sports events, city council and school board meetings at night, being called by the police on a Saturday night to take photos at a fatal wreck, and being asked by a church to take pictures of communion on Sunday morning. You never truly get a complete day off."

To make sure I listened, Dad waved his index finger at me. "Whatever campaigns you conduct for community progress attracts both kudos and enemies, and sometimes you must face those enemies on the small-town streets. I watched my father smile and shake hands with Mayor Johnson, but then go back to the office and pen a critical editorial about one of the mayor's new policies—regarding keeping chickens in town."

Dad learned from watching his father and grandfather as he helped as a teenager. "I learned to do everything, including setting the digital type over my lunch hours when we fell behind and doing page layout. My older brother took the photos until he got drafted and became an Army photojournalist. We covered the local news, including local sports, church events, and the weekly traffic court."

Grandfather O'Connor still served as the editor then and made Dad his managing editor when he and mom married after graduating from Jubilee Junction Community College. When Mark and I were younger, she stayed at home. Sometimes she took us with her to the newspaper office and set up a space for us at a desk, where we would scribble, play with our toys, or do a puzzle while she helped dad. There was a little cot and some blankets in the workroom and a few toys, so we could take naps.

Three years older, Mark was off to kindergarten when I was three. For the next two and a half years, I spent time with Grandma Grace and my great-aunts, going to book club meetings at the library, attending the sewing circle, or running errands. Sometimes we stayed home on the farm. We took care of the kittens, baked cookies, and enjoyed tea parties. I remember taking small sips from my cup and munching daintily on finger sandwiches and scones. How many little girls like "a cuppa Constant Comment tea?" While they entertained me, Mom could go work to help Dad.

I looked around the office now with a fresh sense of resolve. So many generations had sacrificed to keep *The Jubilee Times* going. I'd thought of it as our family business, but always assumed it would continue. Now, I wanted the newspaper to survive—I wanted to share my community's stories with the next generation.

Nine

The Train Trip—Part One

"To travel is to take a journey into yourself."

~*Danny Kaye*

The following Wednesday, I visited Aunt Violet, carrying the shoebox full of tapes, a cassette player, and a small photo album. We sat on her couch to peruse the photos first, flipping back and forth and making comments on the sight of our familiar farms in the 1940s, with old tractors, people dressed in old-fashioned clothing, and a trio of fresh-faced, beautiful girls—the three sisters.

I realized Grandma looked like me—or I resembled the young Virginia Grace. As identical twins, Violet and Vera looked so much alike I couldn't tell them apart at first but decided on the smiling one standing closer to Grandma. Aunt Violet looked pleased when I pointed at her and asked.

"Yes, there I am with Vera. Our mother liked us to dress alike into our teens. We stopped doing it shortly after mother took this picture. Vera took advantage of people when we dressed alike, which was why I didn't like it. She would pretend to be me and nag me to pretend to be her, to fool a friend or distant relative—and once a Sunday school teacher. "Violet's raised eyebrows told me this prank hadn't gone over well.

Her kitty complained about something, so Aunt Violet picked up Beatrix and settled her on her lap.

I studied the picture again and tried to imagine Vera as a teenager. "So, she bossed you around and then tried to make you look bad. No wonder you two don't get along. What an awful sister!"

We turned the page and the three girls stood at the Jubilee Junction Train Depot, alongside three large suitcases with a train in the background. Aunt Violet closed the album. "We'll look at more pictures after we listen to the next tape."

Beatrix became bored and jumped down to take a nap.

We moved to the kitchen table, and I retrieved the tape recorder. Aunt Violet poured glasses of iced tea, and I grabbed the plate of cookies. I inserted the next tape, grabbed a cookie, and pressed play.

Tape #3, Leaving Iowa on The City of Denver
Grandma Grace's voice sounded cheery.

Our parents drove us to the train depot, where I handed my camera to Mama, and she took our picture. Daddy gave us quick hugs and winked as he put $5 bills in our hands. The train arrived, puffing black soot and venting steam, and people got off carrying parcels and bags.

A tired young mother held tightly to a small child as she stepped off the train, glancing around as an older couple quickly walked up and embraced her and took the bags at her feet. Young men in uniform waited for family or friends in the crowd, waving hello or hollering when they spotted them.

A group of passengers boarded the train. I sensed a flash of panic as I looked around at the crowd. Were we crazy to be doing this? None of us had ever traveled out of Iowa before.

Mama hugged each of us tight and tried not to cry. She stared sternly at us. Her gaze drifted to Vera, and then back to me. "You're the oldest, Virginia Grace. You take care of your sisters. I want you girls to write me a letter every week, go to church with your cousin Ed and Mary, and take care of each other. I know you'll work hard and make us proud."

She handed back my camera and smiled through her tears. I kissed her and whispered, "Yes, Mama! We'll be fine. Don't worry!"

Daddy helped the porter lift our three suitcases onto the train before giving us one last wave. "Be good, girls, and have fun!" he called.

We each carried a shoulder purse and our new canvas messenger bags filled with snacks, a small thermos, a book, and other personal items, along with a sweater.

Another porter greeted us, "Welcome to the City of Denver. Right this way, ladies," and he led us to the Frontier Shack.

I took care to put my camera, an Argus AF I'd purchased second-hand for $10, back into the camera case in my bag. For the past year, I had been taking pictures at my country school, and I loved it. I wanted to show my family our adventure in pictures. I brought six rolls of film and planned to buy more in California.

There were eight tables with four chairs around each. We found our seats next to a pleasant-looking older woman who looked up from her book and smiled at us. She introduced herself as Mrs. Jackson, from Davenport, so we introduced ourselves.

The twins took the two seats facing her, and I sat down beside her. We put our messenger bags and purses on the floor. The air seemed cold, so we slipped on our sweaters.

As I glanced around the train car, I saw a dozen young men in military uniforms sitting nearby. Several of them smiled at us, tipping their hats. Two waved and greeted us, calling out "Hello." Violet and Vera attracted more than their fair share of attention, as always, and smiled back. As the protective older sister, I sat up straighter and tried to look stern.

Mrs. Jackson chuckled beside me. "They must be a handful," she murmured.

"Yes, they can be," I whispered. "I'm the big sister. My parents are depending on me to make sure we get to California and back without problems."

She patted my arm. "I have a feeling you'll do just fine."

The conductor came by to punch our tickets, and the train began to move. Outside, I caught one last glimpse of my parent's faces. I waved at them and then the train pulled away from the station, rolling quietly, smoothly, with only an occasional gentle sway.

I shut my eyes and focused my thoughts. For a moment, I didn't pay attention to the chatter of passengers around me or the *clickety-clack* of the train. "Goodbye, mother and father, grandparents, aunts, uncles, and cousins! Goodbye to our beautiful family farms, rolling hills, and Jubilee Junction. Goodbye, little country school and students."

There was some nostalgia at the end of an era in my life—tomboy farm mechanic, old maid schoolteacher, and electrician's helper. I was on my way to building bombers!

I opened my eyes again and tuned back into the chatter all around me. I looked at my sisters, smiling back at the soldiers. I wondered if I could keep the twins in line—well, Vera, really—and make our parents proud. Yet my great anticipation of our new beginnings surmounted everything else.

Violet reached across the space between us then and took my hand. "We're on our way, Grace! I can hardly believe we're here."

Vera pretended not to notice us at first, because she hated shows of emotion, especially when they weren't about her. Then she gave in and smiled. She placed her hand on top of her twin sister's hand. "Yes, watch out California—the three Nelson sisters are on their way!"

Mrs. Jackson glanced up from her book and smiled.

We settled in and watched the changing scenery and surveyed the train car. The flow of conversation around us seemed to ebb and flow as people visited, played cards, told stories, tried to nap, or read a newspaper article or letter out loud to their seatmates.

I watched Violet fall into conversation with Mrs. Jackson as I savored the moment. Vera gazed around the train car and flirted with several soldiers. But I would not let her spoil my good mood. I thought, *This is day one of my new life, and my heart opened to receive every good thing in store for me.* Our California adventure had begun!

That's all for now."

Aunt Violet grabbed a Kleenex. "Shall we listen to the rest of the train trip?"

"Yes, please!"

I switched tapes, and we both sat back. Beatrix slept nearby.

Ten

The Train Trip—Part Two

*"I have found out that there ain't no surer way to find out
whether you like people or hate them than to travel with them."*
~*Mark Twain*

Tape #4, Making friends
*Grandma Grace's voice sounded relaxed as she remembered the
train trip.*

*O*ur trip to California took three days. We traveled through plains, mountains, deserts, and lush green fields. We didn't have the money for a sleeper car, so we sat up for three days, taking naps as we could, thankful for the sweaters our mother insisted we bring. Around us, people chatted quietly, played cards, read or wrote a letter, or napped, while the rhythm of the train gently rocked us all.

We ate in the dining car twice but found the prices extremely high. We got out at stops to buy sandwiches and fruit. Grandma sent along some crackers with peanut butter, sandwiches, apples, and cookies, along with a small thermos for each of us, and told us to drink only clean water. We tried to make our food stretch and splurged on bottled juice and tea in the dining car.

Several stops included complimentary food from canteens. At one stop in North Platte, Nebraska, the volunteers handed us all paper plates with fried chicken wings and legs. With the sailors and soldiers on board, along with those of us heading west to support the war effort, these folks wanted to encourage us with a tasty lunch.

Mrs. Jackson looked after us. We chatted and took turns watching each other's bags to visit the toilet. Soon we relaxed and got to know our other neighbors.

A group of sailors nearby told us they were on their way to California for training before deployment overseas. Very handsome in their uniforms, they joked with the soldiers, headed to posts on the West Coast.

Some sailors—Walter, Paul, Davy, and John—sat directly across the aisle. A group of soldiers—Peter, Jose, Pedro, and Charlie—sat behind us. Jose and Pedro were Mexican Americans and were proud to wear the uniform. From Southern California, they told us what to expect.

Jose enthused, "Orange groves, lemon groves, grapes, and all the sunshine! We have wonderful food. You gotta try Mexican food, ladies—tamales, enchiladas, burritos, and tacos. The ocean, beaches, and beautiful drives along the coast. Yeah, there's Hollywood with all of them stars. Pretty glamorous, ladies!"

Pedro chimed in, "California is a big state, Grace. Maybe you'll get to drive up north, and you'll see farm fields, wineries, and redwoods—enormous trees hundreds of years old—as well as the mountains. Northern California is beautiful and so different from Southern California."

Peter agreed. "You'll love California, ladies! But if you get jobs at the aircraft factories, you won't have a lot of time to sightsee."

Charlie added, "Did we thank you ladies for helping us win the war? We need nurses, secretaries, and factory workers building planes, keeping things organized, and taking care of our wounded soldiers and sailors."

We chatted back and forth. When we rolled into the depot in San Diego, California, we felt tired, but we'd made some new friends and taken care of each other. We gathered our things and followed Mrs. Jackson. Then we stepped off the train, assisted by a porter, Peter, and Charlie, who reached up and helped us down.

Peter and Charlie offered to get our luggage, so we gave our claim tickets to them, and they went to get their bags and ours.

We waved goodbye to the rest of the soldiers and sailors.

Mrs. Jackson's daughter arrived with her three little ones, all happy to see grandma. Mrs. Jackson smiled and looked at me. "Don't you worry, Grace. You're going to make your parents proud. I've enjoyed getting to know you girls." Then she turned to greet her family.

We felt excited, standing there and looking around the big train depot. The soldiers returned with our suitcases and their duffel bags, with the help of a porter. Peter gave him a tip before I could open my purse. I'd never tipped before and watched him carefully.

Peter took our picture with my camera, and I took their pictures, too, and promised to send them a photo. They'd tucked their addresses in our hands earlier. "Maybe you'd have time to write to a lonely soldier?" Violet and I did.

Then Ed walked towards us, waving. Peter and Charlie stayed with us until he reached us and helped carry our luggage to his car, not far away. They shook hands, and he thanked them for taking care of us. Then the two soldiers took off, waving.

Ed looked at us with a smile. "I'm not surprised you three charmed a few soldiers to help with your suitcases. Good work. I wondered how we would manage." He shut the trunk. I got in the front seat, and the twins climbed in the back of his 1940 four-door Ford sedan. We'd arrived in California!

That's enough for now.

I packed up the tape recorder and tapes. "Your trip sounds like fun, especially with all of those handsome soldiers and sailors!"

Aunt Violet chuckled, "Oh my, yes, we liked Mrs. Jackson. But we got tired, traveling like that, without having a bed to lie down in and sleep."

We chatted, drank more tea, and laughed at her kitten's antics. I cleaned up the dishes with her, still chatting.

However, my mind was working overtime. Listening to Grandma Grace talking about her experiences going to California with her sisters had inspired me with a creative way to complete the quilt exhibit. What if I incorporated oral history?

I talked with Carl the next day, and then the administrator of the Prairie View Senior Center, and they loved my idea. I planned to interview the women who knew about quilting, helped create quilts or owned old family quilts. Many of the people who donated quilts to the museum were also happy to be interviewed.

I needed help to do all the interviews, so I asked Tiara, who taught Oral Communications. She worked at the local radio station, KJJW, had a wonderful voice and personality, and had lots of experience interviewing people. We developed a list of interview questions. Then, Tiara recruited a group of her students, and we introduced them to the group of women at the Prairie View Senior Center.

The students captured the remarks of the women answering the interview questions using their digital devices while looking at pictures of the quilts for the exhibit. Several women showed us their treasured family quilts and talked about the stories behind them. Some came to the college for their interviews, while others showed up at *The Jubilee Times* or the *Jubilee County Museum*. Students visited the Prairie View Senior Center for a few of the interviews.

Eleven

The Power of Women's Voices

"Family secrets are like vampires. They never really die, and can always come back to bite you."

~*Alberta J. McMorris*

*T*iara sipped her coffee as she graded papers in the adjunct office. "By the way, my students are still talking about how much fun they're having interviewing women for the quilt exhibit. I'm adding an oral history assignment to the syllabus, and they're going to go back to see their *quilt ladies* one more time and then share their favorite story as a speech, with permission, of course." Then she paused for another sip of coffee. "Girl, you need to apply for the writing position."

I nodded. "I think Shelly should apply, too."

Shelly agreed. "Yes, I applied a few days ago."

Tiara gave me one of her intense looks with her big brown eyes and expressive face. "So, what about you, Gracie? You want to be an adjunct forever?"

I opened and shut my mouth.

Shelly saved me. "Time for class." She packed up her bag.

Gratefully, I did the same while Tiara chuckled as she bent down to pick up her bag, her long natural curls shifting.

I'd tried to do an application, honestly. More than once I brought up my resume on my laptop and attempted to compose a cover letter. I stared at the screen for twenty minutes, looking at the two job ads. Certainly, I wanted a full-time job someday, with benefits. Didn't everyone? But I didn't think I wanted either of these jobs.

A move to Des Moines? A full-time writing job, with all those papers to grade and committee work? Giving up the museum and not being able to help at the newspaper?

I focused on juggling my three jobs and kept making my to-do lists each day. But somehow, I never crossed out "do the application for the Des Moines job" and "do the application for JCC job."

In the meantime, Steve didn't text or call, and I didn't contact him. Life seemed too short to argue every time we spoke. I talked to Shelly about the situation.

"Steve should know he can't dictate your career. He probably believes he knows best, and you would love the job and be closer to him. I'd love to see you get a full-time job here, but you wouldn't be in the adjunct office anymore, you'd have a lot of committee work, and you'd have to give up the museum job. I don't have to ask how you feel about that, do I?" Her kind blue eyes made me want to cry.

"I don't want to leave town. I'd like to have benefits, but right now I'm doing okay. I love Steve, but he makes me crazy every time we're together," I managed.

Shelly dug a stack of papers out of her bag. "Trust your instincts, Gracie." Before I could reply, a student came in asking for her help with an essay.

I walked into my literature class looking forward to our discussion of "A Rural Community," a short story by Iowa author Ruth Suckow.

As the slideshow came up, Jimmy asked, "Uh, Miss O'Connor. Do we get extra credit for this one? I mean, this story is twenty pages long!" Others laughed, while Sarah spoke up, "But I loved the story."

"Yes, twenty pages is a lot for a short story," I conceded. "But it's worth it! The story describes the woods, fields, and farmland surrounding this small Iowa town, as well as the characters so well. And bonus—my grandma met Ruth Suckow when Grandma Grace went up to Cedar Falls to attend the Iowa State Teachers College."

A few people looked confused. Jeremy raised his hand. "I thought Iowa State College was in Ames."

I nodded. "The Iowa State Teachers College is the old name of the University of Northern Iowa. Suckow gave a lecture at the college while Grandma attended there. She felt thrilled to meet her favorite author. Grandma read and collected all of Suckow's books, so I read most of them as a teenager."

I started the slideshow. "Ruth Suckow, a minister's daughter, lived in cities across the state, including Hawarden, Grinnell, Earlville, Manchester, Cedar Falls, and Davenport. She authored short stories, journal articles, novels, and poetry. Famous editor H. L. Mencken once declared Ruth Suckow "was unquestionably the most remarkable woman writing short stories in the Republic." While Mencken acted as the editor of two literary magazines—*The Smart Set* and *The Mercury*—he published every story Ms. Suckow ever sent him."

""A Rural Community" is a story about Ralph, who visits his foster parents after many years of being away. A journalist, he has traveled the world. Remember, she wrote this story in 1924, so he must have covered the news from World War One. He gets off the train in the morning and must ask the stationmaster for directions to his parent's house because they moved into town after retiring from farming, and he hasn't been there before."

I put the discussion questions up on the projector and walked around the room, hearing comments from the small groups.

"This story begins and ends with the guy getting off and back on the train," Jacob pointed out. "That was cool."

"I laughed when his dad talked about Ralph's high school girl-friend. Man, I could see my parents asking me about my old girlfriend if I showed up thirty and single," Jimmy grinned at his group members.

"His adopted brothers and sisters seemed shy, but his parents were sweet, and his Mom kept telling him he belonged to them because he was one of their kids." Samantha's comment deserved attention.

I stopped walking. "Yes! This is important. What do we find out? This couple raised him. He left home because he didn't know if he fit in. But talking to his parents, what does he discover?"

Sarah spoke. "He's connected to his family, and they are all connected to the land." She looked around, and her small group nodded in agreement.

"If he gets tired of traveling, he can come home," suggested Jeremy. "Yeah, and there's a place in the cemetery for him, too."

"His parents didn't forget about him. His mom kept all his articles in a scrapbook," Ryan remarked.

"The description of the countryside, the trees, and the sky made me feel like I'm in church, sort of, if I'm making sense," Sarah mused.

I asked, "Have a favorite descriptive paragraph?"

Two people raised their hands.

Jimmy's hand shot up, so I called on him.

Jimmy read:

And he knew the food! The platter of fried chicken, the mashed potatoes with the butter making a little golden hollow, the awkward bowl of gravy, the big slices of good home-made Iowa bread, the cucumber pickles, sweet pickles, beet pickles, red jelly, honey, corn relish, in a succession of little glass dishes that kept him so busy passing he hardly knew when to eat.

He leaned back in his chair. "Grandma makes all those pickle things, and I like most of them." A couple of people laughed and nodded.

"Let's hear from Sarah next." I turned to her.

"The last sentence is my favorite. I can shut my eyes and pretend I'm on a train at night, moving past my grandpa's farm."

Then, she read:

But all night long, as he lay half sleeping, swinging lightly with the motion of the train, he was conscious of that silent spreading country outside, over which changes passed like the clouds above the pastures; and it gave him a deep quietude.

Several people nodded. "Cool."

"The last sentence is one of my favorites too." I continued. "One reason I love this story is it's descriptive, not just of the Iowa countryside, but of his family. Their connection to the land makes him feel connected, too. Remember the line, *Somehow it pleased him now to think of how deeply rooted they were.*"

And then, I thought of my ancestors, breaking ground for four generations here in Jubilee Junction. I felt connected to them and to the good Iowa farmland my family-owned, and Uncle Vern and my brother Mark still farmed.

We skipped ahead a few pages to the end of the story.

"This is the opposite of an action-adventure story," I told them. "It's a quiet, internal kind of story. Ralph gets back on the train, but what has happened to him? He's reconnected with his family, and the Iowa countryside." Then I read the last passage.

But he was aware that since he had stepped off the train in the morning, the current of his thoughts had been changed. He felt steadied, deeply satisfied. He looked toward the dark pastures beyond the row of dusky willow trees. They widened slowly into the open country which lay silent, significant, motionless, immense, under the stars, with its sense of something abiding.

"Now, for your assignment. Please write a couple of paragraphs about how this short story made you feel about living in Iowa, what you noticed from our literary terms—can you identify ten?—and why the story seems to connect with us, even after 100 years. Turn it in online and then we'll talk about your responses in small groups next class."

Students left in twos and threes, still talking about the story. I smiled as I walked to the office to switch bags. I was going to enjoy my literature class this semester.

Twelve

More Drama with Aunt Vera

"Above all, be the heroine of your life, not the victim."
~Nora Ephron

$\mathcal{I}$ worked hard and collapsed each night on the couch, where Agatha let me know she felt neglected. My freezer held a few Lean Cuisine frozen meals, and when I tired of them, I stopped by Aunt Shirley's Cafe for takeout or a quick meal there.

On Monday evening, I finished up my taco salad and stood up to put the takeout container in the trash. I finished refilling Agatha's water dish when my cell phone rang. I didn't recognize the number, and instantly regretted picking up, as a familiar voice assaulted my ears.

"Gracie? This is your Great-Aunt Vera. My sister Violet moved into some fancy retirement place in town and cleaned out the farmhouse a few weeks back. I figure she gave you the big wicker basket and quilt."

I exhaled. "Oh. Hello, Aunt Vera. It's so nice of you to call."

I heard her shrill bark of laughter and then her voice, harsh and insulting. "Yes, I'm sure you're delighted. Now, look here. All the stuff in the basket belongs in the trash or better yet, the burn barrel—especially the California quilt—if you ask me. No sense stirring up trouble with talking about the past."

"I don't know what nonsense Violet is telling you, but I'd be happy to send you some money to ship the basket and quilt to me at my daughter's house. Your grandma Grace had no sense at all giving the basket to you—it should have been mine!" Her voice grew angrier with each sentence until she shouted the last sentence.

I realized my hand trembled as I held the iPhone away from my face. For a moment, I felt five years old again. Then, I thought, *Wait a second. Did Aunt Vera just say her sister Violet was telling me nonsense? Grandma Grace had no sense?*

In the space of two sentences, I went from being afraid to being angry and stood up straighter. "Aunt Vera, you can stop talking right there. Yes, I have the basket with the quilt, and I'm keeping it. Aunt Violet would never tell me lies, and neither would Grandma Grace!"

I almost dropped the phone because my voice shook. My whole body trembled with emotion. My curls were vibrating. Agatha meowed, sensing my discomfort.

Another voice said something in the background, and Aunt Vera said petulantly, "I'm making this phone call—you can't stop me!"

Then came a scuffling sound, and an exasperated voice, "Mother, you're getting yourself worked up. Just sit down there, please?" I recognized the voice as Donna. "Gracie, dear? This is your cousin, Donna. I hope my mother didn't upset you. I told her not to call. She's been fuming ever since we were down to visit you folks."

"Oh, Donna, hello." I sat down in the nearest kitchen chair, my anger dissipating but still trembling. "I'm sorry she's upset."

"Don't you worry about her. You tell your sweet Mama hi for me, won't you?" In a softer voice, "and Aunt Violet, please? Alright, I need to go. Mother? I'm coming."

I waited a few minutes for my heart to stop pounding, made myself a *cuppa* chamomile tea, and called Mom.

She sighed. "I'm so sorry! We thought we did such a decent job keeping the sisters apart when Donna brought Vera to Iowa, but Aunt Vera's held a grudge about that basket, and only she and Violet know why. Donna is a wonderful daughter—she doesn't deserve this nonsense. I'll call her tomorrow and see how she's doing. How are you doing?"

I picked up my cup of tea with a trembling hand and felt foolish. "Aunt Vera has such a nasty, demanding voice. I didn't like the way she talked about her sisters. She told me that the things in

Grandma Grace's basket should all be burned, and we shouldn't talk or stir up the past. She would pay me to ship them to her. As if I would ever listen to her. I feel so sorry for Donna. How does she put up with her?"

"She's a strong woman. Her father would be so proud of her. I can't imagine it's easy to have her mother living there. Are you okay?"

"I'll *be* okay, Mom. Thanks for listening. How did Grandma Grace and Aunt Violet deal with her all these years?"

After I got off the phone, I wondered briefly about Donna's father. He died in World War Two. Donna was raised by her mother and a second husband named John, who died many years ago. She had two half-brothers and two stepbrothers, and like me, lots of aunts, uncles, and cousins.

The next day, I stopped by Aunt Shirley's Café for supper. Aunt Shirley listened to my story over a steaming bowl of her chicken noodle soup and a large corn muffin.

She remembered, "My mother told us to stay away from Vera at big holiday dinners or family reunions. She always struck me as a selfish woman who did whatever she wanted to do for most of her life and then paid the price. She seemed nothing like her sisters."

Before making eye contact with me, Aunt Shirley scanned the counter to be sure no one needed her. "Did I ever tell you what she saw when Donna was just a little thing, only three years old? She woke up from her nap on Grandma's bed after Thanksgiving dinner and wandered out into the living room. She saw Aunt Violet sitting there and reached up with those tiny arms, so Violet picked her up and cuddled her."

"I would pick Aunt Violet any day!" I tried not to slurp my soup.

Aunt Shirley nodded and continued, "Meanwhile, Vera complained something fierce about something in another room. There's something wrong with the woman when even her daughter preferred Violet. Don't worry, Gracie. I can't think of anyone in this family who would defend her!"

As she turned away, she gave me a naughty grin. "Don't worry about your Great-Aunt Vera. She's too old to drive herself down here, so she shouldn't bother you anymore."

I almost choked on my soup at the thought of my elderly aunt driving her daughter's big truck from Minnesota to Jubilee Junction.

I giggled. "Thanks, Aunt Shirley."

When I got home, Mark called, and he was angry. "Mom told me about your phone call the other night. Aunt Vera had better stay away from you and Aunt Violet. No wonder she moved to Minnesota. None of her family can stand to be around her. Uncle Vern told me a few stories, and she's always caused trouble." As always, he went into big brother mode, ready to take on anyone who threatened his younger sister, bringing back memories I didn't like to think about.

Then, on Wednesday I visited to Aunt Violet. When I told her about the phone call from Vera, her facial expression changed.

"Becky mentioned the phone call. My sister has some nerve calling you and wanting you to pack up the basket and ship it to her—the basket would make for quite a bonfire now, wouldn't it? I'm going to have to talk to Vern."

Then she gazed at me. "She upset you, didn't she? But you're your grandma's granddaughter—and your mama's daughter, too. You're tougher than you know. Your whole family would stand up for you, and Vern and I won't let her bully you."

I mentioned the story Aunt Shirley told me, and her eyes grew warm with the memory.

"I wanted to take Donna home. This was before we had children. Bob brought us a blanket and covered us up, nice and cozy. Donna sat there and snuggled for another half hour before we left. We cuddled at several family dinners before our own babies came along. She was such a sweet little girl. I'll call her tomorrow. Now, let's listen to our next tape."

I felt better because Aunt Violet knew just what to say. Aunt Vera was an angry old woman who knew how to push people's buttons, including mine.

I poured tea into the cups Aunt Violet set out, and she placed freshly baked brownies on small plates. We settled into our chairs, and I pressed *play* on the tape recorder.

Thirteen

The Sisters Arrive

"The beginning is the most important part of the work."
~*Plato*

*Tape #5, Checking into the Boardinghouse
Grandma Grace sounded excited.*

Ed drove us to Chula Vista, to the boarding house, a large three-story home with a big porch. Half a dozen people sat in wooden chairs as we walked up the steps with our suitcases. They called out a cheery, "Hello."

I took a second look, grinned, and called out "Mary!" as a young woman with wavy blonde hair stood up, holding Eddie, a sweet little boy with his daddy's blue eyes and dark blonde hair.

"Hi, hi, hi," he called and clapped his hands. "Daddy!"

The front door opened, and Mary's Aunt Mae and Uncle Henry Hamilton greeted us. Ed did the introductions.

Mrs. Hamilton laughed. "Call us Aunt Mae and Uncle Henry. And here's Hank and Helen." Two teenagers appeared and waved hello. Hank and Helen looked to be thirteen or fourteen years old. "I imagine you're hungry."

We followed Aunt Mae to the big dining room table, where she laid out a feast of a hearty vegetable beef soup, crusty bread, and fresh fruit, while Mary and Ed sat at the table and chatted with us.

They'd just moved back into the boarding house themselves. The Navy needed Ed's mechanical skills, and he'd leave for boot camp in a few weeks. Mary and Eddie would stay with Aunt Mae and

Uncle Henry while he deployed. They had plenty of room with three empty bedrooms upstairs vacated by their grown children when they went off to war. Mary would have the car and family nearby, and Eddie loved the boarding house with so many people to entertain him, including his teenage cousins, Hank and Helen.

After we ate, we signed our rental agreement and paid for the first month, plus meals. We also handed over our ration cards so Aunt Mae could buy groceries for our meals at the boarding house. The two teens each grabbed a suitcase, and Uncle Henry grabbed the third. We carried our purses, sweaters, and messenger bags. Aunt Mae and Mary followed us up the stairs to the second floor to show us our rooms and the bathrooms.

The twins shared a room, so I got the smaller room across the hall. A bathroom was at either end of the hallway, and the boarders in the eight bedrooms on the second floor shared them. Aunt Mae provided sheets, blankets, pillows, and towels, so we made up our beds and put our few clothes into the closet and the old chest of drawers. We set our Bibles and the picture of our family on the top of the dresser. Our suitcases fit neatly under our beds.

My room had a twin bed, a small dresser, a tiny table and chair, and a small closet in the corner. There was a window over my desk, where I could sit to write letters home. I could see the backyard with the double clotheslines and victory garden. The scent of oranges and lemons, neatly trimmed grass, and lots of exotic flowers enticed me. California looked and smelled beautiful!

The twins' room was larger, with a window looking out at the front of the house and the street, along with two beds, two dressers, a table, two chairs, and a shared closet.

We walked back downstairs, and Aunt Mae gave us receipts for the first month. She welcomed us and told us a few things about the boarding house and her rules. Rent was due on the first of the month. Men weren't allowed upstairs, but we could visit with gentlemen in the downstairs sitting room. There would be simple choices available for breakfast, with a pot of oatmeal on the stove, cold cereal, fruit, and bread for toast.

We could make a bag lunch of a sandwich and fruit. Supper was at 6 PM. Quiet time was after 9 PM. We could sign up to use one of the two washers in the basement and hang our clothes on the clothesline outside.

We walked upstairs to get ready for bed, suddenly weary.

In the morning, Ed drove Vera and me to the Bartlett Aircraft factory. He introduced us to Mr. Patterson, the manager in charge of hiring. We filled out the paperwork and waited for a brief interview. By the end of our interviews, Mr. Patterson hired Vera as a secretary, helping to organize invoices, inventory, and payroll.

He hired me as well, and because I knew about electricity, engines, and using tools, I secured a spot using a jig and a riveting tool called the Chicago Squeezer. Later, a photographer took pictures of a woman riveting and nicknamed her *Rosie the Riveter*. Then Ed took us shopping. I needed to buy some slacks, shirts, and heavy shoes. I also found some red ankle socks and a couple of cute headscarves. I added them to the pile and spent $40 of my cash. I purchased a toolbox and just a few of the tools on the list and spent another $17.00.

Ed told me he'd give me a couple of spare tools and when he left, he would give me the rest. If my lead-man needed me to have anything else, I could buy them at the company store. I hid $150 of Grandpa's $200 and another $150 of my savings in a pocket of the suitcase under my bed, so if I needed something, I could buy it. The money belt had another $50 in it. I determined to use my money sparingly.

Mary asked Aunt Mae and her daughter to watch Eddie and took Violet on the bus to the hospital at Camp Kearney. The head nurse hired Violet immediately for the surgical unit. She needed several uniforms and sturdy shoes, spending $30. Vera acted smug because her new job required no outlay of cash for clothing. However, she loved to shop, and bought two new skirts and three blouses and found some nice low heels, spending $25 of her cash.

We ate supper at our boarding house and got to know some of the other women staying there, including two women who worked at Bartlett's, a woman named Maria, and a girl my age named Reva. Two other girls worked on the base. Aunt Mae's teenagers helped serve the meal—a delicious chicken and noodles dish—and cleaned up.

The next day was Friday. We walked around town with Maria who didn't work until the third shift. We took a bus to the base so Violet could drop off some paperwork and then we walked around the parts of the base open to civilians. Finally, we took another bus back to Chula Vista, which once boasted of having wonderful lemon orchards, according to Aunt Mae. I sniffed and thought I still smelled a citrus aroma in the air.

Maria told us about the town on the bus ride. She'd lived here for a year. Chula Vista's population exploded from 5,000 to 10,000 with the relocation of Bartlett Aircraft in 1941. The company employed over 9,000 workers and, as more men deployed, women took their places and kept production up. The people in my building worked on the structures around the engines, called nacelles, of the B-24 bombers, sometimes called the Liberators, and the B-17 bombers, also called the Flying Fortress.

Riding past the front gates of Bartlett's aircraft factory, we saw a group of women dressed in slacks and shirts, with scarves tied around their heads. They wore heavy shoes and carried lunch buckets and small toolboxes. Another stream of men and women walked past them, changing shifts.

We got off the bus and walked to the Mission Federal Credit Union and opened checking accounts. Then we took the bus back to the boarding house feeling like kids waiting for the first day of school. Mary showed us the bus schedules.

Saturday, we took in a movie, *Mrs. Miniver*, downtown with Ed and Mary. We munched on popcorn and drank pop. A newsreel reminded us of the dangers of war.

We did our laundry and wrote our first letters home, proudly telling our parents about the boarding house, the town, and our new jobs.

Ed and Mary took us to their Methodist church on Sunday, and we enjoyed the friendly, warm fellowship of the congregation, now a mix of newcomers and local families. We felt at home. Faith had been the cornerstone of our family for many generations. Mary's aunt and uncle belonged to the congregation and sat with us along with Reva. We passed Eddie back and forth and kept him quiet and happy. The service featured lots of singing, a brief scripture reading, some announcements, and a heartfelt sermon about the Good Samaritan.

Pastor Martin and his wife greeted us and welcomed us to the church. He told us he and his wife came here from Illinois eight years ago. We met a few more people in the fellowship hall and then left with Ed and Mary and drove back to the boarding house for lunch.

Afterward, Violet and I sat in one of the big sitting rooms downstairs. Ed and Uncle Henry discussed Ed's orders. After boot camp, Ed would join one of the navy's ships assigned to do repairs on other ships. Uncle Sam needed Ed's mechanical skills.

Ed took me aside later Sunday afternoon. "Grace—will you do me a favor and look after my girl while I'm gone? I know she has Aunt Mae and Uncle Henry, but I feel better knowing you girls are here, too."

"Mary is a wonderful girl and stronger than you think. But yes, we're family, and we'll do everything we can to help her with Eddie and whatever. Don't worry."

"I know she's strong," Ed looked at me. "But if something happens to me, I feel better knowing she has you girls, too."

I promised, and my cousin said, "Let's see if little Eddie is up from his nap yet. I want to teach him how to catch a ball."

As he walked away, I thought, *Mary has a great guy*. I would do all I could to help her while he deployed.

That's enough for now.

Fourteen

A Surprise Date

"My mother told me to be a lady. And for her, that meant be your own person, be independent."

~*Ruth Bader Ginsburg*

The tape clicked off. We grinned at each other. Grandma's voice sounded excited.

"I love all the details. I feel like I can see those rooms in the boardinghouse and the people, too."

"She loved telling stories." Aunt Violet smiled.

We looked at a couple more pages from the photo album. First, a group of soldiers standing in a depot, the three girls with their suitcases with Cousin Ed, another one of a large train depot, and a group of sailors posing for the camera.

She laughed at the photos when I pointed out their short skirts. "That was the style back then. Plus, they needed the fabric for all those uniforms."

Then Aunt Violet raised her eyebrows. "You look tired. Are you feeling all right? You must work day and night. Do you have time for these tapes?"

"I'm fine. This is a busy time of the semester. Plus, we're almost ready for the exhibit to open. You and your friends are all invited, of course, and will be our local celebrities."

"Oh my. You're treating a bunch of little old ladies like celebrities. What would your grandma think of all this fuss? We're all excited, too."

Aunt Violet walked me to the door and gave me a brief hug.

"Don't worry about Vera. You focus on the exhibit. Grace would be so proud of you."

I turned to open the door and saw her kitty saunter down the hallway and then stop behind her. She chuckled, "I think she's getting trained not to go outside."

I walked to my car, a baggie with three brownies in one hand, my purse and the shoebox in the other, weary to the bone but energized after spending time with Aunt Violet—and Grandma Grace.

Saturday afternoon, Steve surprised me by texting he wanted to take me to dinner and a movie. Dressed in sweats, relaxing with Agatha, I'd planned to splurge on pizza and grade papers, so I had to hustle. I showered, did my makeup, and threw on a nice outfit. Then I straightened up my small living room. I was slightly out of breath when I opened the door to greet him.

The date started well with dinner at one of our favorite places, Ruby's, the steak house near the highway. They have the best steaks, salads, homemade rolls—and homemade pies from Aunt Shirley's Cafe.

Then we headed for the theater to see a movie. I settled down, munched on popcorn, and tried to relax. But Steve seemed impatient, and by the time we left, I knew what we would have for dessert.

We walked out of the theater in silence, and he turned to me. "So, did you hear about the job in Des Moines? Set up an interview yet?"

"I checked out the job, but I decided not to apply."

He looked skeptical and hurt. "Why not? I told the HR guy there you would be the ideal candidate."

"You called him? Why? Steve, I don't need someone arranging things for me. I'm not fifteen."

"I tried to help, Gracie." His voice was tight.

We stood in the parking lot by his car and continued to bicker like that for another ten minutes, his voice getting angrier and more impatient by the minute. Then it continued in the car. By the time we reached my house, Steve was shouting, and I'd started to cry.

As soon as he pulled into my driveway, I opened my door and

got out, grabbing my jacket and purse. Steve continued yelling and opened his door to get out. I waved him away, then hurried to my front door and let myself in, while he slammed his car door and took off a little too fast.

I made myself a cuppa tea and called Shelly once I'd calmed down. "Is this too late to talk?"

She sighed. "No, at all. The kids are down for the evening. I graded for an hour and decided to have a glass of wine. Hubby's watching TV. What's going on?"

I sat down at my kitchen table and took a big breath. Agatha sensed my agitation and jumped up on my lap. I found myself unable to speak, beyond saying, "Steve just left."

"Gracie, what's wrong?" she asked as she poured wine into a glass.

I tried not to cry. "Steve just left, angry, because I didn't apply for a job in Des Moines. I thought I loved Steve, but I get so stressed when we're together, I don't know if we're right for each other anymore. He just spent twenty minutes yelling at me." Then I told her about our awful date and argument. I took a tentative sip of my tea.

"Oh, dear. Are you okay?"

"Yes, I will be. I don't know what to think about our relationship anymore."

"Well, I'm not surprised." Shelly took a sip of her wine. "You met at Iowa State. You've grown up since then. Is he a part of your past or your future? Do you share the same goals? I've been wondering how your relationship was doing with you and Steve separated."

"I used to think we were perfect for each other."

"Oh, Gracie—no one is perfect for anyone." Shelly laughed. "We're all self-absorbed. Marriage is demanding work, even between two love birds. College is a wonderful place to meet someone, but you can't compare college to real life. You're not living together and figuring out who cooks and does laundry, pays bills, and gets up in the middle of the night with a sick baby."

Wishing I liked wine more and possessed a bottle of it, I sipped my tea. "I suppose it's crazy we've dated for so many years off and on and never talked seriously about getting married, huh?"

"Well, this thing with your dad's heart attack sort of changed your plans. You might have stayed in Ames otherwise. You could have gotten engaged and moved to Des Moines by now. Who knows?"

After a few minutes, we told each other goodnight.

Shelly had planted a seed in my head. I kept thinking about our conversation and wondering if my relationship with Steve was over. Did I want it to be over?

The next day, I ran into Mark and Kathy at Aunt Shirley's. Kathy walked over to say hello, then sat down when she saw my face. I told her about our terrible date and Shelly's questions. She listened.

"Steve hasn't called or texted since our fight. I can't decide if I want him to or not."

Kathy sighed. "Shelly's right. Coming back to Jubilee Junction, set your life on a different path. You two have broken up several times over the past four years. His patience is running out."

She peered at me more intently. "I remember when you two talked about getting a place in Ames and moving in together. Can I ask something personal? Have you ever been intimate with him?"

I blushed. "No. I told myself I wanted to wait until marriage at first. But looking back, I was afraid. A friend in high school walked down the graduation aisle pregnant. We planned to finish up at Iowa State. She has four kids now, and I'm sure she's happy. But Emily wanted to go to Iowa State with me to study journalism. I didn't want to give up my dreams."

"I understand. One of my friends from high school graduated pregnant, too. But you and Steve seemed to be closer back then, getting along better."

"Yes, we had talked about getting a place together. But then dad suffered his heart attack. Of course, over the past four years, Steve shifted his career goals from being a small-town lawyer to running for political office. He's a state senator's chief of staff right now and learning all he can. I don't want to spend my life going from one political campaign to the next, and I don't want to live in Des Moines." I tore my dinner roll into small pieces.

Kathy looked at me. "Gracie, what *do* you want?"

"He wants more than I do right now. Every time we try to talk about this, we fight. I don't want him to yell at me like that again. I want him to agree to live between here and Des Moines, so we can both do what we want."

She smiled gently. "Don't you think you better try to communicate with him what you just told me? You are in the Communications Department, right?"

I smiled back, despite myself. "Thanks for listening, Kathy."

Mark waved from their table. "Food's here. Hey, Gracie."

I pondered her advice as I finished my meal, my thoughts churning. I waved goodbye and headed home to grade papers and check email.

Later, I climbed into bed and turned off the light. Agatha jumped up and took her place beside me. Silly kitty. She enjoyed sleeping with me more than in her cat bed. As I tried to relax, one question kept coming back to my mind. *Is he part of your past or part of your future?*

Kathy's gentle words echoed, *I think his patience is running out.* I could no longer deny we'd grown apart.

When I finally fell asleep, I dreamed someone brought me a big box of quilts to add to the exhibit at the last minute. Then I was riding on a train with Grandma and her sisters and talking to handsome young soldiers in World War II uniforms. Then, I was interviewing for a job with a stern-looking man from HR who wanted me to fill out a stack of forms. Suddenly, Steve sat behind the desk, demanding I move to Des Moines immediately. And Aunt Vera marched in and started looking for the basket, and she was carrying matches!

I sat up in bed in a panic, half asleep still. What a confusing nightmare. Agatha complained about me disturbing the blankets.

In the morning, I tried to remember the dream. I gathered my things for school, the museum, and the newspaper, and petted Agatha. As I drove to college, I knew I needed to figure out what to do about Steve.

Fifteen

David Visits the Museum

"Character cannot be developed in ease and quiet. Only through experience of trial and suffering can the soul be strengthened, vision cleared, ambition inspired, and success achieved."
~Helen Keller

As September gave way to October, I received half a dozen phone calls and twice as many email messages in response to the insert about the quilt exhibit in last week's issue of *The Jubilee Times*. *The Des Moines Register* planned to send a reporter to the opening of the exhibit. *Iowa Public Radio* wanted to interview me.

When I arrived at the newspaper office, Dad told me he'd received phone calls and email messages from media outlets around central and northeast Iowa as well, so he felt happy.

People purchased extra copies of *The Jubilee Times* edition with the exhibit insert and sent the newspaper to their friends and family who lived out of town. Dad ran extra copies of the insert, pleased for the business.

Family members had suggested he offer print shop services, since the closest place to make copies was thirty miles away in Prairie Falls, but he'd resisted. Now, he talked to Carl about printing a special edition of the newspaper for the exhibit. Several local businesses wanted to include ads in the special edition of the newspaper. He also wanted to create some postcards and a brochure about the exhibit and share the proceeds.

I recruited students to help us with the exhibit, reviewed the details for the reception, borrowed extra chairs and tables, and checked off the items on my list.

I wasn't going to the grocery store for anything more than cat food and milk. I ate many of my meals at Aunt Shirley's café. She knew about the exhibit and told me how proud grandma would be, using the simple power of storytelling to make the quilt exhibit even better. "We can't wait for the exhibit to open, Gracie."

Mom reported chatting with Donna, who apologized for her mother's phone call. They talked for half an hour. Mom assured her no one blamed her, and they promised to check in more frequently.

Then Uncle Vern called me. "Gracie, Becky told me my sister Vera called you last week about your grandma's big basket. I called and chatted with Donna, who told me she was sorry her mother upset you. I told Donna not to worry. Afterward, I talked to my sister and told her directly to leave you alone. She has done enough damage to my family."

I thanked him and assured him I felt fine.

"Good for you. Vera broke our mother's heart with her escapades in California, and whatever happened out there hurt Violet, too. After the war, we didn't talk about those years. Hold on, Aunt Maggie wants to say hello."

Aunt Maggie's voice warmed my soul. "Gracie, love, how are you?"

"I'm better now, talking to you and Uncle Vern. Thanks, Aunt Maggie. Aunt Vera said some terrible things about Grandma and Aunt Violet and made me angry, so I stopped being scared." I confessed. "You'll be proud of me. I made a nice cuppa tea and then called Mom."

She sighed. "Vera has always troubled me. She has such a sense of entitlement. I'm glad you got angry. Better anger than fear, I always say. Fear paralyzes us. Anger gets us moving. I learned to use anger to keep moving during the war when German planes were dropping bombs on us. Here's a hug over the phone! See you soon."

"Thanks, Aunt Maggie." I told her, "Here's a hug back."

As I refilled Agatha's water dish and folded some laundry, I reflected on how special Uncle Vern and Aunt Maggie were to me. Uncle Vern held me on his lap and gave me my first taste of chocolate ice cream while Grandpa Richard took photos, and then they switched, and Grandpa fed me some strawberry ice cream and Uncle Vern took photos. According to Aunt Maggie, I waved the spoon, "Yum," to both. Now that my grandparents were gone, I appreciated Aunt Maggie and Uncle Vern even more.

The next afternoon, I worked downstairs, looking at several new quilts and updating my spreadsheet. David called to ask if I would be at the museum today because he wanted to look at our archives. He was researching Iowa's involvement in World War II and wondered whether German prisoners of war had worked at any local farms.

I met him at the front desk. We walked back to our archives room where I helped him locate some materials about POW camps in the area, and we chatted about mutual interests.

"How are you liking Jubilee Junction?" I spread half a dozen resources out on the long table.

"I'm liking the area a lot. I've checked out some of those walking trails, and I enjoyed the old Train Depot's Visitor Center. I'll probably go back because I love old trains—I even love movies about old trains."

I was caught off-guard. "Really? Like *North by Northwest?*"

David looked up. "You're a fan? Yes, *North by Northwest* is one of my all-time favorite movies. Hitchcock was a genius."

"Me, too. Growing up in Jubilee Junction and hearing all the stories about the role the railroad played in the 1860s, transporting troops and supplies, and then again during the two world wars, I was probably more interested in trains than the average person. As a teenager, I would fantasize about being Eva Marie Saint and going west to Mount Rushmore to meet Cary Grant."

Then I blushed, feeling silly. "Of course, I loved all the footage onboard the train and at Mount Rushmore, too."

David chuckled. "Me, too. I fantasized about the movie, too. Not so much about *meeting* Cary Grant, of course. More like *being* him. Handsome, cool, resourceful, you know? Hey, he could hide inside the nose of one of our presidents at Mount Rushmore, and he got the girl. He wasn't a nerdy teenager—awkward on the basketball court and better at the debate club."

I laughed. "We could have hung out as teenagers." He skimmed an article and nodded.

"We also have the Historical Society in town. I could call for you to see what they have on World War II and German POWs."

He looked up. "Thank you. I think I've found a couple of articles here."

Then I mentioned the newspaper archives at *The Jubilee Times*, and his eyes lit up.

"They might have some articles about the German POWs. I can also ask my Great-Uncle Vern what he knows. He'd just graduated from High School during World War II and ended up in England in the Army Air Force. Vern served as the navigator on a B-17 Flying Fortress bomber and brought back a British war bride, my Aunt Maggie."

"I'd like to see those archives, and I would love to meet your uncle and aunt. They lived through the war. What a remarkable perspective. Thank you."

I showed him the photocopier in the corner and promised to ask Dad and Uncle Vern about the archives and get back to him. He gave me a business card and promised to come back to see the exhibit. Then, one volunteer raised her hand, and I walked over to help, tucking the card in my pocket.

Sixteen

Avocados and Bus Rides

*"We learned about dignity and decency—that how hard you
work matters more than how much you make... that helping
others means more than just getting ahead yourself."*
~Michelle Obama

$\mathcal{I}$ visited Aunt Violet on Wednesday. She
frowned when she saw me.

"Are you taking care of yourself, Gracie? You look tired. Are you
up for this today?"

"I'm okay, Aunt Violet. I want to hear the next chapter!"

She had arranged tea and cookies on the table, and we settled
down in anticipation. Beatrix played nearby, ignoring us.

Tape #6, Settling into New Routines
Grandma's voice was relaxed and happy.

Violet and I loved living in Chula Vista and figured out which bus to
take to get to the aircraft factory or base, where to go to buy clothes
or shoes, and who to trust at the boarding house. You didn't need a
book or radio program to be entertained in the downstairs sitting
rooms. Just sit by one of those girls, wanting to hear your radio show
or the news about the war, and you would get an earful of gossip
about who is running around on her husband, spending too much
money, or keeping a bottle of wine under her bed to help her sleep.

Mother frowned on listening to gossip and warned us girls about
the risks of gossiping, and now I understood why. We had a few

minor incidents of gossip at the boarding house, but Aunt Mae kept an eye on the girls most likely to offend.

Aunt Mae soon became like a second mother. She made sure we ate properly and took care of ourselves. She possessed an uncanny knack for knowing which of her boarders needed some extra attention, and who might be a troublemaker. I saw her watching Vera with a worried eye several times.

Having Ed, Mary, and Eddie around helped us adjust to life in California those first few weeks. As we spent time together, Eddie grew fond of us, and we loved him dearly. He called us "Gwace, Bilet, and Bewa."

After our big shopping trip, the three of us girls sat down with notebooks and pencils and tried to calculate our budgets. We would earn about $120 a month, and I might make more with overtime. We made about $.75 an hour, which doesn't sound like much to you, but the money stretched further back in the 1940s. Our rooms cost $40 each per month. Bus passes cost us $5 a month to get to work. We spent another $20 a month for breakfast and dinner at the boarding house, and packed our lunches to work, for $65 in expenses, leaving $55 to save, and spend carefully.

We were proud to be three young women in the workplace earning our keep, but we were part of the home front, building planes and taking care of injured sailors. I brought home around $33 a week. Violet made $35 a week, and Vera made $32 at first, but we all got a raise in a few months. We knew we weren't earning as much as the men did, but we were happy. Remember that a dollar back in 1943 would translate to about $16 today.

Life fell into a routine for us. During the week, we got up early, ate breakfast, packed lunch, said hi to the family, and caught a bus. After work, we cleaned up, ate supper, played with Eddie, visited with Mary, Aunt Mae, or Reva, read a book, or chatted on the porch. We would clean our rooms and do laundry on Saturday morning and catch a movie in the afternoon. Movies only cost thirty cents, and for another quarter, we could get popcorn and a drink. Translate that into today's dollars and the thirty-cent movie would be about five dollars in 2008.

We attended church with Uncle Henry, Aunt Mae and their children, and Reva in one car, and Ed, Mary, Eddie, and the three of us in another car. We ate lunch with the whole boarding house family, wrote letters home, and got our clothes ready for the new week ahead.

Monday morning, I got up at 5:30, grabbed breakfast downstairs, packed a simple lunch, and headed for my bus to get to the factory by seven. Reva and I took the bus together and enjoyed chatting on the way to and from work. She worked in another department, but we worked the same hours. Sometimes Vera rode with us, but most of the time, she took the next bus since the office didn't open until 8:00.

Reva and I grew to be close friends. She came from Los Angeles, and her grandparents farmed near a small town called Escondido, about thirty-five miles away, where they grew avocados and oranges. Reva came to work at Bartlett's six months before we arrived. Two of her brothers had deployed. Reva possessed a sweet, friendly personality and offered to show us around town.

Violet's hours depended on which shift she worked at the base hospital, so we rarely saw each other until dinner unless she worked the night shift. Violet loved working at the base, however, because she was learning so much.

Vera and I made friends with other women at the boarding house. After supper, we took turns helping with the dishes, reading, or writing letters, listening to the radio with news about the war, and getting our clothes ready for the morning.

After we received our first paychecks, we felt independently wealthy. We' deposited them in our checking accounts at a Credit Union a couple of blocks away, set up frugal budgets, and focused on our new jobs. We paid Aunt Mae for our rooms ahead and treated Ed and Mary to a movie and fish sandwiches down on the waterfront. Aunt Mae's daughter, Helen, offered to watch the baby.

I took pictures of the boarding house, our cousins, our rooms, the view from our rooms, the outside of the factory, the church, and the ocean. California was a magical place—and so different from Iowa. Chula Vista means *cool view*, and when I walked around our neighborhood and downtown, I felt amazed. The trees and flowers seemed so different from the Midwest. Palm trees, exotic flowers, and towards the marsh, tall grasses, a beautiful coastline, and all the bustling of a larger city with the industries supporting the war effort. I started a photo album, and dropping off a roll of the film became one of my favorite splurges, with double prints so I could send some home.

Reva and I took a bus ride one Saturday to visit her grandparents. The ride took about an hour, and I enjoyed the scenery on the way there and back. Reva's grandmother's eyes were the same beautiful shape and color as her granddaughter's, and her grandfather seemed proud of all his children and grandchildren. He showed me photos of them, including photographs of her brothers and cousins in their uniforms.

Then we walked around the farm. They didn't have animals or row crops as we did back in Iowa. The avocados grew on beautiful trees, and I took pictures of them, amazed at the sight. They also managed an orange grove. Their way of farming differed greatly from the farming I was used to and smelled better! I took pictures of Reva with her grandparents in the orange grove.

I'd never eaten an avocado before and found the buttery and mellow flavor delicious. Reva's grandma served us chicken salad sandwiches, along with a simple salad of chunks of avocado drizzled with olive oil, balsamic vinegar, salt, and pepper over lettuce. We took four ripe avocados with us back to the boarding house along with a small bag of oranges.

Six weeks after we arrived, in mid-July, Ed left for his basic training. Afterward, he would go through another eight to ten weeks of specialty training, and then deploy.

Mary and Eddie saw him off with Uncle Henry on Monday morning. Eddie waved "bye-bye Daddy," and Mary tried not to cry. Uncle Henry held the little boy. "Let's look at the big bus from over here," and gave her a moment to collect herself.

When Reva and I walked into the boarding house Monday afternoon after work, Eddie was playing with a couple of toys in the sitting room while his mother helped Aunt Mae with supper, and Helen watched him. He ran up to us. "Daddy go bye-bye big bus."

Uncle Henry sat reading his newspaper nearby and looked up at us. "He's been saying the same thing all afternoon."

Reva and I put our work bags down and got down on the floor to play with him.

"Hi Eddie. We're home from work. Did you show Uncle Henry your car?"

Eddie squatted down, grabbed the car, and made a face. "Zoom zoom. Unkie Henwy lookie me."

Uncle Henry put down the newspaper and smiled. "Why yes, your car goes fast."

Helen and Reva both laughed and clapped for Eddie. I walked out to the kitchen to say hi to Aunt Mae and Mary. I hugged Mary and asked how she was doing.

She sighed. "I'm so glad to have family here." She looked at Aunt Mae, who smiled as she stirred something. "Keeping busy helps."

I nodded. I wrote letters home each week and told my parents not to worry. We were working hard, going to church, and making friends. It was wonderful living at the boarding house, with Eddie and Mary, and Aunt Mae and Uncle Henry right upstairs.

Their little birds were spreading their wings and flying!

That's enough for now.

Seventeen

Audio Clips & Phone numbers

"Every broken heart has screamed at one time or another: Why can't you see who I truly am?"

~*Shannon L. Alder*

*T*he tape recorder stopped. Aunt Violet had a few tears in her eyes. She grabbed a Kleenex, saying, "I'm all right, Gracie. I'm just remembering those days. We felt happy to be helping our boys defeat the enemy, and in my case, taking care of the injured soldiers and sailors." Beatrix, who was sleeping in her lap, woke up, yawned, and licked its tiny paws.

I helped Aunt Violet clean up from our snack and boxed up the tape recorder and tapes. I loved hearing Grandma's voice. I found myself caught up in the story, wondering what was going to happen next?

After leaving Aunt Violet's house, I stopped by the newspaper to work on a couple of ads. I felt panic creeping in, no matter how many items I checked off my To-Do list. With just a week until midterm, the semester seemed to be slipping by more quickly than seemed possible.

Mom came out of her office, and we chatted, catching her up on the story revealed by the tapes.

"Oh, the story is like a soap opera. I can't wait for you to call me and tell me about the latest adventure. I've listened to the first few tapes, and you can pick them up. Your dad listened with me. We loved the train trip! I made my copies. These are so precious. We need to digitize them. Your dad is researching options, of course."

Then Mom inspected me. "Are you alright? You look tired."

"My quilt exhibit opens in two weeks. I promised to write a column last week, but Steve came down to Jubilee Junction over the weekend and wanted to take me to a movie and dinner. I hadn't expected to see him, so I was *in a pickle*, as Grandma Grace used to say. I'll be okay. I just have a lot on my plate."

"Don't worry. We can fill in something else for the column. Everyone's excited about the exhibit. How are things going with Steve?"

I hugged her. "Look, I need to get to work. I'm not avoiding the question. But things are fine with Steve. Don't worry."

Several days passed, and I still didn't get a text or call. We texted several times a day until our argument Saturday night and usually spoke by phone three or four nights a week. I decided not to contact him until I could sort out my mixed emotions. My parents wisely decided not to comment, and I busied myself with midterm grading and the last details of the quilt exhibit.

I checked out the writing position at the college and decided not to apply because it involved teaching five sections of two different writing classes. I loved teaching my literature class and didn't want to give up my jobs at the museum or writing for *The Jubilee Times*, because I enjoyed them.

When I told Tiara about my decision not to apply for the writing position, she nodded. "I wasn't sure if the position was a good fit for you. But girl, keep your eyes open!" She gave me one of her famous looks.

I asked myself, *Should I be afraid or amused?* I settled on humor and saluted. "Aye, aye, Captain."

Tiara rewarded me with a small smile as she looked back down at her stack of speeches to grade.

By Tuesday there was still no word from Steve. I felt depressed. Did I miss him or just the idea of having a boyfriend? I didn't know, which also troubled me.

I walked to the campus library to return a book. David sat at one of the computer stations using a database. He looked up and greeted me. I sat down, and we chatted for a few minutes. Before I left, he asked me for my phone number and gave me his.

"So far, you and Carl are my only friends in Jubilee Junction, along with Aunt Shirley, of course, and my landlord," he explained. "I don't want to make Carl or Aunt Shirley feel bad, but you're a lot prettier and better company." He grinned, and we both laughed.

I headed for the museum around noon. I was meeting six students from Tiara's speech class today to edit the audio clips for the quilt exhibit. One student, Clay, found the best software for editing audio and showed up with the software loaded on his laptop.

"Hey, Miss O'Connor. This software's going to work great. I played with it last night," he said as he entered the back door with his backpack slung over his shoulder.

"Hi, all. Clay, that's great news! And thank you for finding something free."

Two students who carpooled with him came in and followed us down the hall. The other three students arrived, and we walked down the steps together, talking. I'd already downloaded the software to three museum laptops.

We settled ourselves around a large table in my basement workroom and divided up the files between the three computers.

While they worked in pairs, I walked around to answer questions or preview an audio clip. In between, I fussed with my clipboard, showing the layout of the ten stations with netbooks, listing the women interviewed, along with the quilts being displayed.

At the entrance to the exhibit, we planned to have signage with quotes about quilts, including Grandma Grace's, "Every quilt has a story." As we worked on the audio clips, the students told me about their experiences helping with the interviews.

"Your Great-Aunt Violet is friendly. I enjoyed meeting her."

"Mom brought out an old quilt from her grandma, and we talked for an hour."

"I didn't know they could make quilts in different ways—Janice kept talking about tying knots."

"I thought quilts just kept you warm. There's a lot of history and storytelling involved."

We finished work, uploaded files to a Google Drive folder, and relaxed for a few minutes, then I checked my watch. "Let me show you some changes I made since last time," I suggested, and we walked upstairs to look at the exhibit mockup in the workroom.

Wednesday morning, Agatha played with her toys and mewed loudly as I headed for the front door. I reached down and petted her. "Have fun! I'll see you later. You have plenty of food and water."

When I walked into the adjunct office, Tiara looked up and smiled good morning.

"You have a minute?" I asked, as I set my travel mug down on the desk, dropped my bags, and sat down. I swiveled around to face her.

"Sure, what's on your mind?"

"I have a red and white Drunkard's Path quilt, which I thought was symbolic of the women's temperance movement, but it's also part of the Underground Railroad patterns. We have three other quilts with patterns mentioned in the same article. I didn't think the Underground Railroad came through this part of Iowa."

"There are many quilt patterns with special meaning for slaves seeking freedom." Tiara took off her glasses and rubbed her nose thoughtfully. "Grandma Sally always told me that one of my ancestors made the trip to Iowa before slavery ended, and he used quilts hung in the windows to find help his way. I'd love to see those quilts, Gracie."

"Sure. Come over to the museum any afternoon, and I'll show them to you. I feel like I should do a follow-up exhibit to this one."

"That's a great idea. Including them now might generate interest and motivate people to dig out more of their quilts," Tiara pointed out. "I'll send you a couple of links to excellent resources about the Underground Railroad in Iowa and quilting."

I pondered the situation as I prepped for class and decided for now to include the four quilts and consider doing another exhibit later. I thought again about Tiara's grandmother's story. I'd love to find a Civil War connection to Jubilee Junction—and the arrival of a free former slave before slavery ended would be historic.

I drove over to see Aunt Violet and felt as though I was hooked on a soap opera. I had never thought about Grandma Grace and

Violet—even Vera—as young women before. I'd looked through the black and white pictures of the three girls in California the night before. The sisters posed for pictures at the train station with a couple of soldiers and sailors, at the boarding house, on the navy base, and out in the parks and streets of San Diego and Chula Vista. Some pictures showed the girls with Ed, Mary, and Eddie, Aunt Mae and Uncle Henry, the teens, church people, or people at the boarding house. Some pictures didn't include Vera.

As I stepped out of the car, leaves were falling.

Aunt Violet opened her door. "I'm so glad to see you. Your mother dropped in with the cookies over her lunch hour." She hugged me, then we walked down the hallway to her kitchen.

We sat down at the table, and I retrieved the tape recorder and selected the next tape. She poured the tea, and I put the plate with several cookies on it between us. I pressed *play* and then reached for a cookie. Her kitten nudged her ankle and mewed, and Aunt Violet picked her up.

Eighteen

Violins & Piano lessons

"You may encounter many defeats, but you must not be defeated. It may be necessary to encounter the defeats, so you can know who you are, what you can rise from, and how you can still come out of it."
~Maya Angelou.

Tape #7, Nickel Raises & Internment Camps
Grandma Grace's voice sounded cheerful.

*V*era and I got nickel raises! Don't laugh. A coke cost a nickel at the movies or on a break at work. Later, Violet earned a raise, too. The twins turned twenty in July. Aunt Mae baked a cake for them, and our parents sent a package. Eddie helped them blow out the candles. The package included birthday cards, new outfits for the twins, some embroidered handkerchiefs, and several pieces of hard candy for each one of us, along with a small stack of letters and cards from family and friends.

We ate a lovely birthday supper and sat around and talked afterward. Vera told us that women now made up more than half of the workers at the plant, and they could not keep up production without us. Later, we learned that over 5,000 women worked at Bartlett Aircraft by the end of the war.

Violet talked about what she'd learned at the base hospital and how her student nurses were progressing. It was a rare evening of sharing the spotlight.

As the months passed by, Reva and I became close friends. She told me about life in a big city, and I told her about life on a farm. I thought she seemed sad, but decided it concerned her loved ones being off at war.

Then one day, on our way to work, I noticed Reva looked especially troubled. I asked her what was wrong.

"I'm worried about my friends Harry and Lily. The authorities sent their family to one of those internment camps because they're Japanese Americans," Reva told me.

Before I could react, she sighed. "I know the Japanese attacked us at Pearl Harbor, but my friends aren't soldiers—they're students. I don't think it's moral to put people in these terrible camps. Lily and Harry Namimoto aren't spies, and neither are their parents. The Namimoto family ran a flower shop. Mrs. Namimoto taught at my mother's school, and their uncle owned a big greenhouse and farm outside of town."

"How awful. Have you been friends for a long? How did you meet?"

"Lily and I became friends when we took piano lessons from one of my neighbors. My lesson came right after hers, so I would sit and admire her piano playing. They both attended my high school, and the Namimoto family lived near us. Lily is a year younger than I am, but Harry's my age, and we were in high school and had a lot of classes together. He's a wonderful writer and loves to read. Harry also plays the violin. Lily and I've been writing letters to each other, and I haven't gotten a letter in three weeks. I'm worried about them." Reva looked on the verge of tears.

I didn't know what to say. Coming from Iowa, I didn't have any non-white friends. "I'm so sorry, Reva." I put my hand on her arm, trying to reassure her. "I'm sure you'll get a letter soon."

"The authorities only gave Mr. Namimoto two weeks to sell his flower shop and their house and cars. My father overheard some men talking about it, and they planned to offer Mr. Namimoto a fraction of what the properties' value. My father confronted them, and they acted like it was just business."

"How horrible. Is that even legal?" I asked.

"I don't know. My father is a Methodist minister. He thinks the problem is people's prejudice and fear against the Japanese, even though they are Americans. My father helped find people to rent their house and the greenhouse and farm, but they had already sold the store. And what did it accomplish? The government hasn't prosecuted anyone who helped in the Pearl Harbor attack."

I thought before I spoke . "I think your father is right. People were afraid of people who didn't look like them after the attack."

"Lily and Harry came to see me before they left, and they were afraid. They couldn't take a lot of their possessions, so my father and mother are storing their things in our basement. I have Harry's violin under my bed, back in LA, and some of Lily's piano books, a box of her notebooks and paperbacks, and some stuffed animals." Reva was close to tears.

I felt shocked. I didn't know families had to sell their property. "Your family did the right thing to help them. How long have they been gone?"

"The Namimoto family left last summer, along with hundreds of others after the President's Executive Order, so it's been almost a year and a half. Harry and I should have graduated together last June. They were sent to a camp at Manzanar, which is over 300 miles from here and over 200 miles from Los Angeles. Harry started a weekly newspaper, and Lily teaches piano to children. Their mother began teaching classes for children, and their father grows vegetables and flowers for the camp."

I didn't know what to say. I'd read about the internment camps in the newspapers, but they didn't seem real, somehow, until now. Reva thanked me after I handed her a fresh handkerchief. "You're the only one I trust here, Grace," she told me finally.

In September 1943, I could put together seventeen cowl flap assemblies in a day, which I have been told was a local record. This task required very precise work. I'd learned a lot since the first day, back in June, when the leadman walked me to the department making cowl flaps. An older woman taught me what to do, and I fixed half a dozen sets of cowl flaps under her supervision. The cowl flaps are part of the structure around the engine that opens to cool it down.

The leadman watched me work the first week and then took me down a couple of tables to a young woman named Josie, a thin, dark-haired girl who answered my questions. Josie grew up in Chula Vista and had several family members serving in the military, including a brother, an uncle, and several cousins. "I thought about taking some bookkeeping classes, but I like this better," she told me, grinning.

Josie was a skilled riveter with a year of experience at Bartlett's. I learned a lot by watching her. She showed me how to drill holes and use the Chicago Squeezer to rivet by hand. The leadman contrived a jig for me, which held the pieces in place, and showed me where to drill the holes to join them together. I liked my job. However, there was a half-inch hole I needed to drill with the large half-inch drill motor. When the drill kicked through the hole, the drill gave me a good kick in the chest where I held and supported the drill.

My right breast began to hurt. Soon, I felt a lump! Josie asked if I was okay, and I told her my breast was hurting from the drill. She called our leadman over and told him I needed to see the nurse, and he agreed.

I explained the problem to the nurse, who made an appointment for me in San Diego, where I saw a specialist. He examined me and wrote a note, recommending I be taken off the half-inch drill operation. He thought the problem was a bruise swelling, and it might be temporary, and go away. Fortunately, it did.

Mr. Peterson, our leadman, assigned a man in our section named Joe to do the half-inch holes. Joe was grudging at first, but as he watched me work, he became friendlier, and we worked together just fine. In making my cowl rings, I first put the parts in my jig and drilled the smaller holes. Then each piece required sanding, or deburring, until smooth on the ends so they fit well.

I enjoyed working with my hands, learning new things, and meeting new people. I enjoyed having a challenge and proving myself as capable as any man doing a job. I was helping to build B-17 bombers for our fighting men.

Nineteen

Reva's story

Tape #7, continued. Japanese Americans and Internment Camps

Evacuees must carry with them on departure for the Assembly Center, the following property:
(a) Bedding and linens (no mattress) for each member of the family;
(b) Toilet articles for each member of the family;
(c) Extra clothing for each member of the family;
(d) Essential personal effects for each member of the family.
All items carried will be securely packaged, tied and plainly marked with the name of the owner and numbered in accordance with instructions obtained at the Civil Control Station. The size and number of packages is limited to that which can be carried by the individual or family group."
—Wartime Civil Control Administration, evacuation procedures for Japanese American residents of Military Area No. 1 in California, May 17th, 1942.

*R*eva looked worried as we sat on the big porch at the boarding house together one evening. She held a letter from Lily in her hand.

"Why are you worried about Harry?" I asked, picking up from our conversation on the bus ride home.

"Lily thinks Harry is enlisting in the military, with the other boys at the camp, in a special unit called the 442nd. They're all second-generation Japanese Americans, or Nisei, and they're proving themselves to be fierce fighters, even if their country seems to have turned against them," Reva told me.

I nodded. "They're remarkable if they want to fight for their country. I imagine your friend Lily is worried about her brother, and it sounds like you are, too."

"Yes, I am. Thanks for listening, Grace." Reva looked around. "But please say nothing at the plant, or here at the boarding house. Most people think all Japanese Americans should be kept in those terrible camps. I tried to educate a few people, but they became angry, so I stopped trying to explain. I've been afraid to talk about my friends here at the boarding house." She slipped the letter into her pocket.

"You can talk to me anytime, Reva. I'm sorry your friends are going through this." My heart ached, and I wondered how Americans could be so cruel to each other.

We walked upstairs to our rooms, but I thought about two teenagers I'd never met and wondered what life was like in an American internment camp. Violet walked by around the time Mary stopped by my room for a chat, and we talked about the order to take Japanese Americans to the internment camps.

Mary sighed. "I agree with Reva, but standing up for the Japanese Americans has become difficult. When we first moved out here, we lived next to a Japanese American family. Hardworking and friendly, they owned a restaurant, and we loved their spicy noodles. But when the executive order came down, they had to sell or rent their property and left with just a few bags."

"My Aunt Mae and Uncle Henry tried to help them and were shocked by some of the hateful talk in town. I don't know where they were sent, and I'm not sure how to find out. The attack at Pearl Harbor killed a couple of local boys, and we grieved for them. But being mean to Japanese Americans who look like the attackers is just prejudice."

Violet looked stunned. "Oh my, Grace. The journey to California has made me realize just how small our world was back in Iowa. We read about the executive order, but not knowing any Japanese Americans, it didn't seem real, somehow."

I nodded, trying to think of what I could do to help Reva and her friends. Violet and Mary read my mind. "Grace, if you want to be her friend, let her talk," Mary told me, and Violet nodded.

So, Reva and I continued to ride the bus to work together and chat about her friends.

I got to know some of the other men working at the plant, and most treated me kindly, though a few seemed skeptical at first. I tried to imagine the dramatic changes in the workplace over the past two years, when suddenly, women made up half or more of the workforce. Most of the younger men went to war, so the men at the factory couldn't pass the physical or may have been too old for the draft. Many of the men inspected planes and trained and supervised new hires.

Joe warmed up to me. One day he told me gruffly my cowl flaps were top-notch, his highest praise. Another day he commented, "I'm glad you're here. Josie needs a friend. She's a hard little worker."

I nodded as I handed him several cowl flaps needing the hole drilled. We became proficient at timing our work, so I wasn't tying up too much of the shift with Joe waiting for me. As we talked, I got a better picture of how the different departments worked together. Each plane required teamwork and lots of hard work.

Every day, I walked to my department with a lunch bucket in one hand and a toolbox in the other and was proud to be here. Seeing all the women in trousers—with their hair held up with colorful scarves—handling tools, working side by side with their male coworkers, I realized they did most of the jobs on the assembly line once done by men.

I made friends with several women married to enlisted men, and they told me sixty of the widows from Pearl Harbor contacted the plant and asked to get jobs there because they wanted to support the war effort. Bartlett's now depended on the skilled work of women from farms, small towns, and big cities alike, from all over the country—women like Reva, Vera, and me. Violet was doing important work at the base hospital, caring for wounded troops. I couldn't imagine being anywhere else. Although I looked back on my country schoolhouse and children with fondness, I was needed here.

Our factory consisted of three enormous warehouses, with high ceilings and lots of things moving above our heads. When we finished work on the power packs, they were lifted up and moved to another area of the plant where workers constructed the shell of the plane, as well as the instruments, equipment, and seats, and put the engines and power packs into place. The factory was noisy, with all the equipment, an assembly line, and people. Our factory didn't have all the safety gear you would see today in modern factories, and from time to time, people got injured.

Once the planes were completed, the inspectors checked them over for problems, and then the WASPs (Women Airforce Service Pilots) flew them to bases using the runway on the west side of the plant.

I sat near there on my lunch break because I loved to watch the graceful take-offs of the giant birds as I munched on my sandwich and drank some tea. I imagined flying in one of these planes.

I knew about the WASPs, of course, but you needed to be a licensed pilot before applying to the program. It seemed like an impossible dream for this farm girl. I settled for watching other people fly the planes I helped to build and prayed the war would be over soon.

Once Mr. McCabe—Mac—the supervisor, saw me manage tools, he took an interest in me. I told him my father had treated me like one of the boys growing up, and I worked on engines in the tractors and trucks on the family farms. Then I told him about my adventures as an electrician's helper the previous summer, and his attitude became noticeably more friendly.

One afternoon, Mac came to get me. He nodded at my lineman and then took me to the part of the plant where they did the last checks on planes before flying them to a base. He showed me a plane that had one of its engines sputtering, but the inspector reported they put it together correctly. Mac and I did some adjusting, testing, and figured out the problem, using the tricks my father taught me about listening to the engine. From then on he'd stop by to see if I could go check an engine. As long as I kept my numbers up, my leadman was satisfied.

Vera told us she was enjoying herself as well. Her eye for detail proved useful to her boss on a few projects. Mr. Patterson gave her more responsibility, and she seemed to flourish. She was making friends with another secretary at work and a woman at the boarding house. Vera seemed to smile more at work.

Without her twin around, Vera was a different person. She wasn't as competitive or sarcastic. However, I was busy with my job and only caught glimpses of her at the factory. She and I didn't ride the same buses, so I didn't get many chances to see the other side of my difficult sister.

Violet was busy at the hospital on base, taking care of patients and helping mentor a group of five nurses who didn't get to finish their training before the war was declared, and their instructors all got recruited to go overseas. Violet and another nurse offered to take them through the remaining material in the last few classes and answer their questions. The library at the hospital had medical books, and Violet and I worked together to structure the material into manageable chunks, with short quizzes periodically, and step-by-step instructions.

The headlines continued to encourage us, as in May, when the British and American forces defeated the Axis forces in North Africa, and then in July, when the Allied forces invaded Sicily. However, in September, the Germans took control of the Italian Army, freed Mussolini, and set up a puppet government in northern Italy. We worried even more about our soldiers, sailors, and airmen all in harm's way.

Letters from home continued to convey news of local boys being wounded, shot down, and missing in action, or pushing onward with their units. We got the news about what was happening in Jubilee Junction, or tidbits about our brothers from our mother, aunts, and grandmas, who enclosed newspaper clippings with their brief notes. I sometimes had a sense of dread when I opened Mama's letters. All too often, the news was grim. My heart ached as I cried over those letters, thinking of the parents, spouses, children, and friends left behind to mourn. Violet and I read our letters together and cried together. Vera frowned when she saw us and tried to ignore her stack of mail.

"What's the point of reading something if you'll cry or get depressed? We can't do anything about it. We're doing what we can to help win the war," Vera told us rather matter-of-factly one afternoon and walked away.

Violet sputtered, "What's wrong with her?"

I think Vera wasn't as tough as she wanted us to think she was. Maybe she rationalized that if she didn't read the bad news, she wouldn't get upset. She didn't write home much, either.

"I'm sure you two girls are telling Mama everything, and she's a busy woman. I send a postcard once or twice a month," she waved her current postcard at us.

Violet and I continued to read our letters together and sometimes cry together. Then we'd talk about work and the people we met. I told her about working at Bartlett's, my coworkers, and dreaming about flying. She told me about how much she was learning about different types of injuries, surgeries, rehab methods, and medications. We shared our dreams and supported each other.

That's enough for now, Gracie.

Twenty

Uncle Vern's Story

"Character cannot be developed in ease and quiet. Only through experience of trial and suffering can the soul be strengthened, vision cleared, ambition inspired, and success achieved."
~*Helen Keller*

*T*he seventh tape ended. I felt as though a time machine had brought us back to today. "Grandma worked with a woman whose friends ended up in one of those camps?" I asked. "We saw a presentation about the internment camps in high school with lots of terrible pictures. They put some of them in horse stables."

Aunt Violet looked sad. "Yes, I believe putting those people into internment camps put a terrible stain on our nation. We put over 120,000 Japanese Americans in those camps, and I don't recall one being charged with a crime."

"And what about the children who spent several years in one of those camps? It would traumatize them for life, I would think." I was fighting tears.

Aunt Violet stroked the kitty in her lap, thinking. "Children are resilient, but those families had little choice but to move and start over."

I sighed. "And how could they start over? Many of them sold their property for a fraction of what it was worth. If you ask me, those people who took advantage of them, buying their property on the cheap, were the real criminals."

Aunt Violet nodded in agreement.

I stood up and cleared the table, then Beatrix woke up and

yawned, stretching and arching her back. She jumped down from Aunt Violet's lap and sauntered to her water dish.

I packed up, ready to leave. "These tapes are giving me a lot to think about."

I thought Aunt Violet looked sad, and I regretted upsetting her. She stood up and put a few cookies into a small zip-lock bag and handed it to me. She commented, "I know, dear. They're bringing back memories for me—mostly good."

Then we walked to the front door. I gave her a big hug, and she patted my back.

"See you next week."

"Yes," I replied, deep in thought. Instead of finding answers, my list of questions was growing.

The next day, my literature students and I discussed "The Death of the Ball Turret Gunner" by Randall Jarrell, published in 1945. The poem packs a lot of terror into five lines, describing the death of a gunner in a Sperry Ball turret in a World War II bomber.

In just five lines Jarrell captured the horror of the war in the skies, ending with the remains of the gunner being washed from the turret with a hose. Tragic, to my way of thinking.

We discussed the poem, with many of the boys liking it.

"Man, what a way to go!" Jimmy exclaimed.

"Yeah, the poem makes me think of those air battles in *Star Wars*," Jacob commented.

"So, the frozen fur is the fur collar on the bomber jackets, and the planes actually flew six miles up in the sky?" Samantha asked. "Wow."

"The comparison of the turret and his mother's body is sad," Sarah pointed out. "I wouldn't want my son to go to war."

We discussed the contrast of the experience of war from six miles up to the fierce hand-to-hand combat of the Second World War.

"Either way, people die. You just don't see them from the airplane," Jimmy observed.

As I walked to my next class, I wondered, *What did Uncle Vern experience during the war? Was he the navigator? If so, he must have known a few gunners.*

Later, I told my parents about the poem we'd discussed.

"Didn't Uncle Vern serve as the navigator on a bomber?" I asked.

"Yes, but I've never heard him talk about his experience. He must have gotten injured to meet Maggie in the hospital, since she was a nurse. All I know is his crew got shot down."

Mom nodded. "Now I'm curious as well, Gracie."

I called Aunt Maggie from the newspaper office and told her about the poem we'd studied.

"Do you think Uncle Vern would talk to me—talk to us—about his experiences in the war? I asked. "I don't want to upset him, but I wish I knew what he experienced."

Aunt Maggie paused. "I'll talk to him. He doesn't talk about the war, unless he's around other veterans, and most of those friends have died. When they were younger, they'd go to these reunions and have a few beers and tell their stories. The wives got together and had a few drinks, and talked about our men, our children, and moving on from the war. I recall meeting at least two other war brides, and it was especially nice to chat with them over tea."

She sighed. "After the war, most of us civilians just wanted to forget the horrible things we witnessed, especially those in Britain. Such death and destruction. Fresh out of nursing training, but nothing could have prepared us for the horrible things we saw in the war—bombings, injuries, deaths. However, some memories stay with you, don't they?"

"Aunt Maggie, I would love to hear your story, too," I told her.

"Yes, let's plan a family meal. I'll call your mother up. We should learn from your grandma Grace's example. It's time for our family to hear our stories while we're here."

Later, Mom called and put me on speakerphone.

"Aunt Maggie called." Mom paused. "We're going to have supper on Saturday. Vern will tell his story and let us record him. His children have asked him questions over the years and think this is a great idea. Your comments made a difference."

Dad got excited. "I've been wanting to know more for years.

Vern was a teenager, right out of high school, when he enlisted. Ten months later, he was on a B-17 bomber crew as the navigator. Imagine taking a kid who has never been on an airplane, never been out of Iowa, and suddenly he's on a giant ship headed overseas. Then he's living in England and flying missions. I'm looking forward to our meal. Great idea, Gracie."

Saturday night, we gathered at Aunt Violet's new apartment for a potluck supper, with several of us eating at the kitchen island or coffee table. Beatrix hid and only came out once we finished eating.

After our meal, we turned our chairs towards the living room, and a few people sat on the couch or floor. I grabbed my iPad while Mom found a fresh cassette tape and grinned as she placed it into her old-fashioned cassette recorder.

Uncle Vern sat in a dining room chair. He looked around at all of us, cleared his throat, and unfolded a couple of pieces of paper from his pocket.

"Gracie asked me about my experiences during World War II and mentioned a famous poem, "Death of the Ball Turret Gunner" by Randall Jarrell." He looked around the room, then continued.

"I enlisted at 18 years old, right after high school. Ten months later, I became the navigator and radioman in a B-17 Flying Fortress Bomber crew in England. My best friend was Jimmy, our pilot. Our squadron lost half a dozen young men in the ball turret, and the poem describes the scenes of battle well, talking about the flak, the terror, being up six miles, and the frozen fur. The ball turret gunner was always a smaller man, and they hunched up something fierce for five or six hours.

"My crew ditched in the ocean twice. I met Maggie after the first water landing. The first thing I saw when I woke up was this lovely creature with beautiful red hair saying my name and holding my hand. She was taking my vitals, mind you. But I saw her beautiful smile and those green eyes, and I was smitten. Still am.

"They let me out of the hospital a couple of days later. I suffered a mild concussion, but fortunately, everyone in our family has hard heads."

All of us chuckled.

"Our gunners needed weeks to heal up. Jimmy came through without injuries, but the co-pilot cut his hand, trying to get Doug's body out of the ball turret, and needed stitches. So, we'd lost four men out of a ten-man crew.

"Jimmy and I drank the beer he promised with the rest of the boys a few days later. We asked permission to wheel the three injured men outside and handed each a warm British brew. Our remaining crew members joined us. We drank to Doug and his bravery. We drank to freedom. We drank to our lost B-17 Fort—and we drank to taking down those two German fighters before we ditched.

"Then Jimmy grinned. 'Well, boys, I have news. We're getting a new B-17. Can you believe it? Back home if I wrecked a car, I'd be walking. But here they give you a new ride.'

"He saluted the injured gunners and co-pilot. 'We're going to miss you fellas, and you too, Fred. Hope you all heal up fine.'

"Two weeks later, we had four replacements for our injured crew members and a new Flying Fortress. We flew several training flights, and then we completed another nine missions without incident. However, on the twentyth flight, German fighters hit us with flak, and we lost two engines. Not only that, but they also wounded the co-pilot and killed the top gunner.

"Jimmy did a second water landing in rough seas, breaking his arm while trying to operate the controls. I dinged my noggin and hurt my leg on a broken instrument panel when we hit the water. We got ourselves and our injured out of the sinking plane and into the life rafts, which we lashed together. One of our new crew members injected me with a syrette of morphine from his first aid kit once we all got into the life rafts. Then he did the same for Jimmy. Good lad and quick thinking.

"Soon, a rescue boat arrived. I don't remember the boat ride to shore, or the ambulance ride to the hospital. They put me and Jimmy in the same hospital room. They took him to surgery and me to x-rays.

"I fell asleep, and when I woke up, this nurse, Maggie, was fussing with my pillows. 'You don't have to keep getting injured to talk to me, you know.' She brought me a cool drink of water and steadied the glass at my mouth, so I could take a few sips from the straw.

"I found my voice, finally, and asked for her name.

"'Margaret Rose Smith, but you can call me Maggie,' she told me in a lovely British accent as she left the room.

"I laid back in my bed, muttering her name—Margaret Rose Smith—until Jimmy groaned. 'Vern, are you nuts? You sound like you're sixteen and want to take her to the high school prom.' I didn't know he'd returned from surgery.

"We healed up, got a new Fort, and more crew members, and Jimmy and I flew a half dozen more missions. Then, finally, the war ended.

"Maggie and I courted and married in England before I returned home to Iowa."

Then Uncle Vern sat down and smiled at Aunt Maggie. "Your turn, dear."

Twenty-One

Aunt Maggie's story

"Dreams are lovely but they are dreams. Fleeting, ephemeral, pretty. But dreams do not come true just because you dream them. It's hard work that makes things happen. It's hard work that creates change."

~*Shonda Rhimes*

*A*unt Maggie looked at all of us and then down at her notes.

"I grew up near Cambridge, where I took some nursing classes, starting at seventeen. I wanted to be a nurse because my father was a doctor.

"He was also an Air Raid Precautions Warden. One evening during the Blitz in 1940, he heard children screaming in a bombed-out house and rescued them. A falling beam trapped their mother, and she begged him to rescue the children and the baby, and he did. He made two trips in to get the children, who sobbed for their mother. He and another rescue worker went back in with crowbars to free the mother, but all three died when the building collapsed.

"I rarely tell this part of the story, but I was there at the scene. Mother asked me to take coffee and sandwiches for my father. He brought the children out to me, told me he loved us but needed to save the mother. I held the baby and prayed as the two little ones clung to me and wailed.

"Someone called the children's grandma, and she arrived shortly after the building collapsed. She put her arms around all of us, and we wept together. Then she thanked me for her grandchildren because, without my father, she would have lost all of them.

"My mother, two brothers, and I moved into my paternal grandparents' flat above their grocery store. Living through the Blitz was terrifying. We didn't have time to grieve. We tried to carry on a day at a time, but I remember being cold, hungry, frightened, exhausted—and angry.

"I was fortunate to get a job at the 163rd General Hospital at Wimpole Hall in 1943 because they didn't have enough American nurses yet to staff the hospital. We kept busy, and I liked to think that I was making a difference.

"I remember the first time I saw Vern, after that first water landing. He looked so young and handsome in the hospital bed, with gauze and a bandage around his head. He woke up as I took his vitals, and looked amazed, watching me take his pulse, and I got flustered. His plane had ditched in the ocean, and he'd been injured while helping another crew member exit the plane.

"I liked Vern's smile and laugh. He was a Yank but a handsome one and so charming. But something else, though. As I got to know him, I realized he possessed a kind heart, a wonderful sense of humor, and strong faith.

"Mother met him and liked him. 'Listen to me, Margaret Rose. If Vern proposes, you do not worry about me. I'll be fine, and so will Johnny and Peter. This is your chance for happiness, my love, and your father would agree with me.'

"When Vern proposed, I realized I couldn't imagine living without him. I came to America on an ocean liner full of war brides in 1946, and Vern met me in New York. We took the train back to Jubilee Junction, and I enjoyed the journey through this unknown country. I loved Vern's family, the Iowa countryside, and living on a farm. I took naturalization classes at the college and became a citizen, then took more nursing courses, and worked. Later, we started our family."

When she finished, Maggie smiled and looked at all of us. "I'm so happy you all wanted to hear our stories."

I put down the iPad and clapped, and others joined me. Vern and Maggie looked surprised and then pleased.

"Good job." Aunt Violet dabbed her eyes with a Kleenex. "We prayed for you every day, Vern. Maggie, your father was such a brave man. He did a remarkable thing, saving those three children."

Dad told them, "Wonderful! I'd love to print excerpts in the newspaper around Veterans Day. I'd like yours to be the first, Vern."

Mom dabbed her eyes. "I enjoyed hearing Maggie's story, but to lose a father so young, and to be there. Thank goodness for your grandparents and mother."

I walked over to them. "Thank you both. I'll never read the poem with my students without thinking of you, Uncle Vern. Your friend Jimmy sounds like a great guy. And, Aunt Maggie, I can see the scene in my mind of your father rescuing those children. I can't imagine how you dealt with so much grief and stress, but I'm so happy you met Uncle Vern."

Mark and Kathy crossed the room and hugged them. Mark told him, "You entered the service as a teenager, Uncle Vern, but you did some pretty courageous stuff. We'll write it up. I want the rest of the family to know your story, too."

Kathy told Maggie, "What a remarkable story. I can't believe all you experienced, between the blitz and losing your father. He died a hero." She embraced Maggie, and they both cried.

Vern looked pleased as he choked back tears. "We were just young men—soldiers—trying to win the war. You don't have to carry on so much. Thank you all." He blew his nose. "Any dessert?"

Maggie hugged Kathy and then turned to her husband. "We'll have a nice cuppa tea and cake, dear. You did a wonderful job."

My parents and I walked into the kitchen and returned with a tray of slices of chocolate cake with whipped cream cheese frosting, small plates, napkins, and forks. That's my family—always up for cake.

We were setting up the quilt exhibit, and I couldn't have done it without my volunteers. We ended up with thirty-six quilts ranging from the small quilt meant for a baby to several quilts double or queen-size. The display took up our large exhibit gallery and spilled over into the hallway leading to the smaller exhibit hall, which has several more stations with quilts, along with photo collages about the quilters and the quilt pattern, estimated dates of when the quilts were completed, and other information.

Throughout the space, we positioned ten netbooks. Our visitors could listen to the voices of local women talking about the individual quilt patterns, their history, their significance, their memories of working on quilts in groups, and the role of quilts in telling their family history.

As we searched for quotes about quilts, I found a quote comparing authoring a book to making a quilt. "And books, like quilts, are made, one word at a time, one stitch at a time," according to Sena Jeter Naslund.

Another quote came from one of my favorite writers, Anne Lamott. "We stitch together quilts of meaning to keep us warm and safe, with whatever patches of beauty and utility we have on hand." I used both quotes for our signage.

I thought about all the work going into making a quilt. A person must choose the pattern, pick out colors and fabrics, and stitch together the blocks or pieces making up the quilt. I could see that a quilt was a work of time and patience, and required a keen understanding of patterns and colors.

All the quilts in our exhibit came from quilters in Jubilee County and ranged from the late 1800s to the 1990s. A few quilts came from one skilled quilter, several resulted from several family members' work, and others came from church groups or quilting clubs.

Carl and I discussed many ways to organize the exhibit: chronological, by pattern, by the maker, or by a group. We decided to be eclectic. We displayed two or three quilts by the same family or quilter. In other cases, we put several quilts together with the same pattern to show the various skill levels and techniques used to create the quilts.

We discovered four of the quilt patterns fit with the Underground Railroad theme, and I needed to decide if I should pull those quilts and build the next exhibit around them or leave them in the current exhibit.

Tiara came over the previous week and walked through the

exhibit with me, excited when she saw the four quilts I identified as possibly relating to the Underground Railroad. She made a few phone calls and found Mrs. Bernice Johnson, an elderly black woman in her church, who talked about the symbols on the quilts. Clay edited her interview, and we updated our exhibit materials.

"You've done an excellent job here, Gracie. You leave room for the possibility of another exhibit focusing on the American Civil War era and the Underground Railroad." Tiara looked around and smiled.

"Clay found the software and figured out how to use it, and the exhibit came together nicely," I told her, looking around.

"Also, Tiara, I need another favor. We'd like a program on the patterns and symbols in quilts for the museum. We only have sixty minutes, so how about doing an adult coloring activity? You would introduce the common patterns. I'm not a quilter, but I'd like to color in some of those patterns, including those for the Underground Railroad and The Woman's Christian Temperance Union—WCTU." I showed her some patterns I'd found.

Tiara chuckled. "I like it. I think the program sounds like fun. Some women should do a quilting workshop for the adult education program at the college, but this would be a wonderful way to talk about the meaning behind those quilt patterns. Let's talk more and look at our schedules."

Twenty-Two

Skirts Vs. Slacks

"We stitch together quilts of meaning to keep us warm and safe, with whatever patches of beauty and utility we have on hand."

~*Anne Lamott*

*W*hen I had time between my jobs and household chores, I thought about Reva's story about her two Japanese American friends. I searched online and found pictures showing families in the internment camps, which made me more upset, or as Grandma Grace would have put it, *all riled up*.

"Remember the actor George Takei, Sulu from *Star Trek*? His family lived in horse stables, at one of the worst camps, in California," I told Tiara and Shelly one day in the adjunct office.

Tiara nodded thoughtfully. "I've read his story. What his family suffered—what all the Japanese Americans suffered during World War II in those camps illustrates man's inhumanity to man."

Shelly shivered. "I can't imagine being told you have to sell everything and go off to a camp just because you look a certain way or worship differently or fill in the blank."

I put up my hands in defeat. "Yes. What did those families do when the camps closed? Many families had lost everything. I read the authorities gave them $25 and a bus ticket, but their homes had been sold, their businesses sold, and they were probably afraid they wouldn't be welcomed back into their communities."

Shelly asked, "Didn't they get some kind of compensation decades later?"

"Yes." I brought it up on my laptop. "It took 45 years to get an apology, and they got $20,000 each, which is so unfair."

Tiara sighed. "Yes. I can relate, girls. Abraham Lincoln's General Sherman promised my people forty acres and a mule after the war, but Lincoln was assassinated. We've been waiting for the United States government to make good on its promises for 150 years. Imagine if the freed slaves had been given forty acres and a mule at the end of the Civil War? What would our country be like today?" She waited for a beat.

Shelly and I looked at each other. "More small businesses and property in the hands of Black families? More Black farmers?" I guessed. "Less poverty, more generational wealth?"

"I would hope so. If only President Lincoln had served out his term, we might've received the money. But President Andrew Johnson reversed the decision. The House of Representatives apologized in 2008, but the Senate chose not to pass it." Tiara seemed calm, but we could see the fire in her eyes.

"Oh, Tiara. I'm sorry for going on and on about the Japanese Americans. They're not the only group that faces discrimination. I feel like an idiot."

Shelly sighed. "Gracie, you aren't the only one. We need to beef up our curriculum for teaching American history to cover more about the Japanese American internment camps, slavery, White Supremacy, women's contributions to history and struggle for equal rights, as well as the civil rights movement. Our deplorable treatment of Native Americans doesn't even get mentioned most of the time."

Tiara looked at us, "Makes you wonder how a Black man with a funny name got elected our president, doesn't it? Oh yes, and make that twice!" She smiled because we knew she was a huge fan of President and Michelle Obama.

Shelly nodded. "Yes, we have a Black President. I think he's wonderful, and he's done a lot of smart things. And yet we still have racism. Look at those people marching with Nazi flags and the KKK being named the oldest American hate group. It's frightening."

I sighed. "How do you not explode, Tiara? I'm worked up about something from World War II when there is still prejudice and racism today."

Tiara looked thoughtful. "Girl, I'm a Black woman, a mother, an educator, and a community activist at heart. I've learned to pick my battles. I try to educate my audience on the radio—and in the classroom. There are hundreds of fierce Black women we don't read about who worked for Civil Rights. Google Dr. June Jackson Christmas, one of the first Black women to graduate from Vassar, a psychiatrist focused on community mental health. During World War II, she spoke out against the interned Japanese Americans. Then, there are Black suffragists like Ida B Wells and Mary Church Terrell. What we learn from them is patience, persistence, having a plan, and finding like souls." Tiara looked warmly at us, and I felt a deeper sense of appreciation for her.

Aunt Violet welcomed me at the front door on Wednesday afternoon. I handed her a white pastry bag and noticed her kitty behind her.

"She follows me everywhere."

We walked down the hallway and sat down at her kitchen table, where a teapot was already there, with cups and plates. She placed the scones on a plate.

I put the tape in the tape recorder and pressed play. We settled back to listen.

Tape #8, Inappropriate Behavior on Busses
Grandma's tone was thoughtful.

Gracie, here is something to think about in your day when women can be doctors, astronauts, senators, or about anything they want to be. Vera wore skirts to work as a secretary. I wore slacks since I worked in the plant and did a lot of bending and stooping. I noticed the difference in how soldiers and sailors treated us when we rode the bus together. Sailors said rude things to me, especially when I worked overtime and traveled alone in the early evening. The situation made little sense to me.

Why did they act like I was some easy woman? I grew up wearing some of Vern's overalls on the farm and liked them for comfort, especially if you bent down and worked on engines.

Vera just sniffed when I asked her why the men acted so rude. She got her way, so if we got on a crowded bus, she just looked at a man, and he would jump up to give her a seat. It left me standing, holding onto a strap overhead and trying not to fume, while she sat there smugly with her purse on her lap, flirting with some poor sailor.

I started carrying a book to read and then I could ignore any unwanted comments or looks. While this wasn't the first time in my life when I'd reflected on the way society treated women, I began thinking about what folks would call social justice today. Their response seemed to go beyond fashion. I tied my hair up in a pretty scarf and tried to look presentable. Before I left the factory, I always washed my face and hands. I couldn't understand why I was more deserving of rude comments simply because I was wearing trousers.

I tried to take the same bus as Reva. Having the two of us together, wearing trousers, didn't seem to make us such a target. Violet wore nursing uniforms with skirts, and she exuded a gentle magic. Violet didn't treat men the way her sister did—as some creature designed to treat her nicely and then go away. When we rode the bus together, men gave her a seat as well, and often commented, "Thanks for taking care of our soldiers and sailors, ma'am!" Violet would smile and say, "Thank you. Here's my sister. How about a seat for her? She's building bombers for you boys," and then someone would acknowledge me, and I took a seat as well.

One evening, Violet heard some of the nasty things the men called out to me when we rode the same bus. She turned around, her cheeks blazing with anger. "Shame on you! Why are you talking like that to my sister? She's a good Christian girl. She's building bombers for you boys. Please apologize and remember the next time you pick on some girl wearing slacks—she's someone's sister, someone's daughter, and someone's girlfriend or wife. Would you want your sister or girlfriend to be treated so rudely?" My gentle sister glared at them. She was the sweetest person you would ever meet, but very protective.

The three sailors looked down, ashamed. One of them lifted his cap. "I'm awful sorry, Miss. We think we're tough guys; sometimes we take our teasing too far."

Other people around them gave them dirty looks, and an older woman glared at them. "Thank you, miss! I get sick of hearing these comments, even if they are not about me."

From then on, I held my head higher. Sometimes I ignored a few comments. More often, I looked the offender in the eye and said, "What did you say? I didn't hear you," in my best stern schoolmarm voice. If I did that, the man or men would look ashamed and apologize.

I kept thinking about my conversations with Reva, about her friends Harry and Lily. They were judged based on their race, which seemed wrong, but I felt helpless to do anything to change it. Likewise, I was being judged because I wore my slacks to and from work. I did not deserve the crude comments.

Women had been voting for several decades, and the three of us girls considered ourselves equal to our brothers, even if our mother worried about me being a tomboy, wearing Vern's overalls. People in our small town knew my family and treated us with respect. This experience in California was something new, and I didn't like it. If I ever married, it would only be to a man who treated me as his equal and a partner. And when I saw injustice, I would speak up and act.

I kept writing home, and my mother sent us letters faithfully, with news about our brothers. Victor got injured in Italy, recovered, and returned to his unit. Vincent completed training in engineering and helped build pontoon bridges, preparing for amphibious landings, and other tasks for the army. Virgil, sent to the Pacific, saw action in several battles and was doing well.

Mama told us Vern completed his training as a navigator and deployed to England with the 8th Air Force. He wrote home with tales about eating lots of mutton and dreaming of Mama's good pot roasts. "We drink a lot of warm beer, but we try not to complain. The Brits have been in the war much longer, and we can see the signs of destruction from the bombing. We're living in Quonset huts with coal heaters and some of them are living in apartments known as cold water-flats, with no hot water at all."

Our church in California—full of women whose husbands, sons, and brothers had gone to war—continued to reach out to those who have lost loved ones. Volunteers visited the base hospital, organized dinners for the bereaved, and put together little packages for the local soldiers deployed overseas.

As we helped sort donations into small boxes and wrapped them up one Sunday afternoon, Reva looked somber. We talked about the toll the war had taken on all of us.

"I know it's discouraging, but we can't give up hope. So many have already sacrificed their lives for our country. Surely, we have seen the worst." She seemed sad.

I wasn't sure how to respond or what to think. Finally, I tried to smile. "Yes, I agree. I hope we see the end of the war soon." However, I had mixed emotions. The entire world seemed to have gone mad. So many people had already died. I prayed for my brothers and friends fighting abroad. "Please God, protect my brothers and bring them home. End this war, dear God."

From what I knew, we civilians were all doing everything we could, but now the war's end lay with our troops, and as Uncle Henry put it, "Unfortunately, the war will only end after a bloody slog through two battlefronts." Mary's uncle fought in the Great War, so he knew something about war.

We needed to stay strong for them, do our jobs, and keep praying. Well, as Mama says, "that's enough for now!"

Twenty-Three

Sorrow & Celebration

"Each time a woman stands up for herself, without knowing it possibly, without claiming it, she stands up for all women."
~*Maya Angelou*

The tape stopped, and I shook my head. "I'm glad you and Grandma could be there for each other. When you stood up for her on the bus, I loved it. I wouldn't want to be one of those sailors."

"Women have to stand up for other women, especially sisters," she explained, and then looked troubled.

I wondered if the troubled look was about her twin. "Vera didn't think she needed to defend her sister?"

Violet nodded. "I didn't understand her back then, and I still don't."

"Should we listen to the next tape?"

"Are you sure you have the time?"

I nodded as I popped out the old tape and inserted the new. "Well, we still have cookies." She smiled.

Tape #9, Frances gets Visitors
  Grandma's voice was thoughtful.

I'm thinking back to the fall of 1943.

On October 15, I turned twenty-two. We ate a good meal at the boarding house, and everybody wished me well. I got a cupcake with a single candle on it at supper, and they sang "Happy Birthday."

Eddie sat on my lap and helped me blow out the candle, bouncing with excitement. Uncle Henry backed up a little as he held the cupcake safely away from Eddie's hands.

Mother sent a box with a new outfit, letters and cards, candy, and a new handkerchief. Mary and Eddie gave me a pretty bracelet. Uncle Henry winked as he handed me a small package with the last tool I needed for work. "Your cousin Ed wanted me to give the tool to you." Violet and Vera gave me small gifts as well.

Reva and I ate lunch together, and she updated me about her friends. Harry was now a member of the 442nd Infantry Regimental Combat Team, finishing his training at Camp Shelby, Mississippi. She and Lily wrote to each other faithfully, and Reva's mother put together a small box to send to the camp.

The mood became more somber as the headlines announced the movement of the Allied Forces against the Nazi regime, with fierce battles and many casualties. After supper, I escaped to the porch with Reva, who shared my frustrations and fear. One evening, my normally stoic friend broke down.

"I'm so worried about my friends and brothers. Jimmy, my oldest brother, is in the Navy, and he's over in the Pacific. My younger brother Billy is in the Army, and he's in Europe. We have boys from high school scattered across the globe." She faltered.

I patted her arm, trying to think of something soothing to say. Reva looked at me. "I'm just being silly, aren't I? We all have loved ones deployed, and we must have faith, just like the pastor says." Tears trickled down her cheeks.

"You're not being silly. I'm worried about my brothers and friends from back home. They're all over Europe and East Asia." I put my arm around her while I found a clean hankie in my pocket. She thanked me for the hankie and wiped her tears.

"Thank you, Grace. Sometimes I get tired, don't you?" she asked, and I nodded.

"Yes, of course, I do. We need friends, cups of tea, and conversation. I think I'd explode, otherwise."

We kept working, and we kept praying, and the days passed by. In the fall of 1943, Italy surrendered to the Allies. The heads of the Allies—Roosevelt, Churchill, and Stalin—met at the Tehran Conference to plan an attack on Germany.

Then, one Saturday afternoon in October, Frances, one girl at the boarding house, had visitors. A chaplain and a Navy officer marched up the steps of the boarding house and asked for her. Her husband was stationed on a ship in the Pacific and had died in a submarine attack.

Frances collapsed, screaming "No! No! Not Fred." The chaplain and officer caught her and gently helped her to the couch in the front room.

Someone fetched her a glass of water and a hankie. Frances sobbed in her roommate's arms while the chaplain quietly talked to her. Finally, Aunt Mae asked several girls to take her upstairs, and one stayed with her until she cried herself to sleep.

The chaplain and officer spoke briefly with Aunt Mae regarding the arrangements and left because they needed to make other visits. I shuddered, praying my parents wouldn't have visitors bringing sad news about one of my brothers.

Several days later, her parents arrived at the boarding house. They came to take her home for the memorial service. Frances told them she was returning afterward so she could help build planes, and she did. We all feared it was not the last official visit to the boarding house, however, since most of us had loved one's serving overseas, including the Hamiltons.

We enjoyed our Thanksgiving dinner at the boarding house, which we set up as a buffet. It was a scaled-back feast, done with our combined ration cards, and supplemented with Aunt Mae's victory garden out back, but still a feast. I still remember that wonderful roasted turkey, and the bowls of mashed potatoes, gravy, string beans, peas, citrus fruit salad, rolls, and bread and butter pickles.

The entire meal tasted delicious, but we all especially enjoyed the ice cream Aunt Mae brought out at the end with fruit turnovers. Eddie clapped his hands in excitement and opened his mouth when Mary fed him the first taste of ice cream. "Mo!" And we all laughed. Then we took a bite ourselves.

"Oh, my goodness, this is good!" Mary licked her spoon.

We all agreed, with several people vocalizing their pleasure as moans.

"It's delicious! What is in it?" I asked.

Aunt Mae looked pleased. "I found the recipe for the honey ice cream in a booklet about how to make desserts without sugar. It's the easiest recipe ever. Take one quart of cream and mix with three-fourths cup of honey and freeze until solid. I made four batches for us, so I'm glad you like the ice cream."

Mary licked her spoon. "One of Aunt Mae's neighbors is a bee-keeper. One of our friends at church has an acreage with a few dairy cows. They each got some, so that leaves two for us!"

Violet scooped up the last spoonful in her dish. "Delicious! Thank you."

Several girls cleared the table, others stored the leftover food, and the Hamilton teens swept the floor and took out the garbage. Then, we listened to the Glen Miller Band's "In The Mood" and the Andrews Sisters' "Boogie Woogie Bugle Boy" on the radio while Vera, Reva, Violet, and I washed the dishes. Mary and Aunt Mae sat, drank tea, and chatted with us while they rested with their feet up on a kitchen chair. They did the bulk of the cooking. Uncle Henry sat around the corner, reading the newspaper. Eddie fell asleep after lunch, and Uncle Henry gently placed him in his playpen in the opposite corner.

When we'd finished the dishes, Violet and I did an impromptu dance to a few of our favorite songs on the radio. Vera grabbed Mary to join us. Reva grabbed another girl. Uncle Henry grabbed his wife for a dance. Eddie woke up from his nap in his playpen and squealed in delight as we all danced around the kitchen, so Uncle Henry grabbed the little boy and danced around with him in his arms. Girls in the sitting room jumped back up to dance with us. What a wonderful afternoon. We'd become a family.

November turned to December. The aircraft factory arranged for Christmas music and some chocolate bars, and then we headed back to work. In early December, Edward R. Murrow delivered his "Orchestrated Hell" broadcast over CBS Radio, describing a Royal Air Force nighttime bombing raid on Berlin. "Berlin was a kind of orchestrated hell, a terrible symphony of light and flame."

Violet's five student nurses finished their coursework, took their tests, and passed in December. Violet seemed modest about her contribution to their success, but her supervising nurse and the head of nursing both acknowledged her in the ceremony.

We celebrated Christmas with our California family of Mary, Eddie, Aunt Mae, and Uncle Henry. A package arrived from home, with some molasses cookies, hard candy canes, and a few small gifts. Mother included letters from our brothers, and we sighed in relief they all were all right, despite a few minor injuries. Mary got several letters from Ed and sent him a package for the holidays.

At the boarding house, we combined our ration cards for a holiday meal. We ate spaghetti and meatballs, lettuce and tomato salad, fresh fruit cups, breadsticks, soft molasses cookies, and more of the wonderful honey ice cream for dessert.

On New Year's Eve, we attended a church service with Mary, Reva, and Aunt Mae. Eddie stayed home with their teens. As we prayed, Violet and I reached for each other's hand, and Violet also reached for Vera's hand, who sat beside her. On my other side, Reva and I held hands. I took a breath and visualized my brothers, my childhood friends, Ed, and classmates now in harm's way.

The pastor led us in prayer, and tears trickled down my face as I reflected on the lives already lost in our farming community and the ripple effect of those losses in their families. Would our brothers come through the war safely? How long would this war last? Could the Allies prevail over the Nazis and the Japanese?

But that's enough for now.

Twenty-Four

Tragedy at Anzio

"I would like to be known as an intelligent woman, a courageous woman, a loving woman, a woman who teaches by being."

~Maya Angelou

$\mathcal{I}$ looked over at Aunt Violet, and she nodded. I flipped out the old tape and inserted the next one.

Tape #10, Tragedy & Telegrams
  Grandma Grace's voice was strained.

Gracie, 1944 started with lots of drama. The Soviet Army routed the German Army surrounding Leningrad on January 27, ending one of the longest and deadliest sieges in history. The Russian people had endured for two and a half years, but at the cost of over one million soldiers' and civilians' deaths.

Battles broke out on both the European and Pacific fronts as the new year began. Letters from home brought news no one wanted to hear. Violet and I cried every time we opened a letter, while Vera tried to be stoic.

Vern's plane was shot down, and he and his crew did a water landing. He survived but injured his head. Victor was wounded in battle, but no one knew the details. Virgil's unit came under heavy fire, and he was one of a handful not seriously injured. Uncle Paul's battalion moved through Italy to assist in the fight there.

Then, in early February, we received a telegram from Mama, and it broke our hearts. Victor had died as the result of his wounds at Anzio. We grieved, thinking of our parents and grandparents.

Vera walked in, and we showed her the telegram. "He died fighting for our country." She looked sad. "He was a good big brother." She walked to the twins' room.

Violet and I shook our heads, blew our noses, and took a breath. "I think we should call Mama," I suggested, and Violet agreed. We gathered our coins and walked downstairs to the telephone booth across the street. Having seen the chaplain and officer visiting Frances, Violet and I knew all too well what poor Mama and Daddy had endured.

When Mama answered the phone, we talked between tears. She told us to stay in California. She wasn't sure if they could have a funeral.

After a few more minutes, she told us, "Here, Daddy wants to say hello." Her voice broke, and my father sadly greeted us, "How are my girls? I want you to know we're proud of you, and we're proud of your brothers. God bless Victor. He was such a brave young man. I hope a friend held his hand at the end. I hope he didn't die alone."

We cried our goodbyes, dried our eyes, and returned to the boarding house, where word had spread. Reva, Mary, Aunt Mae, and Uncle Henry greeted us with hugs and offers of sympathy. We sat down for a cup of tea and talked around the kitchen table. Mary tried to hide her anxiety for Ed, and I whispered, "We're all praying for Ed."

Later, we walked up to our rooms, and Violet lingered in mine for an hour, our broken hearts full of memories. Victor gave us piggyback rides when we were young. He was kind, generous, and thoughtful. When it snowed, he checked on us at the schoolhouse with his big wagon and drove everyone home. I could hardly bear to wonder how he'd died. I hoped Daddy's wish came true, and a friend held his hand.

One day, Reva seemed excited about something on our bus ride to work. She was waving a letter from home. "Grace, my father got permission to take some packages to the internment camp, and he saw the Namimoto family. He gave Lily my package." Reva's face glowed with excitement.

"Great news. How is she doing? How is her family?" I asked.

"Dad thought they looked good. He took pictures, and she looks wonderful, considering the awful circumstances. The whole family enjoyed seeing him. They miss Harry and worry about him. Dad is returning and hopes that I can go along too," Reva said.

"What did you send her in the package?" I asked.

"I told my mother to pack up some of Lily's piano books, along with a couple of her novels, and add some stationery, envelopes, pens, and stamps. Mom added a few things for Lily and her parents, too. A few Hershey bars, hand lotion, nice soap, shampoo, toothbrushes, toothpaste, and nice toilet paper." she giggled. "Dad had to find a bigger box. Mom is such a practical person, but they liked it."

"Great choices," I nodded. "I remember you mentioned they have a piano in the chapel, right? I think she'll appreciate the fact you are thinking of her."

I thought of how lucky Lily was to have Reva as a friend, and how lucky I was, too. Reva made our stay in California much better. Not only did we ride the bus together, but we shared our worries and dreams, and in doing so, we became good friends. She and her grandma also introduced me to avocados.

Suddenly, spring made itself known. We admired the flowers, even as we read about more battles, more bombing raids, more victories, and setbacks. Later, we found out that we had sent one and a half million American troops to the United Kingdom by May 1944. Operation Overlord, or the Battle of Normandy, began when 1,200 British bombers dropped 5,000 tons of bombs on German gun batteries on the Normandy coast to prepare for D-Day. The first Allied troops landed in Normandy. The next day, D-Day began with over 155,000 Allied troops on the beaches of Normandy in France. They pushed inland, as Hitler attacked England with V-1 flying bombs.

The newspaper headlines announced the latest war news, and so did the newsreels at the movies. Across the country, American families gathered around their radios to listen to the President's Fireside Chats when he gave updates from the wars in Europe and the South Pacific. We didn't have your internet, Gracie, but people read, listened, and talked.

One evening, Reva told me about her latest letter from Lily, with tears in her eyes and a trembling voice. We walked out onto the porch for privacy. Lily wrote to her about another unit, made up of Japanese American Nisei, the 100th. They cleared out the German troops to liberate Rome but got orders to remain roadside while other troops marched by in a slap in the face. Reva sighed, telling me the story.

Then the 442nd Regimental Combat Team arrived, with Harry's unit, and the two groups combined. They cut off the Germans in Belvedere on June 26, 1944. They destroyed an entire SS battalion and got the Presidential Distinguished Unit Citation, the highest award for a military unit. Harry saw fierce action, getting wounded, but refused to leave his unit until after the fighting stopped. He recovered in an Army hospital and returned to his unit.

With a shock, I realized my brother Victor fought during the first phase of the battle for Anzio, and Reva's friend Harry and his unit finished the job. I tried to explain to her, my voice suddenly shaky. I couldn't stop the tears as I struggled to explain what happened, and what it meant to me.

Reva put her hand on my arm in comfort. "So strange, isn't it Grace? Two soldiers who never met, and one finished the battle the other one started so bravely."

I nodded, genuinely moved by the intersection of my brother's unit fighting for Anzio and her friend's unit securing Anzio months later. I realized then again how much I loved Reva and appreciated her friendship. She understood me.

I grabbed my handkerchief and willed myself to stop crying. "Yes, you're right. Harry sounds like a wonderful young man and a fearless soldier," I managed at last.

"And so does your brother, Victor. Lily says his parents are so proud of Harry, and she is too," Reva told me. "But she worries about him, of course, and so do I."

We embraced and walked upstairs to tell Violet about Lily's letter. I wanted to write to my parents and let them know what I had just learned. I thought the news might comfort them, somehow, to know such fine young soldiers fought the battle.

We told Violet what Reva learned from Lily's letter and read it aloud for her. We shed a few more tears. Violet responded the same way I did. She thanked Reva. We sat down and wrote a letter to our parents, copying details from Lily's letter.

Later, I slipped over to see Mary and relayed the news. She hugged me. "What an amazing story."

So far, Ed's ship hadn't been in any battles and kept busy doing repairs.

That's enough for now.

Twenty-Five

War-time Memories

"Give sorrow words; the grief that does not speak whispers the o'er-fraught heart and bids it break."
~*William Shakespeare*

Aunt Violet looked sad, prompting me to speak up. "I'm so sorry. I didn't know you lost a brother in World War II. He sounds like a wonderful guy."

She told me, "Victor was a wonderful brother and too young to die at 24. He gave us piggyback rides when we were little girls. When it snowed, he checked on your grandma. He'd hitch the tractor to a farm wagon, drive up to the schoolhouse, and take her and the children home."

Then she stood up and bagged up a few cookies. "See you next week. I know you've got a lot to do, so go get it done!"

We walked to the front door. Her kitty following us.

I was glad Aunt Violet had Beatrix for companionship—and comfort. I hated to leave. "See you soon, Aunt Violet. Bye, Beatrix."

I called my parents and offered to bring sandwiches to *The Jubilee Times.* Mom fetched her tape recorder, and we listened to the recent tapes. Dad smirked at the stack of four new tapes. However, he sat and listened to the first two, looking somber by the end. Then his phone rang, and he left the room.

Mom looked at me with tears in her eyes. "This takes me back to when your brother deployed in the war in Iraq."

I nodded. "Yes, me too. I remember worrying about Mark and wondering if he was in danger and if he received our latest care package yet."

"I still stop when I see beef jerky and his favorite granola bars in the grocery store. I want to buy them for the next box, and then I remind myself he's home now, safe."

Then, Mom told me, "I didn't know my mother's big brother died at Anzio. How awful not to bury him in the family cemetery. Although there is a military plaque there, just no headstone."

"Was Anzio an important battle?"

Mom thought. "I think so, yes. Your grandma certainly thought so."

It was quiet as we thought about Grandma's brother dying at Anzio.

"I can't imagine how horrible it would be to not have my boy's body come home. I just realized what the military plaque meant." Mom looked teary-eyed.

I put my hand on hers and tried to lighten the moment.

"What did you think of Grandma Grace and her sisters wearing skirts and slacks?" I asked her. "And the reaction to her wearing slacks on the bus?"

Mom looked thoughtful. "We couldn't wear slacks to school, even during the winter, until I was in high school. They just built the new JJ High School in 1969, and the School Board actually debated whether the girls in sports could use the facilities for their practices." I did an eye roll, and Mom told me, "Yes, really."

She continued, "I remember the school sending home a note to the parents to not drop off their daughters wearing miniskirts too early. Some girls stood in front of the doors for twenty minutes or more and then were sent to the nurse complaining of pain, with chilblains on their thighs. We've come a long way, Gracie."

"What a crazy fashion choice, wearing miniskirts in an Iowa winter! Why not let girls wear slacks? Let me guess. Men were in charge, right? Male school board members, male coaches, and male administrators."

Dad walked through the break room and grabbed a brownie. "Are you girls trash-talking men? We aren't all savages, you know."

Mom replayed the part of Grandma's tape where she talked about skirts and slacks. Dad listened. "I apologize. It sounds like your grandma met a few rude men. I've seen it happen when men get together. Take three guys and on their own, each one is a great guy. But put them together and watch out. Suddenly, they're acting more like a pack of feral dogs than civilized people. Of course, add in plenty of alcohol, and there you go. I'm sorry they made crude remarks to her on the bus and happy to know she learned how to deal with them."

Mom played the tape about her brother dying at Anzio.

Dad sat down. "I've wondered about your great-uncle. I've seen the military plaque. Anzio was an important battle, bloody, and drawn out."

He looked at us. "These tapes are bringing back my American History classes and a lot of memories of your Grandma Grace. I grew up knowing her, you know. She was a wonderful woman. Non-traditional—Grace loved wearing a work shirt and jeans, putting her hair in a ponytail, and working on an engine with Richard."

Mom smiled, remembering. Dad put his arm around her.

I listened, wishing I'd known my grandparents in those earlier days. What a romantic gesture to help your girlfriend pilot a plane to Iowa from California, and then show up with your plane and propose. My grandparents had been an extraordinary pair. My parents were another. Would I ever find someone who loved me that way?

I kept busy the next few days, between classes and the museum.

Carl liked the final layout of the exhibit, and the quilts looked lovely, as did the signage. However, the oral history aspect pulled it all together.

We did a preview tour for the museum board of directors. They walked around, listening to the audio clips of women talking about quilts at each of the ten stations. They looked at the signage, with quotes about quilting, names of quilt patterns, and the person or family who donated the quilt to the museum. At the end of the tour, they gave us feedback, several digging for Kleenex. They liked it.

I created a virtual preview for the museum website, with highlights of the tour, and uploaded it. I picked up the brochures from the print shop at *The Jubilee Times*, and my follow-up article about the quilt exhibit appeared in Friday's newspaper.

Other area media outlets contacted me for interviews and promised they would be there for the opening. I found five new advertisers for *The Jubilee Times* and developed fresh ad campaigns for two of our current clients. My parents seemed pleased with my work. I felt like my journalism degree paid off!

I'd invited Steve to attend the opening of the exhibit, but didn't know if he would come. Things continued to be strained between us.

I got a series of text messages from Stephanie, his younger sister, who called Steve a jerk. He'd talked to her about me and our fight.

As I folded laundry late Tuesday night, I looked forward to tomorrow's visit with Aunt Violet. Agatha stretched out in her usual spot on the couch, watching me. I scratched her ears.

"What do you think, Agatha? Will Steve show up? Do I want him to? Why is life so complicated?"

Suddenly, another image popped into my head—David. What if David showed up at the opening? I realized I really liked him, which was a problem if I had a boyfriend.

I tossed and turned, worrying about my relationship with Steve. Finally, I acknowledged to myself that the only way we could be together would be on *his* terms, not mine. I'd live and work in Des Moines, a big city where I didn't know my way around. I'd leave behind my family, friends, and the rolling hills I loved. I wouldn't be able to escape his temper if we were living together. Then, I remembered how angry Steve got the last time we were together, and how frightened I was. I didn't want to see him that angry again. So, what did we have to discuss?

Aunt Violet met me at the door the next day and took a critical look at me. "You look tired. Want to skip today?"

"I'm fine. It's been a busy week."

"Are you getting enough to eat?" She motioned to a plate of freshly baked blueberry muffins. She poured the tea.

Her kitten played on the floor nearby with a new toy, batting it around with her little paws, sniffing it, and looking alarmed when it rolled around.

"I haven't slept enough, but I'm young. I couldn't miss today."

I turned my attention to Beatrix. "Hello, kitty. How are you two getting along?"

"She's such a sweet companion. I'm glad to have her. She keeps me entertained."

"Those muffins look yummy." I sat down at the table and inserted the next tape in the machine. Then I put a muffin on my plate and pressed play.

Twenty-Six

Cowl Flaps & Fireside Chats

"You must do the things you think you cannot do."
~Eleanor Roosevelt

Tape #11, Celebrating a Year in California
Grandma Grace's voice was excited.

During the summer of 1944, we'd been in California for more than a year. We worked hard, worried about the headlines, and heard less from some of our soldier friends.

Mac, my new friend at work, the manager at Bartlett's aircraft, watched me work and seemed impressed with my ability to troubleshoot engines using some tricks I'd learned from my father working on those tractors. I assumed everyone else heard what I heard—the sound of a good engine with everything adjusted just so, as compared to an engine begging for someone to do some tweaking.

He knew I'd taught school and asked me to help train a few new girls while still getting my seventeen cowl flaps put together a day. I worked a few extra hours, and I didn't mind. I wanted to contribute something.

By now, you're wondering—what is a cowl flap? Let me explain. Our department made the cowlings, or engine nacelles, the cooling structures around the engine for the Boeing B-17 Flying Fortress. The cowlings could open or shut, as needed, and looked like a bunch of metal flaps in a circle.

So, I made the individual cowl flaps, and so did Josie. Then she and Joe fastened the cowl flaps to the nacelle, a circular structure housing the motor. The two-person job involved one person using a rivet gun, while the other person used a metal rod to push against it to ensure a good fit. As the motor got hot, the flaps would open to cool it down. Others in our area worked on motor mounts, plumbing, electrical harnesses, and everything else to hold a bare engine to a wing.

When the United States became involved in World War II, our company secured a contract with Martin Air to build power packages for the B-17 and B-24, rolling off assembly lines. As the men began being drafted or enlisting, the company realized they needed to replace them with women, starting in the late spring of 1942. Women made up more than half of the workers for both companies. By the fall of 1944, 12,000 workers helped build planes.

Before the war, I thought I would be a schoolteacher who helped Dad work on engines on the side. Now, I loved working with my hands, making cowl flaps, and helping Mac troubleshoot engines. I also enjoyed training new workers. My Iowa country schoolhouse seemed a million miles away.

Reva and I ate lunch together every day. One day, she looked excited and told me about going along with her minister father on his latest visit to Manzanar last weekend. Reva took the bus home to Los Angeles on Friday and then joined her father for a long car ride. But it was worth it because she saw Lily and her parents. Reva helped with a church service, which allowed her to see Lily and talk afterward. Lily gave Reva a picture of Harry in uniform.

Reva's father chatted with the Namimoto family and assured them he was collecting rent, and once released, they would have funds to restart their lives. He also took pictures of Reva with Lily, and of Lily and her parents, and Reva took an envelope out of her bag to show me the pictures. She and Lily stood side by side, their arms around each other, faces glowing with happiness.

The summer passed with a few movies, several trips to the beaches, and two bus rides to visit Reva's grandparents, who welcomed us. Each Sunday, we attended church with Aunt Mae, Uncle Henry, Reva, Mary, and little Eddie. We enjoyed the sense of family there.

In Italy, the Germans slowed our invasion, but by June 4, the Allies entered Rome, and my brother Vincent marched with those troops!

President Roosevelt announced he would run for a fourth term as U.S. President in July.

Then we heard the tragic news of a failed plot to assassinate Hitler conducted by a handful of Germans, including Col. Claus von Stauffenberg. The plotters and their families suffered at the hands of the Nazis.

The news sounded better by August 1944 with the liberation of Paris, but there had been much bloodshed, and there would be much more. I cut out the articles about the war for my scrapbook.

Bartlett's aircraft factory now sponsored a daycare center for its workers. Several women we work with dropped their children at the daycare before coming to work, and we recognized how essential affordable daycare was for working mothers. I walked by one day and recognized a co-worker.

"If we were back home, my grandma and great-aunt would help," she told me. "I couldn't stay there. With my husband deployed, I wanted to help build planes."

I agreed with her. I couldn't imagine having children and a husband off to war, but if I did, I would want good childcare and thought the daycare centers were a great idea.

At the factory, we celebrated a milestone with the completion of the 40,000th bomber. However, we went back to work after a burst of patriotic music and some Hershey bars. Our boys needed every plane we could build.

At the boarding house, we gathered in the two front sitting rooms to listen to the President's Fireside Chats on the radio. We admired his strong, confident, and defiant attitude. We felt reassured and told each other we had a powerful leader. FDR was known for his wisdom, sense of humor, and sharp political knowledge. Here are three of my favorite quotes:

"The only thing we have to fear is fear itself." Roosevelt's First Inaugural Address.

"There is a mysterious cycle in human events. To some generations much is given. Of other generations much is expected." Franklin D. Roosevelt.

"Yesterday, December 7, 1941—a date which will live in infamy— The United States of America was suddenly and deliberately attacked by naval and air forces of the Empire of Japan. As Commander-in-Chief of the Army and Navy, I have directed that all measures be taken for our defense. With confidence in our armed forces—with the unbounded determination of our people—we will gain the inevitable triumph—so help us God." President F.D. Roosevelt. 8 December 1941.

That's all for now.

Again, when the tape stopped, I looked at Aunt Violet. "I've learned a lot so far. It's one thing to read about the war in a textbook, and another thing to listen to Grandma Grace describe what you girls experienced living through the war and working on the home front. It's amazing to think of all the women workers at her aircraft factory, building planes."

Aunt Violet stared at me. "Don't forget the base. Women filled a lot of positions there, too. Nurses, a few doctors, nurses' aides, X-ray techs, secretaries, drivers, cooks, janitors, and ambulance drivers, to name a few. Then, you have women working in stores, running the business their husband or father left behind, driving the bus, subway, or train. I became convinced that women could do any job." She stroked the kitty in her lap, thinking.

Aunt Violet looked up at me. "Sometimes it feels like a lifetime ago, and some days it feels like just yesterday. Some of my patients were so horribly injured." She glanced down at the sleeping kitty in her lap. "War is a terrible thing, Gracie. It tears families apart."

"I keep remembering when Mark deployed to Iraq," I told her softly.

I packed up my tapes and tape recorder. Violet motioned at the cookies, and I bagged up a few. "I can see myself out." I kissed her cheek.

I walked down the hall and heard her whispering to the cat.

Twenty-Seven

A Family Meal

*"The most beautiful people I've known are those who have
known trials, have known struggles, have known loss, and
have found their way out of the depths."*
~*Elisabeth Kubler-Ross*

I barely made it to the car before my phone
pinged with a text from Mom.

How U today? Supper?

I giggled. She rarely used abbreviations in her text messages.

I called her. "Hey Mom, I'm just leaving Aunt Violet's. Want
me to pick up supper?"

"No need. We have pizza here and I made a salad."

"Sure, I'll be right there," I replied.

When I walked into *The Jubilee Times*, Mark and Kathy were chatting with Aunt Delores. "We came for the free pizza," Mark grinned.

"I hope they got the extra-large, then," I teased him.

We gathered around one of the long tables in the workroom,
passed the breadsticks, salad, and two kinds of pizza—one veggie
and one loaded with meat.

Afterward, Mom passed around brownies, and I told them about
the recent developments in the tapes, including the death of grandma's brother.

Mark commented, "I'm sorry to hear about Grandma's big
brother dying at Anzio. It seems like family members have served
in every war from what I've seen in the cemetery. What stories
could they tell, huh?"

Mom looked at Mark. He held up both hands. "Mom, I can read your mind. You want me to sign up for a family tell-all session about serving in Iraq, right?"

Kathy teased him, "You have a lot of memorable stories, Mark, like the guy in your unit with the giant pet spider he kept in the jar. Thankfully, he put some holes in the lid."

Mark nodded. "That camel spider was the size of my fist. My friend needed a bigger jar, and we all got nervous about it escaping. How about when Mom got mad because I traded my laptop for a Nintendo? They didn't have adequate internet access back then on base, and I saw this kid who wanted a laptop for whatever reason, so we swapped."

Mom remembered, indignant. "Who takes their Nintendo to war?"

Mark laughed. "I saw the poor kid about six weeks later, and he poured sand out of the laptop case. We lived in fancy tents and the wind blew sand around. I'll try to jot down some entertaining stories. Then it's dad's turn."

Mark looked at dad, and I could tell they were thinking about all the veterans in the family. His older brother Patrick, an Army photojournalist, deployed to Viet Nam, and died there, just a few days before his departure for the states. Dad served in the National Guard but didn't deploy. However, he helped after a few natural disasters like floods, fires, and tornados.

Kathy smiled. "With all the digital devices we have now, creating an oral family history is a great idea for a project. I think I'm going to assign something to my high school students."

Later, Mom sent me home with a couple of brownies and a couple of slices of pizza for lunch the next day. I left the last few tapes in her care so she could copy them.

We hugged, and Mom told me, "Thanks for the update on the tapes. Keep listening!"

I drove home, put the pizza in the refrigerator and played with Agatha and refilled her water dish.

I began working on my weekly column on the quilt exhibit. Previous columns covered individual quilts and quilters. I'd also written about the collaboration between the community college students, the museum, and the women who agreed to be interviewed. Now I wrote to invite the community to come to the exhibit.

My mind kept going back to the three sisters in California, Grandma's friend Reva, and Harry and Lily, the two Japanese American teenagers stuck in an internment camp. They all experienced the war differently and made sacrifices. I hoped their families knew their stories and how the war shaped them.

The next morning, I packed my messenger bags and headed to the newspaper office. I finished three brief articles and the column and sent them to my dad. Then, I headed to the museum.

As I walked around the exhibit, I realized I couldn't wait until next week to hear the next tape. I called Aunt Violet.

"Hi Gracie, how are you doing?" she greeted me.

"Can I please come over after work today and hear another tape?" She laughed. "See you at four."

When I arrived, Aunt Violet greeted me. I set down a bag of scones from Aunt Shirley's Cafe and grabbed two little plates from her cupboard. As I walked past the doorway, I saw Beatrix running back and forth on the loveseat out on the sun porch.

Aunt Violet explained the kitty spotted a rabbit running in the backyard, darting in and out of piles of leaves on the ground. "She seems to think they're playing."

I watched Beatrix and laughed. The bunny seemed curious, stopping to look at the small cat on the other side of the glass. It sniffed and then scurried away. Beatrix watched closely and seemed to imitate the rabbit, sniffing and looking and running.

Aunt Violet set the tea down on the table and poured it into our cups.

We sat down, and I plugged in the tape recorder and popped in the next tape. We were laughing at Beatrice while munching on our scones when we heard Grandma Grace's voice say something about meeting a young sailor named Don Anderson.

Aunt Violet's face changed from laughter to sorrow, and she dropped the scone back on the plate. She tried to put a more neutral look on her face.

I mouthed, "Should I stop the tape?"

She shook her head. "I'm sorry—I was just surprised."

Tape #12, Don meets Violet
Grandma Grace's voice sounded somber.

Now it's late August 1944. We worked hard and made friends at the church, boarding house, and work. The sun seemed to shine brighter and more intensely in California.

Then we met a young, handsome sailor at our church in town for a couple of months for special training before his ship left after the holidays. Don Anderson hailed from Minnesota, the son of wheat farmers. Six foot tall with wavy blond hair and blue eyes, Don had a wonderful personality, too. He and Violet warmed to each other on his very first Sunday, which made Vera jealous, of course. They chatted after the service, and I saw Vera's eyes narrow, but she said nothing.

I realized Don might cause problems, even if he seemed like a great guy. He was taking classes as a radar technician on base, and he stopped by Violet's hospital ward to say hello. We saw little of Violet for a few weeks. She and Don took long walks, enjoyed picnics down by the water, and talked and talked. Don possessed one of those wonderful laughs, you know. You wanted to laugh, too.

Meanwhile, Vera dated Jim, a manager from the plant, but she broke it off after three or four weeks. Jim had injured himself in the plant a few years earlier and walked with a limp, but it hadn't held him back.

Are you wondering about your grandma? Did she have a beau? I made friends with a young sailor, and we went to the movies a few times. He and I were friends, and he deployed shortly. I enjoyed spending time with the girls at the boarding house and my friends at church. We worked long hours at the aircraft factory, and I felt no desire to date. I didn't want to get too close to a man because he was likely to get sent off to war and might not come home. But I could see my sister Violet and Don getting closer.

Violet talked about Don constantly. He attended church with us every Sunday and ate lunch with us at the boarding house when he could get away. I saw him and Uncle Henry chatting away like old friends.

Don brought a gift for Eddie the first weekend he spent time with the family, a little package of three toy cars. Then, he and Hank sat down on the floor and played with those toy cars with Eddie, and Eddie adored Don too. He fit right into the family. Violet glowed.

A handsome man in his navy uniform, Don seemed crazy about Violet. Could he be the right man for my wonderful sister? He'd have to survive the war, and the days were ticking away until his ship deployed right after the holidays.

Once he finished training, Don would be a radar man on the ship USS Ommaney Bay, an escort aircraft carrier. As he and Uncle Henry talked, I listened and learned more about his job. The Navy used radar to help navigate and detect enemy aircraft. Don would oversee all of that once done with his training.

I tried to be positive. Don and Violet were obviously in love. Surely, God would spare Don, and they would be together. I took a few pictures of the love birds, thinking I would send some home and give some to Violet.

In the meantime, I prayed for everyone I knew who had deployed. And so, the days passed into October and November, working hard at the factory to keep up with orders, daydreaming about flying, and trying to keep our spirits up.

That's all for now, Gracie.

Twenty-Eight

First Love & Ugly Memories

"A woman with a voice is by definition a strong woman."
~Melinda Gates

When the tape stopped, Aunt Violet looked down at her half-eaten scone.

"Don was *your* boyfriend?" I asked shakily. I recognized the name, then. Wasn't Vera's first husband an Anderson?

She sighed. "Yes. You might say Don was my first love."

"I didn't see this coming. Are you okay?" I thought about asking what happened to Don, but I couldn't. Aunt Violet looked so vulnerable.

She exhaled and nodded. "This all happened a long time ago. Just be patient. Your grandma is going to tell the entire story. Please understand, while I may be upset hearing Grace tell the story, I know it has a happy ending."

We cleaned up from our snack, and I packed up my tape recorder. I lingered for a few minutes and then checked the time. With the exhibit opening next week, I still needed to do a great deal, so I hugged her and left.

I climbed into my car and safely stowed the shoebox holding the tape recorder and tapes on the passenger seat. I thought of getting a salad from Aunt Shirley's Cafe. Then I saw Dad's truck down the street. My parents must still be at work. I called to check on them and offered to pick up supper.

After eating our salads and burgers, I told my parents about the latest developments. Mom looked pensive for a moment and then looked at me with an astonished look on her face. "Are you sure his name was Don Anderson? And he and Violet were dating? Not Vera?"

Dad looked up, also surprised. He put the rest of his sandwich down on the plate.

"Yes, I have the tape in my car. Do you want to hear it?" I brought it in, and we listened to it together on her cassette player.

Dad listened, and held out his hand for the tape so he could digitize it.

Mom sighed. "Poor Donna—poor Violet. Thank you. I see why Mother wanted to save this for you."

I didn't understand. "What happened to Don?"

Mom looked sad. "I'm not sure. Keep visiting Aunt Violet and listening to the tapes. Things are falling into place, but we don't have all the puzzle pieces. Let's keep this to ourselves until we know more, all right?"

I nodded.

I frowned as I got into my car. What happened to him? Violet married an Army doctor named Bob, not a wheat farmer named Don. Did something terrible happen to Don?

Saturday, Kathy called to see if I wanted to grab lunch. We ended up at the Jubilee Cafe and lingered over our Cobb salads.

"How are you doing?" she asked. "These tapes from your grandma sound pretty intense."

"They are. I want you and Mark to listen to them when you have time."

"We would like to hear them," Kathy admitted. "Mark's intrigued even if he calls them episodes from a soap opera, based on the tidbits your parents have mentioned. Speaking of soap operas, have you heard from Steve at all since those apology texts?"

"No, and I think it's for the best, you know?" I stirred the straw in my iced tea.

Kathy stared at me with a fierce look in her eyes. "Gracie, you listen to me. You're stronger and more capable than you know. You'll be fine. Remember, you come from a long line of strong women, like your Aunt Violet and your Grandma Grace."

I nodded, feeling teary. I felt thankful to have Kathy in my life because she'd become my big sister, and I loved her dearly.

"Have you thought about going to see a counselor?"

"No. I should be over this by now." I twisted a strand of hair in my fingers. "Besides, I saw a counselor at Iowa State for a few sessions."

"Those boys assaulted you," Kathy spoke firmly in a low voice. "You did nothing wrong. Fortunately, we found you before anything more happened. But I think you could use a session or two with my friend Charlene."

"I'll think about it. But right now, you're my counselor." Close to tears, I added, "Thank you for keeping my secret all these years. I wouldn't want Mom and Dad to know and worry or be disappointed in me."

"Your parents wouldn't judge you. It happened, and you've moved on. Let's plan a movie night, okay? If Mark is good, he can join us." Kathy looked at me kindly.

We finished our meal twenty minutes later, stood up, paid our bill, and told each other goodbye.

I headed home to tackle some chores, but ended up sitting on the couch with my clipboard to gather my thoughts. I took a breath, drank some tea, and let myself remember. Agatha climbed onto my lap, and I put the clipboard aside to hold her close.

I was away at college, in my junior year, and attended a football game with Mark, Kathy, and a group of his friends. At halftime, we got something to eat. Two guys from the group stood in line with me for hotdogs and recognized a buddy tailgating nearby. They talked me into going over to the party, so we yelled hello, but the group seemed intent on getting drunk. The two guys grabbed a beer and gave one to me, but as soon as I saw a trash can, I pitched my beer into it. We ended up walking around, seeing people, and laughing. I thought we needed to get back to the game. Halftime must be over.

The next thing I remember, we'd walked to an area over by a metal fence, away from people, and I was about to ask why we were here, when one boy grabbed me from behind, pinning my arms, while the other one fondled me, pawing at my clothes, and saying disgusting, sexual things. I yelled for help, but the boy holding my arms told me to shut up.

I kicked the boy in front of me. He slapped my face and sneered, "You might as well enjoy it because we're going to have some fun."

He tugged at my jeans and t-shirt after I heard him unzip his pants. I yelled for them to stop and cried, but they laughed at me. My purse hung down from my arm, and I tried to swing it but couldn't because of being restrained. I kept screaming.

Suddenly, we weren't alone. Someone grabbed the boy restraining me, and I fell forward, but Mark was there and caught me in his arms. A campus security guard grabbed the boy who had assaulted me. Mark asked if I was okay, but I was hysterical.

The security guard then radioed for the Ames Police. Mark held me while I sobbed, and he and his friend glared at the two boys who had assaulted me while they looked down at the ground. The security guard and Mark's friend backed them up to the fence so they couldn't move.

I looked like an awful mess. The one boy had ripped my shirt and torn my bra half off, and I'd felt him fondle my bare breasts. My cheek stung where he slapped me, and he'd unzipped my jeans. I couldn't stop shaking. The other boy had left red marks on my arms.

Mark took off his jean jacket and put it around me, after first furiously inventorying the bruises on my arms, the state of my clothing, and that his so-called friend had unzipped my jeans. Mark hugged me and told me, "I'm here, Gracie. You're okay. When you didn't come back after halftime, I came looking for you."

He called Kathy on his cell phone, and she got there within minutes. She'd been searching nearby. She stared furiously at the two boys, who looked down in shame, while she comforted me. She and Mark drove to the police station with me. I made a statement to the police, but my parents didn't have to be notified because I was nineteen. I decided not to press charges if they stayed away from me. I didn't want to testify in court because I didn't want to be labeled as a victim.

The counselor told me if there was another complaint, the University would expel them. The boys had to go to a session with a counselor and moved to a different dorm. Fortunately, I did not run into them again. But I paid close attention to whom I associated with and where I was all the time.

I'd attended Jubilee Junction Community College for two years before transferring to Iowa State. The incident reminded me I wasn't in my hometown anymore. While I never admitted out loud that the attack was another reason for coming back to Jubilee Junction when Dad suffered a heart attack, I felt safer here. I worried about him and wanted to help mom.

I never told Steve about the assault because I felt ashamed. Suddenly, I realized how I'd pushed him away, in part because of the assault. I seldom drank alcohol because I'd heard too many stories of men sexually assaulting women after being at a party with lots of beer or hard liquor.

I felt a rush of emotions—shame, guilt, and fear. I remembered how angry Steve had gotten and how afraid I'd felt. It triggered that sense of helplessness I'd felt during the assault.

Agatha meowed loudly, and I realized I'd been clutching her rather tightly for several minutes. I felt cold and shaky. I let go of her, and she scampered away, still meowing. Then she settled down at my feet, looking up at me. I breathed out slowly three or four times and grabbed the blanket on the couch and wrapped it around me until I felt calmer and more in control.

I thought again of Kathy's friend Charlene Mason, a counselor in town. I didn't think I needed counseling. However, Agatha might disagree, and if she possessed opposable thumbs, she might be dialing Charlene's number. I'd stapled her business card to the inside cover of my planner. I told myself I'd see how I felt in a few weeks. However, I remembered Mark's arms around me when he found me and Kathy's assurances that I was stronger than I thought. I would always appreciate what they did to help me.

Twenty-Nine

The Quilt Exhibit Opens

"Life shrinks or expands in proportion to one's courage."
~Anais Nin

The following Monday morning, Iowa Public Radio aired the interview with me about the quilt exhibit. I walked into the classroom, and one of my literature students teased me, "Hey, you're a celebrity, Miss O'Connor."

Leaving class, I recognized David in the hallway. He walked towards me and smiled, stopping briefly.

"I hear you're some big-time celebrity now. Excellent job on the IPR interview. I can't wait to see the exhibit." He kept walking, so I called "Thanks!" and kept moving, too. But I smiled all the way to my next class.

Tiara and I chatted in the adjunct office. She felt excited, and so did her students. "This PR buzz about your exhibit has been a real boost for the college, too," she told me. "It's good publicity, and those pictures of my students with your aunt and her friends and the story about the oral history project will help us during budget time next year. I'm adding an assignment to the syllabus, and I want to get some little digital devices to record interviews with software to edit them. Girl, you did a good job!"

Monday morning finally arrived, a gorgeous day with the leaves an array of fall colors and the temperature cool enough for a sweat-shirt. The sunshine held the promise of a magical day.

As soon as classes ended, I dashed to the parking lot. When I arrived at the museum, I saw more cars than expected since the exhibit didn't open for another hour. The bank across the street offered to let us use their parking lot for overflow, and two TV trucks greeted me.

I entered the staff door, checked my make-up and hair, and as I walked into the foyer, I saw Steve standing by the front door, holding a vase with red and white roses. He looked happy to see me, put the vase down, and hugged me.

"I didn't think you would come," I admitted.

"How could I miss it? This is your big day."

My family arrived, as did the reporters and photographers. The crowd milled around in the entryway, impatient to get into the exhibit. I saw museum volunteers standing at a desk in the corner taking money and bagging up merchandise as people bought postcards featuring the quilt exhibit, t-shirts, other gifts, and special edition exhibit guides.

Carl stood up formally and got the crowd's attention. "We planned to wait until 2:00, but we're opening the exhibit early because of your interest. I want Gracie O'Connor to step up here because she's spent hours creating the exhibit, and you're all in for a real treat."

I stood up and looked around.

"Thank you, Director Patten, and thank you all for coming. This exhibit represents Jubilee Junction's history—your history. Your mothers, aunts, grandmas, and great-grandmas created works of art to keep their families warm, brought color and charm to their homes, and crafted treasures to hand down from generation to generation. I want to thank my family members for participating and telling their stories, as well as everyone else who took part in the Oral History project with Tiara Butler's Oral Communication class at Jubilee College—and here they are!" I gestured.

Aunt Violet and her friends from the Prairie View Senior Center had arrived and were met with applause. Several college students stood with them, along with Tiara, and they all grinned and waved.

I explained, "As you walk around the exhibit, you'll hear the voices of local women describe the quilts. Just press the quilt icon on the small computer at each station. Thank you again for the help from the students in editing the oral interviews, and for our volunteers who will stand by to help at each station."

As I spoke, my students and volunteers walked to their stations and powered up the netbooks.

The guests of honor walked around the exhibit first, along with our mayor and city council members. College administrators, the Director of Tourism, store owners, bankers, and others followed them. Steve and I walked around together, with my family close behind.

There was a reception, and as people mingled, I looked around, excited. Aunt Violet and her friends were celebrities and so were the students who interviewed them. I walked over and congratulated her, Tiara, and all the women we interviewed. They seemed happy to be there. A crowd of family, friends, and well-wishers surrounded them.

My parents congratulated me and hugged me.

"Great job, Gracie. You pulled this exhibit together nicely," Dad told me. "This is a good crowd." Then he smiled apologetically and grabbed the camera around his neck. "I need pictures for the paper. How about one with you and your mother? Then I'm going over to get pictures of Violet and Tiara and others."

"I love the way you used oral history." Mom hugged me. "Your grandma Grace would be so proud!" We posed for him and then he circulated the room, taking photos and greeting people.

Steve chatted with Mark and Kathy before joining me and Mom. "Your exhibit's wonderful. Everyone loves it."

Steve spent the night in Jubilee Junction, staying with Mark and Kathy. He never brought up getting a job and moving to Des Moines.

The crowds continued all week and into the weekend. The exhibit provided great publicity for the museum and the community. After going to the museum, people walked up and down the historic area of Jubilee Junction, checking out the town, the shops, the parks, and the Old Depot. They bought books and souvenirs at the Old Depot and postcards and gifts at the county museum shop. They looked for a place to eat. Aunt Shirley ran out of pie, brownies, and her daily special. She was both mortified and tickled and told me so the next time I came into the café.

"I have never run out of pie before!" she told me, scandalized. "But we're doubling our orders for ingredients and keeping up. I haven't been able to leave the cafe to see the exhibit, but I loved the photos in the newspaper insert."

Steve came back to see me on Saturday, and we attended the exhibit again, ate out with Mark and Kathy, and then drove back to my apartment for dessert. We played some board games, and then Mark and Kathy left.

Thirty

Steve's Offer

"A lot of people are afraid to say what they want. That's why they don't get what they want."

~*Madonna*

Steve and I sat on my couch and watched a movie. Agatha curled up beside me, and I petted her.

Steve looked at me. "Does that cat have to be up on the couch?" he asked in an annoyed tone.

"It's my home, and she's on the couch all the time."

He told me, "I think we need to talk about our relationship."

I felt a creeping sense of panic but smiled. "Sure."

"Do you remember how we talked about getting a place and moving in together a couple of years ago?"

I nodded, not trusting my voice, thinking, *So much has changed in the past four years. Like your career goals and anger issues.*

"I see how much you enjoy teaching, writing, and working at the museum. We have museums in Des Moines and colleges and newspapers. We could go back to Ames and look for a house," he argued.

I started to say something, and he stopped me with a kiss. "Just think about it."

We sat and kissed, and I mentally took a step back, and thought that I wasn't buy his sales pitch. He didn't get it. I loved Jubilee Junction.

He whispered, "I could just stay here tonight, couldn't I, Gracie?"

I found my voice. "Oh Steve, Mark and Kathy are expecting you."

I kept my tone light, but the alarm bells went off in my head like the Klaxon warnings in disaster movies. If I let Steve stay, he would see it as an agreement to move to Des Moines. I hoped he wouldn't respond in anger, but he nodded and kissed me goodnight.

The next day we met at church, enjoyed a family dinner, and attended a birthday party for Uncle Vern, so we had few opportunities to talk. He sweetly kissed me goodbye a few hours later. I knew now he would never agree to live in or near Jubilee Junction. His idea of compromise seemed clear—move to Des Moines, or maybe Ames. I decided to not panic and focus on my work.

Monday afternoon I walked around the exhibit, checking the netbooks before we opened. Carl told me people were just delighted with the quilt exhibit. As the doors opened, we welcomed a crowd, and our volunteers moved to the computer stations.

After work, I saw more cars on the street by *The Jubilee Times*. Inside, a small crowd of people walked around the lobby, admiring the view of historic downtown from the windows and asking questions about the town. Dad ran off more brochures for the exhibit, additional copies of the special edition of the paper with my four-page photo essay, a simple map of the town, and postcards with quilts on them. Aunt Delores displayed these materials on one section of the reception desk, with a sign listing their prices.

My cousin Allie talked to people and answered questions as Aunt Delores calmly collected money, bagged up merchandise, and smiled at everyone. I'd never seen this many people here at once.

Mom saw me looking around. "Lots of people are coming to town for the exhibit and stopping in to ask for information—and buying things."

Aunt Shirley's Café's parking lot looked packed, with several people standing in line outside the entry talking, so I decided to visit her another day.

It was Wednesday, so I stopped by Aunt Violet's, and she beamed at me.

"I've taken three phone calls about groups who want me to talk about quilting. My friends feel like celebrities. It's so much fun."

"That's wonderful!"

"Three of us are organizing a workshop in basic quilting techniques for the Adult Education Department at the College," she told me. "Imagine! What would your grandma say?"

"She would say 'Good job,' don't you think?"

We chatted over tea and cookies. Beatrix played nearby, and I realized again what a splendid companion the kitty was for her. I retrieved the tape recorder and inserted the next tape.

Tape #13, An invitation to Fly
   Grandma Grace's voice sounded cheerful.

One Monday morning in early December, as I worked in my area, my leadman told me the plant manager wanted to see me. I finished my work assembling a cowl, washed my hands and checked my hair, and walked to his office. A secretary sat out front. She showed me into his large office and asked if I wanted something to drink. I accepted a small bottle of orange pop and sat down in the chair in front of the desk and admired his view of the runway from a large window.

Then Mac walked in with another man and introduced us. Mr. Bartlett smiled and asked me the most amazing thing. "How would you like to fly in one of those planes you helped build?"

I knew the WASPs ferried planes to bases, but I built planes—I couldn't fly them. I felt thankful I was sitting down, so they couldn't see my legs trembling.

Mr. Bartlett explained he wanted me to help some experienced women pilots deliver a plane, but he also needed a favor. Would I be willing to pose with some other workers for a government photographer coming to the factory next week? The photographer wanted to feature women doing all kinds of jobs for an article about women working on the home front.

"Mac told me what a great worker you are, and how skilled you are with engines. I see you out there, watching the planes over your lunch hour. I think you'd be great for this project. We'd take pictures of you and your friends riveting, as well as all the other jobs we do here at the plant, and then you would help to deliver the plane to an airbase."

Mac explained we would fly a plane to a base a couple hours away in California then take more pictures at another factory, and I would get a bonus for my participation. I didn't tell him I would have paid to participate. After dreaming of flying, I was going to be part of a flight—on a B-17 Flying Fortress! The resulting photos and stories will appear in a national magazine. I couldn't wait to tell Violet and Reva all about it.

Later, I later learned the bittersweet reason behind the photoshoot. The WASP program ended Dec. 20, 1944, after training over a thousand women. These wonderful women pilots freed up male pilots for combat. As I record this, I'm looking at the Wikipedia entry for them, in 2008. Can you imagine such a wonderful resource?

It says the WASPs flew over sixty million miles, transporting all kinds of aircraft. They towed targets for live-fire practice, simulated strafing missions, and transported cargo. During the war, 38 WASPs died, and one disappeared. This photoshoot would honor them and their service and including me and a few of the women in the factory acknowledged the role of women in the aircraft factories and elsewhere on the home front.

That's all for now.

When the tape stopped, I grinned. "Grandma Grace got to fly in one of those bombers and be in a photoshoot? What a remarkable story. Do we have any of those pictures?"

Violet smiled. "The clippings should be in the scrapbook. so, bring it along next time."

Beatrix followed us to the front door, and Aunt Violet picked her up. "I don't want to take the risk of her going outside. Goodbye, Gracie."

Thirty-One

Steve's Proposal

"People think at the end of the day that a man is the only answer [to fulfillment]. Actually a job is better for me."
~*Princess Diana Spencer*

$\mathcal{I}$had a quick dinner with my parents and left the tape there. When I got home, Steve called me and wanted to know if I could come to Des Moines for dinner and stay over at his sister's house this weekend. He sounded excited, which made me suspicious. He reported his parents and little sister would join us for dinner Saturday evening, and my stomach suddenly churned.

Saturday morning I packed my bag, arranged for a friend to check on Agatha, and climbed in the car for the hour and a half drive.

When I called to tell Kathy about my change of plans, she asked, "Do you think he wants to propose? What are you going to say?" She had an uncanny ability to anticipate my concerns.

I answered honestly, "I'm not sure. I don't think we want the same things anymore."

As I drove to Des Moines, I wondered what life might be like with Steve, in Des Moines, if I just gave in—compromised and did things his way. Could he be right—was I wasting my life in Jubilee Junction?

I reached his sister's apartment building and changed clothes. Stephanie apologized because she had to run an errand and would meet us at the restaurant. Steve picked me up, and we drove to downtown Des Moines, to a very fancy place, the kind with lots of vigilant waiters who jumped in to grab plates, refill water glasses, or brush breadcrumbs off the table.

I wanted to talk to him before we arrived at the restaurant, but he kept up a steady banter in the car, and I gave up. Steve wore a new suit, while I wore the new dress I bought for the opening of the exhibit.

I'd known his parents for nearly seven years—his father, William, a successful lawyer and active in local politics, and his mother, Elaine, a high school teacher of social studies. As we chatted, I realized Mr. and Mrs. Smith seemed nervous, too. We ordered our beverages, and Stephanie came in, apologizing for being late. She and I'd become friends, so I felt better seeing her there.

After we ordered our meals, we made small talk. They asked me about the quilt exhibit and promised to see it. I'd sent them the Special Edition with the insert, and we chatted about the pictures. Our salads came, and a fancy breadbasket. I took a warm roll and buttered it, but my stomach suddenly felt full of butterflies, and I wondered what Steve was planning.

The meals arrived, and we began to eat. As I took the first delicious bite of my salmon, Steve looked like the fifth grader who wanted to open the presents at his birthday party and couldn't wait any longer.

I'd barely swallowed that first bite when he stood up with a dramatic flourish and got down on one knee. He whipped out a ring box and started in on a prepared speech. I noticed other diners put down their forks to stare at us.

"Gracie Elizabeth O'Connor, would you make me the happiest man on earth—" he said and paused for dramatic effect.

His parents looked excited. Stephanie glanced at me, and I saw a mixture of emotions on her face, probably mirroring mine.

Suddenly, this scene seemed over the top, given our recent arguments. I stood up abruptly, grabbed my purse and jacket, and looked at him. "I'm sorry, Steve. I can't say yes. We haven't resolved our issues. You spent twenty minutes screaming at me because I didn't apply for that job just two weeks ago. You can't bully me into compromising by proposing in front of your family. I told you—I don't want to live in Des Moines, and I don't want to be a politician's wife."

I apologized to his parents and looked at his sister in a panic. My overnight bag sat on the guest bed back at her house. Stephanie jumped up. "Hey, save my food. I want the cherry cheesecake for dessert. Later, guys."

Steve walked after me, still carrying the opened ring box. "Gracie, stop. Let's talk."

I gazed at him in tears. "Why, Steve? You didn't want me to say anything last time we talked. You asked me to think about moving in together, but you didn't want my opinion. You thought you could bully me into agreeing to do things your way if you waved a ring in front of your parents. I want a partner, not a boss. Our relationship is over. I'm sorry. I don't know what more to say."

Steve fumed. He grabbed my right arm by the wrist, his finger and thumb clamping down. "You walk away from me now, and we're over, do you hear me? I wanted to give you this ring and get you out of Jubilee Junction. We could have a great life together. But if you don't want me, I'll find another girl to give this ring to and believe me, there are a lot of girls I know who would like the life I'm offering. So, I won't wait for you anymore. Do you understand me?"

His voice grew louder with every word, and he tightened his grip on my wrist.

I cried out in pain. Other diners and wait staff looked at us. Suddenly, I felt like a small animal, caught in a trap.

I used my other hand to pry his hand away. "You're hurting me!" I cried. "Let go, Steve. Please."

Several people stood up, unsure of what to do. "Are you alright, miss?" one man called out, and a waiter walked over to investigate and then walked away quickly.

Stephanie came between us and tried to pry his hand away. "Steve," she cried, "You're hurting her. Let go. Stop it!" He didn't listen. Stephanie hit his chest with her hands curled up into fists. She looked at her shocked parents. "Dad?"

Steve's usually kind face hardened, and he shook with anger, as his grip on my wrist became even more painful, and I continued to cry.

His father walked up behind him and demanded, "Steven, enough. Let go of Gracie's wrist this minute." Mr. Smith placed his hand on his son's hand and looked at him, and then at me.

A manager walked up to us, looking flustered, as half a dozen other diners were standing nearby, concerned. "Is everything all right here?"

Mr. Smith nodded. "I apologize for the disturbance." He shook hands with the man, and I saw multiple twenty-dollar bills pass hands. "Could I buy everyone a dessert?"

Steve finally let go, and I stepped away, cradling my injured wrist. His fingers and thumb left red marks on the inside of my wrist, which was throbbing with pain. My mind tried to reconcile the idea that the man I thought I loved had hurt me. I was sobbing now.

Steve stood there, looking dumbfounded, still holding the opened ring box. Finally, he closed the box and put it in his pocket. He walked towards me with his arms out, and I took a step backward, flinching.

His father put up a hand to stop him. "There isn't anything you can say to Gracie now to fix this mess."

Then Mr. Smith turned and looked at me sympathetically. "I'm so sorry, Gracie. We hoped you two would marry and give us some grandchildren." He looked at a server walking by. "Some ice in a small zip-lock bag, please?"

Steve's mother came up, looking shocked and apologetic. She hugged me and whispered, "I'm sorry about your wrist." Stepping away, she looked at her daughter. "Stephanie, please take care of Gracie."

She turned to her son, grief, anger, and disappointment in her voice. "You told us you'd worked everything out, Steven. Did you see the red marks on her wrist from your fingers? Gracie doesn't deserve your anger. We raised you better. It's a wonder the restaurant manager didn't call the police. Now come back to the table." That got his attention.

Steve looked stunned, finally seeing my wrist, stammering out a lame excuse. He turned and followed his parents, his shoulders slumped.

Stephanie stood beside me, shocked into silence, her arms around me. Then she exhaled and stepped away. The diners shrugged and resumed eating their meals.

I winced at the pain in my wrist.

Stephanie put her hand on my uninjured arm. "My brother's a jerk. I hoped you guys could work it out. But that's not happening, is it? You can't drive home tonight, especially with your injured wrist. Stay with me, and take off after breakfast like we planned, okay?"

I nodded, angry with myself. Why had I come? What did I expect to happen?

We stopped by the reservation desk, and Stephanie motioned me to a nearby bench.

I sank, trying to slow my breathing, and wiped my eyes.

A server quietly handed me a small zip-lock bag of ice, which I gratefully applied to my wrist. I looked up to thank her, but she'd slipped away, leaving several Kleenex in my lap.

"Stay here, Gracie." Stephanie walked back to the table and returned with our meals boxed up a few minutes later.

"Mom asked the waiter to pack up our meals to-go. My parents aren't happy with Steve right now for pressuring you—and hurting your wrist. I haven't seen him angry like that for years. They're having an awkward conversation I'm happy to miss. We can pick up some cheesecake at the front counter over there and take it home—my dad paid for it already."

I slipped on my jacket, put the small bag of ice in a pocket, grabbed my purse and meal box, and tried not to cry. Once in her car, I applied the ice again.

Stephanie chatted away, and by the time we drove back to her apartment we'd both calmed down somewhat. We found an old romantic comedy movie, *When Harry met Sally,* ate our dinners, polished off the slices of cheesecake, and ended with mugs of hot tea. Stephanie refilled the baggie of ice, and I kept it on my wrist while we watched the movie, and it felt better.

When the movie ended, she looked at me with tears in her eyes. "I can't believe he hurt you. Let me see."

I obediently held my wrist up. She'd offered to take me to the

ER earlier, but I didn't think they could help me, because nothing felt broken. It still hurt and looked terrible.

The next morning, Stephanie made omelets with cheddar cheese and paired them with cinnamon toast. We ate, and I packed up. After a hug, she followed me to the car with another baggie of ice.

"Call me when you get home, okay? Don't be mad at my parents. Apparently, Steve told them everything was good between you two. They love you and wanted you to be the one, you know?"

I nodded. "We'd just had a horrible fight over me not applying for that job. I didn't think he would try to propose so quickly afterward."

Stephanie shook her head. "It makes no sense. But my parents were upset that Steve hurt you, and so am I. Please get your wrist checked. Let's stay in touch, Gracie. You deserve to be happy. There's a good man out there waiting to meet you."

As I drove home, I realized that Stephanie and I would likely remain friends.

An hour and a half later, I pulled into my driveway. Agatha met me at the door with a reproachful meow. I sent a text to Stephanie and Mom, gingerly unpacked, unloaded the dishwasher, loaded the washer, grabbed my planner, and planned my week. My wrist hurt, so I took some Tylenol.

All the while I craved ice cream, felt depressed, and grieved having spent—no, wasted—almost seven years of my life with a man who'd hurt me. I would never have imagined it.

I told myself the exhibit's opening had gone well and so were classes. I was all caught up with grading. Why was I acting like such a teenage drama queen? I wanted to sit on the couch, hold Agatha, and cry. I wasn't sure Agatha would tolerate being held for long.

My doorbell rang, and I tried to pull myself together as I opened the door to find Kathy and Shelly.

Kathy smiled. "Want some company? Stephanie told me you might need a hug, and Shelly just baked chocolate chip cookies."

Kathy handed me a container of cherry chocolate frozen yogurt, and Shelly held up a Tupperware container.

"We're going to need some bowls and spoons." Kathy hugged me and shrugged off her backpack. "I brought a couple of good movies."

While Shelly set up the movie, Kathy quietly appraised the bruising and red marks on my inside wrist, and I flushed in embarrassment, remembering the scene in the restaurant.

"Stephanie asked me to check on you. She told me what happened. I'm so sorry, Gracie. It looks awful. Does it hurt?"

"It's better, really," I tried to talk but dissolved in tears at her gentle touch.

Shelly walked back over to see Kathy holding me gently and rubbing my back as I sobbed. Then Shelly saw my wrist.

Her face flushed with anger. "I never liked Steve, but I didn't think he would do something like this. Now, I'm wishing that I brought the wine after all, but Kathy said it wouldn't go with the cookies and ice cream."

Shelly's comment struck me as funny, and my friends held me close as I tried to stop crying and laughing and calm down.

I sniffled and tried to joke. "Would it be red or white wine, Shelly?"

She thought. "Maybe red with chocolate chip cookies and white with oatmeal?"

Kathy quietly packed fresh ice cubes into a small baggie and handed it to me, and Shelly found the nearest box of Kleenex.

The three of us polished off most of the ice cream and cookies as we watched one movie, and I kept the ice on my wrist. They needed to get home to their families and get ready for work the next day.

Kathy left last. "You're going to be okay. Mark wants to drive to Des Moines and slug Steve, but he'll cool down. I haven't told him about your wrist yet. Steve shouldn't have pressured you in front of his parents. You're right. He tried to bully you into saying yes, with the whole romantic dinner and his parents watching. But you're tougher than you think."

With one more hug, she left.

I knew Kathy had correctly summed up the situation. A couple of hours later, I nibbled one of the last cookies before folding laundry. I felt tired but strangely peaceful, thinking of the line from "Story of an Hour." *"Free! Body and soul free!" she kept whispering.*

On Monday, my students seemed excited about all the visitors to town, and the exhibit at the museum. Many of them told me their families were getting out their old photo albums and quilts, seeing the exhibit together, then sharing their family stories.

Shelly and Tiara greeted me in the adjunct office.

"How are you doing, Gracie?" Tiara asked. "Shelly mentioned the breakup with Steve. I'm so sorry."

Shelly looked up from her stack of papers. "Sorry—hope it's okay I told her."

I nodded. I felt self-conscious, wearing an extra-long-sleeved shirt today, to conceal the red marks. I was taking Tylenol for the pain. I wasn't sure who else Kathy and Shelly—or Stephanie—might have mentioned my injury to, and I didn't want to cry at work.

"I'm better today, thanks. I have a great support system." Sitting down at my desk, I carefully pulled out my planner and clipboard with my left hand. "It's been stressful, but I'm going to get through this."

Tiara gave me her Queen Tiara look. "Of course you'll get through it. Never doubted it."

Thirty-Two

Betrayal in 1944

"Writing a book, I thought, which men often do, but women only rarely has the posture of sewing. One hand leads, and the other hand helps. And books, like quilts, are made, one word at a time, one stitch at a time."

~Sena Jeter Naslund

*T*uesday, I wore long sleeves again, and the day passed quickly as I checked things off my list. I kept Tylenol in my purse and took it for the pain. On Wednesday morning, after classes and the museum, I headed for Aunt Violet's house.

I knew it was going to be an emotional day as soon as I walked in the door. Aunt Violet had asked me to bring the shoe box with photos and letters in it. I put the tape on, sat down, poured our tea, and noticed my hand trembled a little. Aunt Violet looked strangely vulnerable.

I reached out and took her hand. "Do you want to wait on this one, Aunt Violet?"

She shook her head. "No, not at all. First, let's find the magazine article about your grandma as Rosie the Riveter."

We flipped through the pages and found the article, a five-page spread featuring a dozen young to middle-aged women, ranging from pilots to mechanics to women working on assembling parts of the airplanes, like Grandma.

Then Aunt Violet sat back with a faraway look in her eyes. Her kitty played with a toy nearby.

I pressed play, took a cookie, and sat back in anticipation.

Tape #14, "Marry Me"
Grandma Grace's voice was sad.

This story is hard to tell. I don't like to hurt Violet by reliving these events. Our family would never be the same. While I got more involved with Mac and his boss at Bartlett's aircraft factory, planning the photoshoot, things came to a head with Don and Violet in early December 1944.

On Thursday evening, Dec. 9th, Don and Violet enjoyed a lovely romantic dinner at one of the little restaurants near the boarding house. They lingered over coffee and dessert, having a wonderful time.

Then Don brought out a ring box and proposed, catching Violet off guard. He told her his class had finished, and his orders came early. His ship was to leave on Monday, four weeks earlier than originally planned, and he wanted them to get married before he left—so this weekend.

Married? After dating for only a few months? Violet could hardly believe what she was hearing.

"I love you, Violet. Please marry me."

"Don, I love you. I would be proud to be engaged and wear your ring. However, I want to meet your family and have you meet mine. I'm a proper girl from a Christian family. I can't rush off to a Justice of the Peace. Surely you can understand, can't you?" she pleaded with him.

He didn't. "If you loved me, you would marry me now." He put the ring box back in his pocket.

Don paid the bill, walked Violet back to the boarding house in silence, and stalked off, angry.

He didn't kiss her or turn around when she cried out, "Don, don't leave. Let's talk. I love you!"

Instead, Violet cried in the arms of Reva who was sitting downstairs reading when Violet walked in the front door, sobbing.

"Let me make you some tea." Reva comforted Violet, and they walked toward the kitchen.

Vera overheard her sister sobbing from upstairs—she peeked

around the corner of the second-floor landing. Then, Vera calmly walked to their room, put on one of Violet's dresses, and walked after Don, who was pacing up and down along the street across from the boarding house. He didn't want to return to base just yet.

Mary was sitting by her window, heard the commotion, and saw Vera run down the front stairs of the porch. She asked Aunt Mae to watch Eddie, fast asleep in his bed. Mary followed Vera and overheard most of their conversation.

"Yoo-hoo, Don. I've changed my mind!" Vera called out, waving her arm.

Don didn't understand Vera—not Violet—wanted to talk, and felt tricked at first, but Vera persuaded him to go sit down by the water to talk.

"I heard you proposed, and my sister turned you down." Vera sounded sympathetic.

"Violet didn't want to get married this weekend," Don explained. "She wanted to wait because she wanted to meet my family and have me meet hers before we married."

Vera put her hand on his arm in a comforting gesture. "Lots of couples are getting married before the sailors ship out. I think Violet is a fool to turn you down."

Don told her, "I don't know what to do. I love her, and I expected her to say yes. I've been having dreams I die at sea. I want someone to remember me, to love me."

Vera soothed him, still stroking his arm. "I understand. My sister is too prim and proper. War changes the rules, doesn't it?"

Don turned and looked at her. "You understand me, don't you?"

Vera smiled. "Of course I do. I've been watching you with my sister and thinking she might not be the right person for you." She stroked his thigh as they chatted.

Don put his arms around her, and they kissed, tentatively at first and then more urgently.

They sat there for another half hour, kissing and talking. They embraced with increasing passion, and Mary thought Vera looked bored. Don breathed harder as they kissed.

Impulsively, Don looked at her. "Vera, will you marry me

tomorrow?" he asked, and she nodded yes with just a single tear on her cheek.

He dug the ring box out of his pocket and opened it, but Vera put up her hand. "Let's wait for tomorrow, alright?"

Vera packed a small bag on Friday morning after Reva, Violet, and I left for work. She called in sick and met Don at the court-house, where they married hastily before he deployed overseas. They checked in at the hotel on base and spent three days and nights together. Then, on Monday, Vera caught the bus to work as if nothing happened.

Mary, hiding in the shadows, couldn't understand every word but saw and heard enough to sicken her, and she slipped away, wondering what to do next. She, Eddie, and Uncle Henry planned to leave early the following morning to see Ed's parents in Tucson, Arizona, for five days, so she talked to Aunt Mae before they left.

Violet worked late on Friday and Saturday, because of an emer-gency with a patient, and stayed on the base on Sunday to help when someone else left early, sick. Vera didn't see Don off when his ship deployed on Monday. Don wanted her to go, but Vera told him she was thinking about how she would break the news to her sister.

Instead, Violet went to see Don off at the docks. She walked towards him, hoping to smooth things over from their awkward dinner.

Don saw her coming, couldn't face her, and walked away towards his ship. Around them, hundreds of sailors said goodbye to parents, sweethearts, wives, and children.

Violet walked after him a little faster and put her hand on his arm. "Don?"

Don turned around but couldn't meet her eyes. "I'm sorry. I'm so sorry. Forgive me. Forget me, Violet. I'm no good." He kept walking towards his ship without looking back.

Violet took the bus back to the boarding house in shock.

That's all for now.

I looked at Aunt Violet. She'd shut her eyes. Beatrix lay on her lap, and she gently petted her. A tear or two glistened on her cheek.

She opened her eyes. "I'm all right. Play the next tape. Like taking off a Band-Aid, isn't it? Do it quickly. Yes, these memories make me sad—but I'm here with you, and I'm all right. I had my happy ending with Bob."

I popped in the next tape and took a big breath, as if to prepare myself for whatever lay ahead. I had gotten so upset that I hadn't eaten my cookie. What else could happen?

Tape #15, Violet Confronts Vera
  Grandma's voice was regretful and somber.

I'd been out of town for the weekend for our photoshoot and arrived back on Monday afternoon. Reva met me at the front door and told me about Violet and Don's dinner and breakup. "I don't like to gossip, but Mary saw Vera with Don Thursday night, and then no one saw Vera all weekend."

When I walked upstairs and knocked on the door of the twins' bedroom, I found Vera sitting on her bed, flipping through a magazine.

I asked Vera what happened this weekend, and Vera told me the story as if it happened to someone else. She described persuading Don to sit down and talk, then kissing him and getting more intimate, and his proposal. She wanted to see if she could trick Don into choosing her over her sister and getting married. Now that she had married Don, however, she felt trapped, and her problems were about to get worse. In the middle of this story, Violet walked in, shaking with anger.

"What have you done, Vera? I wanted to see the ship off, and Don wouldn't look at me today—he wouldn't talk to me, except to say he's sorry, to forgive him, and to forget him. He's gone! His ship left today. I told him I would wear his ring and be engaged, but I would not run off and marry him. Now, I see *you're* wearing his ring—*my* ring."

Violet then looked at her bed, saw something, and picked it up—her rumpled dress—and threw it at Vera, who didn't look so cocky anymore. Violet took another step, closer to Vera.

"You wore *my* dress?" Violet looked at Vera. "I will never forgive you for this. What you've done breaks my heart. All my life I've done whatever I could to make you happy—swap hair ribbons, swap clothes, try to make you happy, try not to get us in trouble with Mama, or the teacher, or anyone else." Her voice shifted from anguished to furious.

"You've always pushed me to do things I didn't want to do. I never stood up for myself. *No more.* Do you hear me? You've betrayed me. You've destroyed my chance for happiness with Don. And you don't even love him, do you?"

Violet, my sweet, soft-spoken sister, seemed to grow bigger, and her voice grew louder and scarier, and Vera looked afraid.

She tried to explain. "At first, the proposal was just a joke. Then, I thought, well if he can't have Violet, he can have me! So, we got married."

This didn't help matters.

Violet took a step closer to Vera, who dropped the magazine, stood up, and looked afraid. The dress fell to the floor at her feet.

I felt paralyzed.

Violet took another step, and Vera backed up next to her dresser against the wall. Violet kept talking loudly, and Vera, for once, said nothing.

"You—my twin sister—have ruined everything. I love Don. I wanted to marry him, but I wanted to do it the right way—to meet each other's families, be engaged, and then get married. Are you happy?!"

Violet's words seemed to penetrate Vera's defenses, and she slumped in shame, looking down. Violet stood just inches from her twin. She punctuated her final words with her index finger poking at Vera's chest.

Aunt Mae heard the commotion and came to check on us. She didn't need to knock because the door hadn't been closed. Violet saw Aunt Mae, broke off, and sobbed in Aunt Mae's arms while I stared at Vera, who reverted to her normal defensive and unapologetic attitude. She told me she and Don married Friday morning and spent three nights together before he shipped out.

Several other girls stood in the hallway, hearing everything, but unsure of what to do. Reva was one of them.

Suddenly, I felt I'd failed to protect Violet by leaving that weekend for the photoshoot. Mother put me, the oldest daughter, in charge, and I let the family down. Soon, I was sobbing, too.

Reva and the other girls came in to comfort us. She put her arms around me.

Vera couldn't handle the hostile looks and stormed out.

Reva looked around the room. "Vera cannot come back here." We spent half an hour moving my things into the room with Violet and moving Vera's things into my old room. It felt therapeutic to work together.

Aunt Mae held Violet's hand and talked to her quietly, sitting on Violet's bed while we rearranged the twins' room around them. I saw the crumpled dress on the floor and hesitated before shoving it in one of my dresser drawers. I would deal with it later.

Reva left last. She shook her head. "I wouldn't have believed it possible for one sister to hurt another so badly. Grace, this is not your fault." She gave me a last hug. I sat down on my new bed and tried to figure out what to do next.

Vera returned later, just before curfew. Aunt Mae met her at the front door and told her about the new rooming arrangements, making it clear Vera had violated her trust and her sisters.

At Aunt Mae's urging, Violet sought out our pastor for counseling the next afternoon. Our routines adapted to the new normal, and both twins seemed quiet during our suppers for the next few nights. Reva and I sat together and tried to be supportive of Violet, who spent more time pushing food around on her plate than eating.

I think Vera realized she had gone too far, but her pride prevented her from apologizing, and she withdrew from everyone. The other women in the boarding house made snide comments, expressing their disapproval of her, or giving her the silent treatment. Her wedding ring became a scarlet letter.

While Violet grieved, I fought guilt because everything fell apart the one weekend I left town. I felt anguish at what Violet had experienced. I hoped to come back and talk about my exciting weekend, flying for the first time, doing the photoshoot, and getting to meet a group of women pilots and others who help build airplanes. But my dream of flying seemed insignificant now, and Violet's dreams were shattered, all thanks to Vera's selfishness.

That's all for now. I'm going to walk outside and try to calm down. If I am not there, please hug Violet. I have regretted going on the photoshoot for sixty years, even though Violet has told me repeatedly it wasn't my fault.

The heart remembers such pain.

Thirty-Three

Truth, Texts, and the Shredder

"Hearts live by being wounded."

~Oscar Wilde

*T*he tape stopped, and we both shed some tears. I gave Aunt Violet a long hug, and then I grabbed the box of Kleenex. We sat and drank tea, avoiding the subject until both of us seemed calmer.

We watched her kitten play with her toy, batting it around with her paws. We made small talk. She nodded and tried to smile. I started to ask, but she shook her head.

"Let's talk about this next week, alright?"

I nodded and packed up, and Aunt Violet walked me to the door. She looked tired and every bit her age. I hugged her and told her I loved her.

She responded softly, "I'm all right, really. Love you too."

I left, numb with grief.

I called in an order to Aunt Shirley's and picked it up at the register, not making eye contact with anyone. My messenger bag was slung over my shoulder as I took soup and muffins to *The Jubilee Times* office. I walked into the office and set the takeout bags on the counter.

Mom came out of her office and looked at me.

I sobbed.

She came over to comfort me. "What's wrong?"

I sat down and told her about the latest developments between sobs, and Mom looked at me in astonishment. "Vera tricked

Don into getting married because Violet wouldn't run off to the courthouse?"

"I have the tape in my bag. Have time to listen to it?"

I opened my messenger bag and retrieved the tape, and Mom brought her tape recorder. We listened to it together, eating the soup and muffins, setting Dad's food aside because he'd gotten a phone call.

Mom dabbed her eyes with her takeout napkin. "Poor Donna and poor Violet." She sighed. "I see why Mother created these tapes. Violet could have told us what happened, but I suppose it was too painful. So, my mother's tapes are explaining it for her, helping us understand what happened to the twins and the traumatic impact on Grandma's family."

I frowned. "What happened to Don?"

Dad walked in. "What's wrong? What did I miss?" he asked, looking at our tear-streaked faces.

Mom looked pensive. "Another tape. You'll want to listen to it, but I don't think Gracie needs to listen to it again. It's all falling into place." She hugged me.

Dad sat down to eat the soup and muffin and thanked me.

I waved goodbye, but as I did, my cardigan's sleeve fell back, and Mom saw my wrist. I flushed, hoping she didn't see it, and dropped my hand quickly.

Mom soon dispelled that idea as she hurried up to me, and gently touched my wrist with one hand, and held it in the other. She looked at Dad and he joined her.

"Who did this to you?" she asked.

"Steve," I whispered. I'd told my parents about the proposal blow-up, but not about my wrist.

Mom put her arms around me, and Dad's face darkened. "What happened?"

"Steve grabbed me by the wrist as I walked away from the table. He said some awful things, and he squeezed harder as he grew angrier. Stephanie told him to stop, and he wouldn't. Mr. Smith— his father—stopped him and asked a server to bring me ice cubes in a baggie."

And then the entire story poured out, including Steve's earlier outbursts of anger.

My parents and I sat down, and I cried some more as they comforted me.

"You're done with that man?" Dad asked.

I nodded. "Yes. I could never trust him again."

Dad patted my back like one would comfort a fussy baby, before he pulled away and asked, "Want me to get a posse together and go pummel him? I'm sure Uncle Vern, Uncle Rich and his boys, and Mark would go along. Heck, when I tell them about it, Aunt Delores and Aunt Maggie would join us."

I knew he was teasing, of course. But it got me giggling at the mental image. I exhaled and took the Kleenex Mom offered.

She looked serious. "Get your wrist looked at if it isn't better in a few days. You're icing it?" I nodded.

She grabbed her phone and took a couple of pictures. "I'm going to send the pictures to Delores and ask her what to put on it."

Knowing Mom, she would document it in her diary.

"When she responds, I'll pick it up, and we'll drop it off later," Mom told me.

I hesitated, then asked, "Don't be mad at his family—or Kathy, for not telling you. Stephanie called her and asked her to look at my wrist when I came home from Des Moines on Sunday. Stephanie offered to take me to the ER that night, but I thought nothing was broken, and I felt embarrassed. I'm not sure Kathy's told Mark yet."

Then Mom verbalized my thoughts. "What will he do to the next girlfriend? Break her arm if she doesn't comply with his demands? I never saw that violence in him. He hid it well. But if he wants a career in politics, this isn't a good sign."

I nodded in agreement, thankful to have it out in the open.

Dad looked thoughtful. "These days, everyone has a smartphone. Wonder if anyone at the restaurant documented it?"

I hadn't thought about that. I remembered all the people standing up, not knowing what to do. Did one of them get photos or videos? I tried to push those thoughts away.

Finally, I was calm enough to leave and could see Dad going into his office, probably to call Steve's father.

As I drove home, I tried to redirect my thoughts from Steve hurting me to the tapes and Aunt Violet and Don. When did Violet meet Bob, the Army doctor who became her husband? How does the California quilt fit into the story? What happened to Don? After all this time, I'd gathered more questions than answers.

I drove home, fed Agatha, and tried to focus on grading my composition students' argumentative essays.

The doorbell rang. Mom was there holding a paper sack. She gave me a brisk hug, handed me the sack, and told me to call if I needed anything.

I opened the sack to find a tube of homeopathic bruise relief gel, complete with a sticky note in Aunt Delores' handwriting. "Apply this several times a day, and it'll help with swelling, pain, and discoloration."

A second note from Aunt Delores made me smile. "I have a baseball bat with Steve's name on it. If he comes back to town, let me know. What a creep. Sorry, honey. You deserve better. Love, Aunt D."

I applied the gel and found it soothing. Agatha sniffed it suspiciously and then lost interest. So, I let her play with the paper sack, which she loved to do, with hilarious results.

I played some music while I graded for several hours, trying not to wince. Agatha lay near me, napping, worn out from her antics with the paper sack.

Later that evening, I received a series of texts from Steve. I was thankful he didn't call because I couldn't have spoken to him on the phone. My emotions were too raw.

```
We should see other people.
We can't resolve our differences.
Sorry I yelled at u & sorry for
hurting u.
My family says I was a jerk & u
don't deserve it.
Be happy, Gracie.
```

I hesitated and then typed back my reply.

> I agree.
> The best 2 u.

I wanted to add something about not hurting women, but decided he was part of my past.

Stephanie emailed later. "So sorry your relationship didn't work out, and sorry he hurt you. Let me know you're okay, please. Let me know if you ever need a place to stay in Des Moines."

I replied, thanking her for her kindness.

I sat on the couch and drank tea, half-watching television with Agatha snuggled up beside me. The phone rang.

Kathy asked, "How are you holding up?"

I told her about the texts from Steve, and she sighed. "Well, good for him. He needed to apologize. Now you can move on."

"I hope so. I'm not feeling very trusting."

"Give yourself time. I have a feeling you'll meet a guy who makes you happy. How's the wrist?"

"I'm icing it again. It bothers me to drive, type, and grade. I'm sorry—Mom saw it when I waved goodbye tonight, so my parents know."

"I told Mark, and he was upset. We were just debating what to do about your parents. This is too serious to hide, so it's a relief that they know." Kathy exhaled.

"Mom took photos. She sent them to Delores to get some gel, but I think she's also documenting it in her calendar and diary, like on one of her cop shows."

I told her about Dad's posse idea, and she chuckled.

"Steve better not come back to town. I liked his family, but he tried to control you."

After the phone call, I finished the set of papers and recorded the scores, then I went to my closet for my *Steve box*. It was full of cards, programs from plays we'd seen together, and other memorabilia. I plugged in my shredder and, before I could change my mind, I shredded each card and program. I'd have preferred the drama of a fireplace, but my rental house lacked one, so my trusty shredder was now my weapon of choice. The shredder always freaked out Agatha, and she ran over to see what was happening.

I picked her up and petted her. I thought. *Steve never warmed up to Agatha. The right man will like cats. The right man will see me as his equal and partner.* Agatha ran for the bedroom and hid under the bed until the noise stopped. I kept shredding until nothing remained in the box, and I felt strangely satisfied.

I walked into the kitchen to make myself a cuppa of chamomile tea, then sat down with my planner and *to-do* clipboard and organized my lists for the week. I remembered a line from the "Story of an Hour" as I put my pajamas on and crawled into bed. *"Free! Body and soul free!" she kept whispering.*

Agatha jumped up on the bed and snuggled down beside me. I shut my eyes and fell asleep almost immediately.

Thirty-Four

The Story of the California quilt

"Sisters, as you know, also have a unique relationship. This is the person who has known you your entire life, who should love you and stand by you no matter what, and yet it's your sister who knows exactly where to drive the knife to hurt you the most."

~*Lisa See*

*A*s November began, national politics became the biggest story, with the re-election of President Barack Obama, the first Black President of the United States. My family has always been active politically. My father wrote editorials and articles for *The Jubilee Times* to educate the voters about national, state, and local elections and issues. He promoted voting and was fond of quoting his father, "If you don't vote, don't complain!"

Tiara had actively campaigned for President Obama, and some of her students set up a voter registration table with volunteers from the League of Women Voters in the student union. Dad's mother, Grandma Molly, was the President of the Local League and had been busy with voter registration drives and candidate forums.

The college served as one of the polling places, making it convenient for students, staff, and the public alike to vote. Others drove to the Jubilee County courthouse downtown or the high school.

Tuesday night saw people gathered at the local pub, close to Aunt Shirley's cafe, or Ruby's Steakhouse to watch results. Aunt Shirley served her chili and corn muffins, perfect for warming up on a chilly November evening.

I sat at a table with Mark and Kathy, Shelly and her husband, and Tiara watching the results come in on a big screen TV that was only turned on for special occasions, like football games, the Olympics, or Presidential/Congressional Elections.

As people cheered and raised a glass, I held my mug of hot cocoa, took a sip, and smiled. I wore a sweater over a turtleneck to cover my wrist. I'd taken Tylenol earlier and was trying to celebrate with my family and friends.

Kathy quietly said, "How're you feeling?"

I shrugged. "I'm okay."

"Better days are ahead, I promise," she said.

I nodded, hoping she was right.

Wednesday, I knocked on Aunt Violet's door with a bundle in my arms. She'd called and asked me to bring it. She opened the door, smiled, and hugged me. Her kitten played with a rubber mouse in the kitchen and ignored us.

"Are you okay, Gracie? Your Mama told me you and Steve broke up. She also told me to look at your wrist. I can't believe he would hurt you. So, let's see."

Obediently, I rolled up my sleeve and only winced a bit. It had turned yellowish-green and still hurt.

"I'm okay, really. Aunt Delores gave Mom some natural gel, and I've been putting it on."

She held my wrist and examined it with tenderness and expertise. "You're done with Steve?" she asked.

I nodded.

"He kept you from leaving the restaurant by putting his hand around your wrist?"

I nodded again.

Aunt Violet looked at the wrist again. "You're young and healthy, and it's healing. He didn't break your wrist, and I don't think you need an X-ray. But always remember a man who hurts you once will do it again. Dr. Bob and I tried to help several young women in abusive relationships. Even a sweet little town like Jubilee Junction has its share of sad stories, broken hearts, and sometimes broken bones."

I cleared my throat. "Did you get the women away from their abusers?"

"Yes, and no. We drove one young woman and her baby to Arkansas, to family there. Another young woman bled to death at the hands of a man her family refused to believe could harm her while her two young children watched. If someone asks for help to get away from an abuser, always believe her, Gracie."

The look on Aunt Violet's face revealed such sorrow that pierced my heart. Then she exhaled slowly and looked at the bundle.

"I brought the California quilt."

We sat down, and Aunt Violet looked at the lovely quilt on her lap, the robin egg blue background now faded, and her hands trembled.

She slowly unfolded it. "Gracie, if you look closely, you'll see little discolorations. People cried while we worked on the quilt, so there were a lot of tears on it and a few drops of blood, too. Some tears were mine and Mama's, and sometimes they came from my aunts or grandmothers. There are also some terrible stitches, mostly from Vera, who got so angry I thought she might stab someone with her needle. I haven't touched this quilt in fifty years. Your grandma hid it away."

I put my hand on hers, tears dripping down my face. It was a lovely old quilt, faded from the years, with a patchwork pattern of rows of a variety of fabrics. She pointed out the various patches and identified the piece of clothing they came from, explaining her mother and aunts came up with the idea of making a quilt from clothes they wore in California to bring the two sisters together. The idea failed and created even more stress and grief.

I don't know what I expected—but after all these months of waiting, it was just an old quilt, with a faded blue background, representing the work of a family trying to reconcile the two sisters. Failure seemed to emanate from the quilt, or maybe I imagined it.

Finally, she sighed and set it aside. "Let's listen to the next tape."

I hesitated, and she looked at me. "What is it?" she asked.

"This was at the bottom of the basket, wrapped up in some tissue paper." There was a hint of perfume in the dress I retrieved.

Aunt Violet stared at it for a long moment. "I didn't know your grandma kept the dress."

Suddenly, it hit me whose dress this was and when it was last worn, but she surprised me.

"This happened a long time ago, a lifetime ago. Yes, this is the lovely dress Vera grabbed out of my closet, one of my favorites. I think Grace picked it up and put it away so I wouldn't see it. You can throw it away or use it for rags." She put it down, and I put the dress back in the basket before I refolded the quilt and put it back on the coffee table.

I grabbed the teapot and cups off the counter and placed them on the small kitchen table. As she poured, I grabbed a plate of brownies from the counter. We sat down, and I pressed play.

Tape #16, Actions have consequences
   Grandma's voice sounded tired and sad.

Sorry, Gracie. This episode is difficult.

Vera held her head high at the aircraft factory and worked hard. Since there were only a handful of secretaries, she paid little attention to the gossip about her situation. In the meantime, Violet poured her energy into taking care of her patients, but she cried in her sleep.

We talked every night in our room. She told me the pastor counseled her to forgive Vera, saying, *God's grace is sufficient*, but she was struggling. "I keep seeing the anguished look on Don's face as he turned away from me. He couldn't look at me. I don't understand how he could give her my ring and marry her. Marrying Vera makes no sense."

"He thought he might die in the war. That kind of stress makes people do things they wouldn't normally do." I tried to comfort her.

"I've forgiven *him*. It's *Vera* I am struggling to forgive now. I've watched my twin sister behave as though the world revolves around her for twenty years. She never says she's sorry, never admits she made a mistake, and never stops to clean up her own messes."

I nodded because I struggled to forgive Vera, too. She avoided us, and I felt relieved to not have to talk to her. Vera and I never got along. I realized now she'd been jealous of my closeness to Violet.

My excitement over my first flight remained one of the few things to bring me joy. One night, Violet and I finally found time to talk about it.

"I loved looking down. We flew over the base, the factory, and even our neighborhood with the boarding house."

"It sounds wonderful, Grace. I'm sorry you didn't get to tell me about it sooner."

We attended church with our California family. Vera stayed home, complaining of not feeling well. We think she didn't want to face anyone at church, especially Pastor Martin.

We came back to the boarding house for lunch and then took Mary and Uncle Henry aside to tell them about the weekend. Mary opened her arms to Violet while I held Eddie.

Uncle Henry drove Mary and Eddie to Tucson because Ed's parents were vacationing there, and they arrived back late afternoon on Saturday. They'd enjoyed a relaxing five days, and Eddie charmed his paternal grandparents. They'd missed out on the drama of the previous weekend, or so I thought.

Mary confessed to following Vera and Don. "I didn't know what to do. Neither of you girls was here, and I was leaving early the next day. So, I told Aunt Mae. Just in case Vera denied seducing Don, I saw her kissing him and rubbing his leg. I couldn't hear much, so I didn't know they planned to get married. I'm so sorry, Violet."

Uncle Henry stood up and paced the room in agitation. "How could Vera do such a foolish thing—betray her twin sister?" He shook his head. "Ed will be upset about this. He told your folks he would look after you all, too, and I promised I would do my best. How could Don do something so hurtful? What was he thinking? I'm disappointed in him. However, once upon a time, I was a soldier in the Great war, and I think I understand his emotions." He looked at his wife, who nodded.

"Oh, Uncle Henry, it's not anyone's fault but Don's and Vera's. He was anxious about going to war and did something very impulsive and hurtful." Mary wrapped her arms around Violet. "Her mama and daddy couldn't control Vera for the past twenty years, so how could we do it? Still, it's all I can do but march upstairs and paddle her behind! What a brat."

Violet straightened up and wiped her eyes with her hanky. "I'm sorry for falling apart, everyone. I'm tired of crying and feeling sorry for myself. I loved Don. But Mary's right—it's Vera's fault and Don's, and no one else's."

Then I looked down at Eddie, who looked back and forth from his mother to Violet to me and was looking upset, too. I patted his tummy. "Let's get some toys."

We found his ball and truck, and I put him down on the rug near our feet. Eddie rolled the ball back and forth and made funny noises when he pushed the truck around.

Taking a big breath, I confessed, "It's my fault. The attraction between Don and Violet was obvious to me. I shouldn't have gone to do the photoshoot. I should have stayed here to stop Vera—"

Aunt Mae walked into the room, wiping her hands on her apron. "I wondered where you all had gone. So, you're catching up Mary and Uncle Henry about the mess Vera made?"

Mary sighed. "Yes, and Grace here is trying to take the blame."

Aunt Mae looked at me. "Really? Are you a mind reader, Grace? How do you stop a man from proposing? How could you stop Vera from being Vera? I've been watching her from day one, but I didn't expect this sort of betrayal. Vera's been a selfish girl her whole life and finally, she went too far. Don't you waste your energy feeling guilty."

Mary nodded, and Violet looked at me. "I would never blame you for this, Grace. No one can control Vera. Mary's right."

Mary came over and clasped me to her tightly, patting my back. "You're a good big sister, honey. Your parents will not blame you. This is a mess, and it's all Vera's fault."

Violet came over and hugged me too, and Aunt Mae used her apron to wipe her eyes and joined the hug.

Eddie laughed and clapped at the sight of the four of us women hugging, laughing, and half crying.

Uncle Henry groaned. "We're outnumbered."

He picked up the little boy. "Let's go play with the ball, little man, and let these girls do their hugging and crying without us."

Four weeks later, Violet got a packet of letters from Don at sea, apologizing for being a fool and telling her he still loved her, but could not ask her to forgive him or wait for him. He'd dreamed some weeks earlier he wouldn't survive the war, and he wanted someone to remember him, to love him, but he regretted his hasty decision to marry Vera. A small picture fell out of the letter—of Don in uniform.

Violet picked up his picture, took a long look, and tucked it into the letters without another word.

She didn't know it, but he wrote to Vera, asking for a divorce.

I told Mama and Daddy everything in our next letter home. Our California adventure was like a lovely vase shattered into too many pieces to glue back together.

Christmas of 1944 seemed bittersweet. We ate a subdued meal with the boarding house family. About half of them took the bus home. A smaller group of us attended church. Vera stayed home. She'd stopped going to church services, and finally Rev. Martin and his wife ventured to the boarding house and tried to talk to her. They told her they felt concerned for her spiritual well-being, but they couldn't get through the wall she'd erected around herself.

A box arrived from our parents and grandparents, with letters and small gifts—hankies embroidered with our initials, stationery and pens, candy, and a new blouse for each of us. None of us were up to the celebrations, but we sang carols, wrapped small gifts, and helped to decorate the tree at the boarding house with Eddie, who got excited and wanted to help. Vera kept to herself.

New Year's Eve services came, and Violet and I once again held hands with Reva and Mary at the church. We all prayed for our friends and family members serving overseas, for an end to the war, and for peace. I prayed for my wonderful sister's broken heart and my other sister's cold, dark heart. I prayed for our brothers scattered across Europe and the Pacific—and for my family and friends back home in Jubilee Junction. My heart felt numb and cold with rage and sorrow. I didn't know how to pray for myself.

That's all for now.

Thirty-Five

The Power of Oral History

"One makes mistakes; that is life. But it's never a mistake to have loved."

~Romain Rolland.

*A*unt Violet's face looked stricken. She folded the quilt and handed it back to me. "Now you know why my sister and I could no longer bear to be in the same room and the secret of the California quilt. I felt angry with Vera for having stolen my happiness, for cheating me out of marrying Don. I didn't think I would ever love another man or forgive her."

Beatrix mewed, and she bent down to stroke the kitten.

I put the quilt back into the protective plastic bag and zipped it up, then laid the quilt aside. Lovely and heart-wrenching, it could still inflict pain. I understood why Vera wanted to burn the California quilt, and why Grandma Grace hid it away.

"How did you survive Vera's betrayal?" I asked, taking her hands in mine. Tears streamed down my face. I was heartbroken for Violet, even though I'd loved my Uncle Bob and never knew Don.

"I didn't know I would survive. However, there was a war going on. Every day I woke up and told myself my patients needed me. Vera had betrayed me, but my other sister, your grandma, was steadfast. The folks at the boarding house became my second family. The nurses and doctors I worked with were wonderful. My church family also helped. I attended a weekly Bible Study group of war widows."

I lingered for another cup of tea. I stayed longer than usual until both of us were calm.

Aunt Violet gave me one more hug. "I'm glad you finally know what happened between me and my sister. There were no secrets between me and Grace, or between me and your Uncle Bob. He knew what broke my heart. But he's also the one God sent along to heal my broken heart. Yes, it's upsetting to listen to Grace tell the story, but you'll hear about my happy ending. Don't worry about me, Gracie."

She walked me to her front door, her kitten at her heels. "Keep icing your wrist and apply the gel."

I nodded, but my thoughts were of the young girl she and Uncle Bob tried to save, and how Aunt Violet thought of her all these years later. My heart ached for Aunt Violet and Grandma Grace. Too much sadness in the world, too much selfishness, too much cruelty.

Once I reached my car, I sent a text to Mom. We shared takeout and listened to the tape together. Mom and I were both in tears by the end of the tape, and Dad looked emotional as well.

Mom choked on her words, "Oh my—the puzzle pieces are falling into place. I need to call and check on Donna and Aunt Violet."

"I never liked Vera, and as a good Christian, I felt guilty. But hearing this, everything fits into place. What a terrible, selfish person. Here is my handkerchief, dear." Dad looked angry as he passed his handkerchief over. "Sorry, Gracie. I didn't pack my spare, so you're on your own. Here's a takeout napkin."

Mom and I blew our noses and tried to compose ourselves. I left the tape with her because Dad had been busy digitizing them. She checked my wrist and thought it looked better.

When I got home, I sat on the couch. Agatha sensed my sadness and set her small butt by my feet. She was smart enough not to jump up in my lap, because I might try to hug her again, but she looked up and meowed.

I shut my eyes and remembered the pain in Grandma's voice as she talked about the betrayal of one sister by her twin, and I thought about my own pain. Aunt Violet's broken heart healed, and so would mine.

For the hundredth time, I wished Grandma Grace were still alive and knew how much I valued hearing her voice, her stories, and her wisdom.

I crawled into bed, and a few tears came. I wasn't sure if they were for me or for three sisters who took the train to California—or the poor young woman whose abuser killed her. Agatha meowed and snuggled into my side. Finally, I drifted off to sleep.

With the presidential election over, the exhibit became the talk of the town again. I focused on keeping up with the letters, emails, and phone calls. People wanted to congratulate me or ask questions about their family quilts. Visitors flocked to Jubilee Junction for the quilt exhibit, and then drove downtown looking for our restaurants, stopped at the visitor center at the old Depot, and many came to *The Jubilee Times* office, especially on Saturdays.

I spent much of my time at the museum answering questions, giving interviews, and talking with community groups about the quilt exhibit. We discovered that several of the families who donated quilts reconnected with other family members because of the exhibit.

I talked to Carl Friday afternoon as we watched a group of excited visitors come into the exhibit area. "Did you think this exhibit would be such a big deal?" I asked him. "I hoped the town would like it, but we're getting visitors from other counties."

He thought for a moment. "I'd like to think all our exhibits would attract crowds. But this one's different. You were right. Hearing the voices of these women made this exhibit more personal and captured people's imaginations. Some of our visitors may be related to the people you interviewed. Others just like the quilts. But the popularity has taken us by surprise."

Dad worked with a college student to design a simple quilt logo with Grandma's phrase, *Every quilt has a story,* and the museum sold t-shirts. Dad put together a calendar and note cards featuring the quilts, splitting profits with the museum and Historical Society.

Aunt Shirley's Cafe became a hub of tourism, because of its location downtown, near *The Jubilee Times* office and the visitor center at the old train depot. The museum was a few blocks away.

I received a phone call from The Iowa State Historical Museum, asking if I would like to apply for a grant to take part in the quilt exhibit on the road because several museums would love to host it.

I talked to Carl, who was delighted. "It's great visibility for us. Go for it."

It thrilled Aunt Violet and her friends at the senior retirement housing center to get so much attention. I wrote a series of short profiles of them for *The Jubilee Times,* and other papers around the state wanted to run them too.

After a busy week, it was Wednesday, and time for another tape. Aunt Violet greeted me at the door with a hug. Her kitty sauntered right behind, meowing for attention, so I bent down and petted her. "Hello, Beatrix."

"C'mon in. Your Mama dropped off some oatmeal chocolate chip cookies, and I made some tea."

"Are you doing okay, Aunt Violet? Are you up for this today?"

"I'm fine. This all happened over 60 years ago, so the time has come for my family to hear the story."

"Did you ever listen to these tapes before now? Did you and Uncle Bob tell these stories to your children? I'm still trying to figure out why you and Grandma didn't talk to Mom and Uncle Rich and your children about it."

"Grace told me she was putting together an audio diary, and I was sure she would tell the entire story, but when Bob and I married, we decided to let the past stay there. We didn't want to confuse the children when they were younger, and we didn't want to hurt Donna. Later, we talked about sitting down with the family and sharing the story, but there was never a suitable time." Violet looked thoughtful. "However, yes, they should listen to the tapes, too."

"Dad made duplicates," I told her. "He digitized them, meaning he has them transferred to DVDs."

"Thank you, Gracie."

We settled down at her table, where she set our tea and small plates, and I got out the tape recorder with a sense of dread. I inserted the tape and pressed play, grabbing a cookie. Nearby, Beatrix slept in her cat box, peacefully.

Thirty-Six

Life and Death in California

"The dreams break into a million tiny pieces. The dream dies.
Which leaves you with a choice: you can settle for reality, or you
can go off, like a fool, and dream another dream."

~Nora Ephron

As the tape began, I saw Aunt Violet close her eyes, as if to prepare herself.

Tape #17, Vera's secret revealed
Grandma Grace's voice sounded sad.

By mid-February, Vera had a problem. She threw up at work. Her skirts and blouses looked tighter. Smells bothered her, and she cried easily. Since she no longer shared a room with anyone, she thought she could hide these things from us. But we noticed the changes.

We didn't talk about her symptoms publicly at the boarding house. Violet and I talked about them at night, in our room, and when Reva and Mary dropped by to chat. Vera was bitter and withdrawn. Few people at the boarding house were sympathetic to her, so she took her meals to the front porch, preferring her own company rather than sitting at the big table with the rest of us.

Then, one morning, Vera fainted in the hallway after breakfast. Aunt Mae took her to a doctor and confirmed her pregnancy.

After talking to Aunt Mae, I called home to talk to our parents, who were shocked and more concerned for Violet than Vera at first. But Mama and Daddy assured us they would take care of Vera and the baby. Mama said she'd take the train to California, so we made plans to meet her at the San Diego train depot in two weeks, at the end of February.

Vera gave notice at work and continued to keep to herself. Violet and I felt a sense of relief Vera was leaving soon, and our parents would deal with her. However, I still felt responsible and grieved for Violet—and Vera. I blamed myself, even though everyone else focused on Vera's misdeeds.

After the phone call, we received a long letter from my parents. Father focused on practical matters. He arranged for Vera to stay with his parents until the baby arrived. Mother wrote about an idea she had to create a quilt from the clothing we wore in California. She called it the California quilt, so would we please gather some things she could take back?

Violet threw herself into nursing injured soldiers on base and worked extra shifts. Meanwhile, Vera suffered from morning sickness, looking tired and frail. Each night she shut her door and ignored any attempts to talk to anyone, including her sisters.

Violet and I felt exhausted dealing with her and gave her some time to herself. When we talked to her a few days later, she refused to apologize for hurting Violet. She tried to pretend Don preferred her all along, which only deepened the wound. When I talked to her alone, she told me not to bother giving her advice.

A week later, on a Saturday morning, Vera received the dreaded telegram informing her Don had died at sea weeks earlier. His premonition he would not survive the war proved true. Vera sat down in the sitting room alone, holding the telegram.

Aunt Mae walked in briskly because someone told her the Western Union boy had just delivered a telegram. "I'm so sorry, Vera."

"I'm sorry he died. But I can't pretend to be a grieving widow."

Aunt Mae nodded, but her face said what she would not say.

"You hate me. Everyone here does. You're all judging me—you think I was a terrible person for marrying Don, but it's really Violet's fault. She didn't understand him the way I did. Don wanted to get on the ship as a married man, so I helped him."

Aunt Mae walked away into the kitchen, saying nothing.

Reva was downstairs and saw the exchange. She came upstairs to tell us Vera got a telegram. So Violet, Mary, and I walked downstairs. Vera handed the telegram to Violet silently.

Violet read it and sat down on a nearby chair, sobbing.

I took the telegram. "I'm so sorry, Violet."

Violet look at me, tried to compose herself, and said, "Remember how I got several letters at once, and he apologized? By the time I got those letters, he was already dead."

I looked at Vera but couldn't bring myself to say anything to her.

Several hours later, a car pulled up outside, and a chaplain and an officer climbed the steps of the boarding house and asked for Vera Anderson. They provided more details. Don died when the USS Ommaney Bay suffered damage on January 4, 1945, after a kamikaze pilot hit the ship. Men were trapped below deck. Don volunteered to help rescue his shipmates after the first explosion. Many men died, but he saved half a dozen men. He died a hero, rescuing others, and would get several medals posthumously.

The chaplain tried to comfort her. "I know you are grieving for your loved one, but I hope you will take some comfort in the fact he died serving his country."

Violet burst into fresh tears at the news, but Vera remained stony silent. Mary tried to comfort her, but Vera turned away. "Never mind me. I know you would rather comfort my sister, Saint Violet."

The chaplain and young captain looked confused and startled.

I held Violet's hand and stared at Vera, reprimanding her. "Be quiet, Vera. Just be quiet."

Vera faltered and then shut up. Reva and Mary took Vera to the other sitting room.

Violet continued to sob softly as Aunt Mae and I led her to a couch just inside the front door. Reva found paper and pen and fetched a glass of water for Violet. The chaplain talked softly with Violet and then walked inside and visited with Vera regarding the next steps.

Aunt Mae took him and the officer aside to explain the unusual circumstances, and to be sure Don's parents be notified.

Later, Violet asked Vera to come into our room. Violet showed us the letters Don wrote since deploying, apologizing for his behavior.

Vera finally admitted Don wrote to her, asking for a divorce when he returned.

Vera then walked to her room and brought back the boxes of things Don stored on base, and dumped them on Violet's bed. "I suppose you'll want these things for the quilt," she told us, before turning around and leaving.

Violet and I stared at her. She'd avoided us for weeks.

We gathered a small package of clothing for the quilt to send home with Mama. Violet sorted through the boxes of Don's things. Everything reminded her of her loss, from a dozen paperback books to his extra uniforms to several pictures of the two of them. We packed them up and shipped them to his parents. She kept a few things—the pictures, one book, and one uniform to cut up for the quilt.

Thinking about what lay ahead for Vera almost made me pity her. Her dream since graduating from High School was to leave the farm, to go to Chicago or Minneapolis, and work in an office or courthouse. Now she would be a widow—pregnant—and her dreams were just as shattered as Violet's. Vera would be part of another family now, a family of wheat farmers from Minnesota. Where would she find a place to call home with her baby?

Gracie, I tried to forgive Vera sixty years ago, but my loyalty to Violet won out. I wanted Vera gone, so I didn't have to worry about her next careless comment or hurtful action. So, I counted the days until Mama arrived.

That's all for now.

When the tape ended, we were both crying. I reached over for Aunt Violet's hand.

I stayed an hour, and we talked over more tea, going through many Kleenexes.

"Don was such a fine young man. I look back and remember thinking he was the one, you know? God had a different idea, and Bob was the man for me. Still, I remember how devastating it was to get the telegram that he'd died," she confessed.

"How did you cope?" I asked. "I feel so shallow. Steve proposed, and I turned him down. I never imagined he would hurt me physically, but I feel like I threw away seven years of my life on the wrong man. We should have broken up years ago."

She turned to me. "I know you're hurting, Gracie, but God's grace is sufficient. You didn't waste those years with Steve. You grew up and wanted different things."

I saw her glancing at my wrist, so I let her look at it and gently touch and move my hand around. "Yes, I'm still applying the gel," I told her.

She nodded. "Remember, dear girl, you're one of the lucky ones. You got away from an abusive man."

At the door, she hugged me. "Love is never wasted. I loved Don, and I don't regret loving him. But after he died, I realized I needed to go on. Then I met Bob, and my broken heart mended, and so will yours. Give it time, Gracie."

My parents expected my text. I joined them at the Jubilee Cafe for a quick meal, and then we walked over to the newspaper office to listen to the tape. I knew they could tell I'd been crying, but they said nothing. Once they listened to the tape, however, they both seemed shocked.

"No wonder the family didn't display or talk about the California quilt." Mom shook her head.

Dad agreed. "I see why Vera stayed away from Iowa longer and longer. Her family despised her for what she did to Violet."

As we walked out of *The Jubilee Times* office, they both hugged me. Mom sighed. "Well, we wanted to know what happened between the twins to change everything. Now we know. Let's find an opportunity to discuss this as a family."

My parents stared at my wrist, obviously concerned.

I took off my coat, pulled up my sleeve, and showed them my wrist. "Aunt Violet thought it looked better. I can't imagine a good way to discuss several things right now. Thanks, Mom and Dad."

Suddenly, I felt exhausted. I drove home and crawled into bed with Agatha cuddled up, making soft kitty noises. I cried a little for myself, Aunt Violet, and Grandma Grace. Then drowsiness crept in, and I slept.

Thirty-Seven

Crowds Come to Jubilee Junction

"Letting go gives us freedom, and freedom is the only condition for happiness. If, in our heart, we still cling to anything—anger, anxiety, or possessions—we cannot be free."

~ *Thich Nhat Hanh*

or the next few days, I replayed my conversation with Aunt Violet about broken hearts and healing. I wanted to say God's grace is sufficient, but right now, it seemed like more of a promise than a reality. I knew I'd made the right decision with Steve, but my heart felt heavy and sad. Each time I applied the gel to my wrist, I remembered her solemn warning: *Always remember that a man who hurts you once will do it again.*

I continued to wear long sleeves to cover my bruises. The weather was getting colder, and I was thankful for the chance to wear my favorite sweaters.

Several of Tiara's students stopped me to say hello in the hall and tell me how much they enjoyed meeting the *quilt ladies*.

"The next time I visited Grandma, I asked her if we had any quilters in our family, and we do! She dug out a couple of old quilts, and we talked all afternoon. She didn't think I would be interested. Maybe I wouldn't have been before this project," a girl gushed.

People all over town talked about the exhibit and quilts.

"My cousin moved to New York but follows the Jubilee Junction Facebook page and saw the pictures of the exhibit. She called the other night, and we talked for half an hour. She's been researching genealogy websites and wants to know more about the quilts," a woman told me as I picked up an order at Aunt Shirley's Cafe.

I ran into David at Aunt Shirley's once or twice, and we enjoyed lunch together. I confessed to breaking up with my long-time boyfriend, and he expressed concern, commenting that he had gone through a comparable situation right before moving.

As I graded stacks of essays at home or watched television, David and I texted each other, just to check in. He called me a few times as well. David turned out to be easy to talk to, funny, and smart. I enjoyed talking to him. Agatha was playing with a paper bag one afternoon, so I took pictures and sent one, and he liked it.

Aunt Shirley told me she finally took time to see the exhibit. "It brought back so many memories, watching my grandma and aunts working on quilts."

She slid a bag containing my takeout order and gestured around. The cafe seemed busier than usual. "You see this, Gracie? I haven't seen such crowds since the holidays. Your supper is on me for bringing them to Jubilee Junction. Your grandma Grace would be so proud of you."

Dad told me he hired a part-time person to help with ads, but I could keep writing my column and news when I found the time. He also hired someone to help him run the print shop part-time. Thanks to the quilt exhibit, they couldn't keep enough brochures, bookmarks, calendars, notecards, postcards, and other materials in stock. He'd found a vendor in a nearby town that handled the popular t-shirts.

My week seemed to revolve around my Wednesday afternoon with Aunt Violet. When I arrived, she greeted me, and we found our places at the small table in her kitchen.

"We have cinnamon coffee cake today," she told me. "I made it myself. I thought we'd have some hot tea with it. I have Constant Comment, your favorite."

We sat and ate coffee cake and poured the tea, and the spices in the tea and cake topping lingered on my tongue. I put the tape into the cassette player and pushed play. Beatrix played nearby. I could sense both of us were taking a big breath to prepare for the next events.

Tape #18, Mama Arrives
  Grandma Grace's voice sounded somber.

Mama arrived in San Diego on a Wednesday afternoon, the first week of March 1945. She was tired from the long train trip but resolute. She'd come to take Vera home, where the family would take care of her and her baby. There was a vacant room, so Mama settled into a room down the hall from us.

Mama stayed for a week to help Vera get her things together, do laundry, and pack. She also did some amateur detective work. Mama spent time with Violet, trying to comfort her and understand how this situation happened. She also visited with me, Aunt Mae and Uncle Henry, our pastor, Reva, and Mary to get more perspective. Mama attended church with us, and we ate Sunday lunch back at the boarding house. Vera remained to herself.

Uncle Henry took us for a drive so Mama could see the sights on Sunday afternoon. Violet got called in to work, and Vera begged off. Aunt Mae stayed home with Eddie. Uncle Henry, Mama, Mary, Reva, and I drove past the base and the factory, as well as by the waterfront, talking about each place.

Mama loved seeing the harbor, so we parked and walked around, enjoying the sounds and smells of the water beating against the docks, the seagulls chattering and looking for food, and the inviting aroma of fish sandwiches from a fish shack right on the wharf.

Even though we'd eaten lunch a couple of hours before, we ordered a couple of fish sandwiches and tangy coleslaw so she could have a taste. We sat outside and talked and divided up the sandwiches. I gave Mama the coleslaw with a little wooden spoon.

"It's wonderful," she declared.

Then Mama tried the fish. "I never liked fish, but this is just delicious. I wonder if the gentleman would give me his recipe?"

Mary and I looked at her and smiled, while Reva tried not to giggle.

Finally, I said, "I wouldn't try, Mama."

Uncle Henry looked around at all of us with a half-serious smile. "Aunt Mae doesn't need to know we did this, girls. She'd

be jealous. I'll bring her down here sometime, just the two of us."
We all nodded in assent.

I happily played tour guide, knowing how hard Mama and Daddy
worked to help us prepare for our trip, and how exhausting it would
be to escort Vera home.

A few days after Mama arrived, Vera received a letter from Don's
parents, and Mama asked her to read it out loud to all of us. Mr.
and Mrs. Anderson were confused because Don wrote several
letters about a beautiful young lady named Violet, but then Don
married her twin sister, Vera. They wanted to get to know Vera, so
they invited her to visit their wheat farm, south of St. Paul, Minnesota. They grieved for their son, but felt excited about the baby,
and becoming grandparents.

Mama looked at us and raised her eyebrows, and I almost felt
sorry for Vera, who faltered as she finished reading the letter out
loud. She sighed and threw the letter down on my bed, clearly
surprised. Meanwhile, Violet turned her head and wept quietly.
She'd looked forward to meeting Don's family.

Mama took me aside the night before they left. "My sister Verdeen told me this trip to California would end badly. Vera has
always been a source of trouble. I know you're blaming yourself
and thinking we hold you responsible. But we know Vera, and
she's always been a handful. You're a good girl and so is Violet.
We're so sorry this betrayal happened. Your aunts and grandmas
are quite upset."

She put an arm around my shoulder and leaned in to hug me.
"Violet will be all right. You wait and see. The Lord has another
young man in mind for her—and one for you, too, Virginia Grace."

Vera felt trapped by her circumstances, but she and Mama left
for Jubilee Junction a few days later. Two weeks later, Vera left for
St. Paul to meet Don's extended family. We could only wonder
how her visit went, since Vera didn't speak more than a few words.
to anyone.

Mama sent us a letter telling us about the train ride home. She
had to prod Vera to eat, because Vera became nauseated by the
jolting of the train and all the smells coming from the dining car.

Aunt Mae sent along several packages of saltines, and they helped. At one point, Vera cried and told Mama she didn't want to have the baby. She felt scared, and she didn't know if she could raise a child alone.

Mama was tired, and snapped at her, "Well, maybe you shouldn't have broken your sister's heart and stolen her man. I'm having a difficult time feeling sorry for you. You made your bed, and now you have to lie in it."

Then she tried to be kinder. "Vera, every woman is afraid with her first pregnancy. But you have the next six or seven months to get ready for the baby. You will be fine. You have your family, and Don's family will want to know their grandchild."

Mama kept a close eye on her, kept her hydrated, and got her home, but they were both exhausted from the trip. Mama picked up a suitcase with maternity clothes and took Vera to our paternal grandparents, who welcomed her in a subdued way. Troubled by the circumstances, they tried their best to help their granddaughter prepare to become a mother.

Mama took Vera to see our family doctor, who confirmed Vera's due date of early to mid-August. Mama wrote to us and told us not to worry about Vera anymore because she was looking after her.

We felt blessed to have our friends and family at the boarding house and church. However, I knew things would be easier here without Vera, as awful as that sounds.

Sisters should support each other's dreams—not stomp on them. And that's all for now. Gracie.

Thirty-Eight

Moving On

*"You think your pain and your heartbreak are unprecedented
in the history of the world, but then you read. It was books that
taught me that the things that tormented me most were the very
things that connected me with all the people who were alive,
who had ever been alive."*

~*James Baldwin*

When the tape stopped, I looked at Aunt
Violet. "What a strange situation. Did Don's parents understand
what had happened?"

"I'm not sure, but I think they read between the lines. They corresponded with me for many years and always sent the latest school
picture of Donna."

She stood to pick up the cups and teapot. "They were kind
people—just like their son."

I picked up my plate with half a slice of coffee cake and nibbled on it. I'd gotten so engrossed in listening to the tape that I'd
stopped eating. "This is wonderful. I love the topping and the
pecans," I told her.

"I'm glad you like it, because I'm going to send a few pieces
home with you."

As had become our habit, I ate supper with my parents at *The
Jubilee Times* office and played the latest tape.

My parents listened carefully, Mom and I both getting emotional again.

"I feel like I'm getting to know my grandma Ginny," Mom told me.

"Violet is a remarkable woman," Dad remarked. "I'd no idea of this before. I wonder if Uncle Vern and Aunt Maggie know about all this drama?"

Mom shrugged. "I don't think so. I remember hearing about some incidents when the twins were growing up, but nothing about what happened in California or afterward."

I left the tape to be digitized and headed home.

Agatha met me at the door. After getting her food and water, we sat on the couch and watched something mindless on TV and cuddled before I grabbed my planner. I couldn't focus, however, because my wrist hurt. I took some Tylenol, put on the gel, grabbed some cat toys, and we played for twenty minutes before I attacked chores and grading.

Kathy saw the news first on Facebook, a post with Steve smiling with his arm around a beautiful girl at a Des Moines restaurant in early November. Kathy called me to see if I saw the post. I told her I'd been too busy to check Facebook.

"Gracie, she has shoulder-length, blonde curly hair, and a cute figure. I clicked on her Facebook profile, and she works at the state capitol as a secretary." Kathy was angry. "She looks a little like you."

Stephanie confirmed the news, texting me, worried about how I might take seeing the picture with no warning. According to her, Steve and Ellen began dating immediately after our breakup in October—as in the next day. She was still upset with him, urging her parents to insist he have anger management counseling.

The following day, Shelly sniffed, inspecting the picture on her phone. "Notice she looks a lot like you?"

I looked again. "Really?" But I tried not to worry about the new girlfriend.

Shelly looked at my wrist. "Wonder what he's going to do to her?" She exhaled and unpacked another small box of books and office supplies in her new office. She was the new full-time communications teacher—the teaching job I didn't apply for—and her office was next door to the adjunct office.

Tiara stuck her head in the doorway of Shelly's office, where I'd stopped after class.

"Inseparable,"Tiara looked at our almost matching outfits with a smile. "What's going on with Grandma Grace?"

I summarized the last few tapes for them. "I have one here if you want to listen sometime."

"Let's listen to one, or at least a few minutes. I have an hour." Shelly looked at her watch.

I played the tape for them, and they enjoyed the airplane factory and the drama with the twins.

"David says it's a notable example of oral history," I mentioned, quoting him.

Shelly and Tiara grinned at each other. "David seems to pop up a lot in your conversations lately,"Tiara remarked while Shelly teased me, "When do we get to meet David? I've seen him on campus, but I haven't gotten the chance to say hello."

They both looked at me pointedly, Tiara with her famous squinty look, putting her thumb and index fingers on her glasses and sliding them down her nose.

I gave in, feeling self-conscious. "Yes, he's wonderful. We keep running into each other at the campus library, at Aunt Shirley's, the museum, or the public library. He's a great addition to our faculty here. But it's not like he's asked me out on a date. We just see each other and talk, or we text, or he calls me. I promise to introduce you two. I really like David. He's been a great friend."

"A *friend*? I think he's more like a *boy*friend,"Tiara declared, her expressive face emphasizing each syllable.

"Look, you two, David knows I just broke up with my long-time boyfriend," I confessed. "For now, it's wonderful to have someone to talk to, and we have a lot in common. He's smart, funny, and likes cats."

"Girl, we're happy for you. He sounds like a good man, but I need to meet him and give him the Tiara blessing," she laughed.

Shelly and I grinned at each other, knowing she was only half-teasing.

When I'd finally shown Tiara my wrist, I learned the real meaning behind the phrase "mama lioness."

Her eyes narrowed as she cradled my wrist in her hands. "Steve did this when you broke up?"

I nodded. "I'm sorry. I kept trying to tell you. I wasn't sure if Shelly told you already, and I didn't want to ask, as foolish as that sounds."

Tiara gently dropped my hand, took me into her arms, and whispered fiercely, "That man better stay away from you, because he's gonna have to deal with me now."

During November, I kept busy teaching, grading, and prepping. I wrote my column for the newspaper and fielded calls from people with old quilts who wanted to know more about them. I pondered doing another exhibit, or a series of columns in the newspaper, identifying each pattern and looking for family stories about the quilts.

Visitors came to see the quilts at the museum, and then drove or walked around downtown to eat, shop, and wander around. Dad kept busy printing and selling exhibit-related items.

Wednesday, I drove to see Aunt Violet, with the shoebox in one arm and my purse in the other. We chatted as we walked down the hallway to her kitchen, where Beatrix played with one of her cat toys, pawing ferociously at a small rubber mouse. She picked the mouse up with her teeth and shook her little head as Violet and I laughed at her.

"It's hard not to laugh at a six-pound cat who thinks she's a lioness."

"She's good company and provides me with a lot of entertainment. My daughter and grandchildren visited last weekend and decided Beatrix needed some toys. They called her Trix. I like her new nickname."

"I do, too." Then I handed Aunt Violet a newspaper clipping.

"I found this poem in the shoebox with the photos. I didn't know Grandma Grace wrote poetry, and *The Jubilee Times* published it. You can still see the date, April 1, 1942. "How Long Till it Be Springtime?""

She looked at the clipping and smiled. "I remember your grandma was teaching in a one-room schoolhouse when she wrote this poem. She took the shortcut through our grandpa Carlson's field to the schoolhouse one lovely spring morning. Listening to all the birds just inspired her. She sat down and wrote the poem as soon as she reached the schoolhouse, and only changed a couple of words, I think."

"How did it get published in *The Jubilee Times?*"

"Mama saw it and thought it was good, and she was friends with Mrs. O'Connor. The next thing you know, the editor had a copy in his hands, and he liked it as well."

"It's sort of old-fashioned, but I like it. To think she wrote the poem during the war adds even more meaning to me. Thanks for telling me about the inspiration for the poem." I took the clipping back. "I'm going to retype it and share it with the rest of the family."

How Long Till it be Springtime?
One fair dawning as the meadowlarks were calling
From the dewy woodlands of green willow groves,
I looked down into their peaceful valley dreamland,
Wishing spring could banish all earth's strife's and woes.
All the vale was fresh with green of newborn springtime,
Happy bird land filled the air with melody,
The slow brooklet gently trickled through the hollow,
As it lingeringly took its way to sea.
Yes, 'twas springtime once again when all earth wakens
Yet the world at war caused gladness to depart,
And, instead, my weary soul kept sadly sighing,
Oh, how long till it be springtime in my heart?
Homes are broken, and earth's trials and despairing
Are too heavy for the world alone to hear;
How can birds so gaily sing this war-torn morning,
When for some there'll only be a vacant chair?
Then God seemed to send this thought to me in comfort,
That his gifts of birds, sweet mornings, and spring rain
Give us hope that someday in the hearts now saddened
Flowers will bloom and happy birds will sing again.
So my saddened heart was gladdened with his comfort,
And the dark, cold clouds of doubts seemed to part,
For I know on some sweet day in God's tomorrow
He'll put bright, eternal springtime in my heart.

~Grace Nelson

We settled down at her table, and I poured the tea. Aunt Violet cut slices of chocolate cake and put them on her small cream-colored plates. I inserted the next tape, then pressed play. I nibbled at the cake, enjoying the rich chocolate flavor on my tongue. The women in my family were all chocoholics.

Tape #19, Violet Forgives Vera
  Grandma Grace's voice sounded reflective.

Things settled down for us with Vera gone. I could breathe easier, not worrying about what foolish or hurtful thing Vera would say or do next. I tried to protect Violet and couldn't shake the feeling I'd let her down, even though she insisted I had done nothing wrong.

"Remember, Mama told us Vera has always been stubborn and impulsive? No one could have stopped her," Violet pointed out one evening as we got ready for bed. We crawled under the covers in our respective beds, and she turned out the bedside lamp.

I wasn't ready to forgive myself. "I just wish I'd been here."

"How would you have helped? I wasn't here. Mary couldn't hear all of their conversation and didn't know Vera and Don were going to get married."

Finally, it sunk in. I should not feel guilty about Vera's actions.

Violet accepted what happened, and the two of us shared a special bond. She worked long hours on base at the hospital and told me she didn't want to return home and be the object of pity. "I'm needed here."

I understood.

Fortunately, the women in the church and the boarding house responded with kindness. Reva, Mary, and Aunt Mae made a point of taking care of us both. Reva, Violet, and I talked as we walked the palm shaded streets of Chula Vista on weekends.

The three of us read from the Psalms and found comfort.

Our pastor gave Violet a set of six scriptures to read every morning and night, and she copied them out and carried them with her everywhere.

The Lord is close to the brokenhearted and saves those who are crushed in spirit.

~Psalm 34:18

He heals the brokenhearted and binds up their wounds.

~Psalm 147:3

Even if I go through the deepest darkness, I will not be afraid, LORD, for you are with me. Your shepherd's rod and staff protect me.

~Psalm 23:4

Come to me, all you who are weary and burdened, and I will give you rest.

~Matthew 11:28

Do not be anxious about anything, but in every situation, by prayer and petition, with thanksgiving, present your requests to God. And the peace of God, which transcends all understanding, will guard your hearts and your minds in Christ Jesus.

~Philippians 4:6-7

For I know the plans I have for you,' declares the Lord, 'plans to prosper you and not to harm you, plans to give you hope and a future.

~Jeremiah 29:11

Uncle Henry, Aunt Mae, and Mary were also especially kind. When Mama and Vera left, Violet picked up little Eddie, who sensed her sadness and patted her on the shoulder with his small hands. "Okay, bilet, it okay."

Uncle Henry, Aunt Mae, Mary, and I looked at each other. Uncle Henry responded, "Yes, you're right Eddie. We love Violet, and she's going to be okay."

Several weeks later, a letter arrived from George, one of Don's shipmates and his best friend in the Navy. He was above deck and survived the explosion. George wrote that Don kept Violet's picture with him. As soon as Vera agreed to marry him, he knew he made a terrible mistake. He always talked about Violet. "He loved you, he did, Violet. I just thought you should know."

Violet read and reread the letter for weeks.

Then one evening, I saw her taking all the letters from Don and wrapping a piece of ribbon around them. She placed the packet in a dresser drawer and turned to face me. "I loved Don, and I would have married him when he came home. But he's dead—and he married Vera, not me. I can't change anything or pretend it didn't happen, but I *can* choose not to focus on this drama every day. I've been talking with the Pastor, and I don't know if I can ever forgive Vera, but I'm tired of hating her and being sad."

I looked at my beautiful, strong sister. "You're right. I've been thinking about it, and Vera is going to have a different life than she thought she would. I wouldn't trade places with her for all the tea in China. And I feel sorry for Don's parents for being stuck with Vera. I think moving on sounds good for both of us."

I crossed the room and hugged her.

Gracie, our conversation took place more than sixty years ago, but I still remember the look on Violet's face as she put her grief aside and forgave her sister. I don't know if it's too late, but I would like you to try. Tell Vera I forgive her. I know her life didn't turn out the way she wanted. I think sixty years is long enough, don't you? She hurt my dear sister terribly—she wounded our family.

Before California, your Grandma Ginny used to invite everyone in her family to come to our place for picnics. Imagine a hundred people, or more, gathered outside in the shade of the oak trees our great-grandfathers planted, eating fried chicken and a dozen sides, talking, and catching up on grandbabies and crops. That stopped after we came back from Chula Vista. My parents were heartbroken—and ashamed. We could never get together again as a family without thinking about what Vera had done in California by marrying Don—and betraying her sister. Violet finally stood up to Vera in California, and Vera knew she'd gone too far, but she was just too stubborn to ask for forgiveness.

Donna should know the truth. Her father died a hero in the war, and her mother, a cold, calculating woman, always seemed more concerned about herself than her children. Donna's Minnesota family loved her, and she could turn to her stepdad, John, Aunt Violet, and Uncle Bob. But the three sisters are all getting older, and we need to make peace.

Grandma Grace sighs, and her voice falters.

That's all for now, Gracie.

Thirty-Nine

Grandma Grace's Request

"You know, a heart can be broken, but it keeps on beating, just the same."

~Fannie Flagg

When the tape stopped, Aunt Violet fumbled for a handkerchief in her pocket. She dabbed her eyes and blew her nose, which Trix found very engaging, reaching up with one small paw for the handkerchief.

"What are we supposed to do now?" My voice became shaky.

Violet put the handkerchief away and stroked the cat. "I'm going to call your mother. We should reach out to my sister and Donna."

She noticed my expression. "Your grandma is right. I wish the three sisters could have spoken before Grace died."

I felt unsettled and didn't want to leave. "Let's listen to the next tape, please?"

We sat back down, and I took out the old tape and put in the new one, as Beatrice settled back down in my aunt's lap and licked her paws.

My appetite was gone. I leaned forward to hear Grandma's voice.

Tape #20, Healing the Wounds of War
  Grandma's voice was sad.

During March and April, Violet worked even longer hours as more wounded soldiers arrived at her base in San Diego on big hospital ships. The wounds of war are not only of the body, but of the spirit and mind. Violet said some of the wounded soldiers needed care for both for some time. Many of these young men had suffered horrible injuries, and many had already endured one or more surgeries on the ships and needed more sophisticated medical attention.

Violet looked thinner, and her eyes looked tired, but she said she was fine and didn't want me to worry about her. At the aircraft factory, we worked hard, pushing out a few more planes. In the meantime, the newspaper headlines encouraged us one day and frightened us the next.

Mama's letters came full of clippings, with articles about soldiers or sailors from Jubilee Junction and the surrounding farm towns—dead, missing, injured, or presumed to be prisoners of war.

The allies hammered away at the Germans, who continued to lose ground. The war seemed interminable, with no sure ending in sight. The country waited, prayed, and hoped, and so did we.

The Allies planned their landing in France, but we didn't know about that until afterward. Later, we saw the headlines, with reports of bloodshed on both sides.

In the meantime, our fighting boys kept busy in those early months of 1945. General Patton and his troops in the Third Army crossed the Rhine on March 22, and they liberated some of the concentration camps: Ohrdruf—a sub-camp of Buchenwald, Flossenburg, Dachau, and Mauthausen-Gusen. Later, we learned our brother Vincent marched with those troops.

We felt shocked when President Roosevelt died on April 13, and Harry Truman, the Vice President, became our President. A few weeks later, Hitler and his bride committed suicide in an underground bunker. On May 7, Germany surrendered, and we all celebrated VE day. But more about VE day later.

In early June, your Aunt Violet met a young doctor on base, Dr. Robert Johnson, or Dr. Bob, as she referred to him in her letters home. He'd just returned from being deployed to Europe and saw terrible things, including the concentration camp at Dachau, Germany. He told her about the horrors of the dead bodies stacked up, and of the living who looked like skeletons themselves. Dr. Bob accompanied many of the seriously injured sailors and soldiers on one of the large hospital ships back to the states from Europe.

Dr. Bob was a compassionate, funny man who worked long hours to care for his patients and showed kindness to the nurses. "You nurses are so important. I can do surgery, but you care for the soldiers every day," he told Violet.

Bob and Violet grabbed a coffee on base and chatted when they could. She told me Bob's eyes were blue, his short hair dark blond, and he came from Omaha, Nebraska, originally. He was six feet tall and had an athletic build. They struck up a friendship and chatted when they could between patients.

I met him when she brought him to church one Sunday morning and liked him right away. So did Uncle Henry, Aunt Mae, and Mary. He fit in with our family and our church.

I didn't know what to think. Bob was handsome and seemed like a great guy, but could he be the right man for Violet? Then I saw Violet's smile. I couldn't remember when she'd last smiled. I also noticed sadness on Bob's face when he talked about being deployed to Europe.

Mary and I talked and agreed that if asked, we'd give our blessings. Bob cared about Violet and was protective of her. We liked the way he smiled at her and held her hand. Violet had told him about Don and Vera, and I liked him more for his response, which was to smile and gently say, "Thank you for waiting for me." They worked together and their relationship grew as the war wound down.

Until the end of the war with Japan, we all were working hard, whether building planes or taking care of our injured soldiers and sailors. During the next few months, as the Allies fought to bring the war in the Pacific to a close, we continued to work and pray for our troops stationed there, including two of our brothers and several childhood friends.

And I'm happy, Gracie, to end on something positive. I could tell Dr. Bob would change Violet's life and heal her broken heart.

That's all for now.

The tape clicked. I leaned back and sighed. "I'm so glad you met Bob. I loved going to him for checkups as a child because he made me feel safe, and he always fixed up my scraped-up knees. He was a wonderful doctor and uncle. I'm better now."

Aunt Violet agreed. "Yes, he was a wonderful doctor, husband, and father. I miss him so much. The only person I miss more is your grandma."

Then she took another look at me. "I know you're worried about me, Gracie. Hearing the tapes brought back a lot of painful memories, but I'm all right. I've enjoyed hearing Grace's voice again, and not all the memories are sad."

She gestured for my wrist and inspected the marks left by Steve's fingers, now turning colors but healing.

We cleaned up, I packed up my tape recorder and tapes, and we hugged at the door.

I called Mom from my car, and she told me to come over to the newspaper. She'd ordered a pizza. Mom set the hot pizza, salad, and paper plates and forks on the table when I walked into *The Jubilee Times*. We ate supper and chatted.

After I played the tapes for them, Mom looked at me and then at Dad. "Violet is right. We need a family meeting on the Nelson/Walters side. Violet may want her children to come as well. I'll call her and plan for a meal over the Thanksgiving holiday. Our house can't hold that many people, so where can we have the family dinner?"

Dad suggested, "What about Violet's old farmhouse? She left your Grandma Ginny's large table and chairs there. She has that great kitchen and a big dining room. We'll take a couple of long tables and folding chairs, and ask people to bring sides, while we make a big ham and turkey."

Mom grinned. "What a great idea, Matthew. I'll call Violet and get her okay." She walked to her office, where we saw her grabbing a clipboard and her phone.

Dad looked at me. "This could get interesting. I wonder if Vera will come?"

I got a funny feeling in my stomach again, just thinking of my last conversation with Aunt Vera. I remembered her hurtful words about her twin, Grandma, and the California quilt.

Dad looked at me, half amused. "Getting ready for battle?" he teased.

I sighed. "Aunt Vera is the most annoying person in this family. At least now I understand why I never liked her. Grandma Grace wanted us to reach out to her, and it's the right thing to do. But I'm just not going to listen to any nonsense about Violet or grandma."

Dad nodded and asked to see my wrist. I told him, "Aunt Violet says it's healing up."

He gently inspected it for himself and nodded. "Yes, thank goodness."

I drove home to grade and prep for classes. I needed to write my column, but I also needed some time to process the latest developments with the twins.

Mom called before bedtime, having everything arranged. Violet's other children and grandchildren would listen to the tapes with their mother later, but her oldest son Robert Junior and his wife Elizabeth would join us at Thanksgiving, Nov. 22. She hoped to get word from Donna yet.

Later, I sat on my couch, checking email, and making my list for the next day while half watching a TV show. Agatha lay nearby, stretching and yawning. I wondered how our family meeting would go. Would Vera agree to come, and would she blow up?

Forty

David Gets a Tour

"Friendship ... is born at the moment when one man says to another, 'What! You too? I thought that no one but myself...'"
~*C.S. Lewis*

*D*avid showed up at the museum on Friday afternoon, November16, around four o'clock.

"Hey, Gracie. I wondered if you have time to show me the quilts. My students have been talking about the oral history aspect of the exhibit, and I want to see it—and hear it—for myself." David looked around with curiosity. People walked around, listening to the audio clips at each station and looking at the signage and quilts.

"I've been gathering research for my book, the one about German POWs working on Iowa Farms. Over the last few weeks, I bumped into you a dozen times. I'm sorry for taking so long to follow through. I meant to get here a couple of weeks ago."

I looked at his lovely brown eyes with those golden flecks and felt a little flustered. "No problem, David. I would be happy to give you the quarter tour."

As we walked around, we listened to the audio clips at the ten stations. Afterward, we chatted about the exhibit in the lobby.

"You did a wonderful job here. I see why the exhibit engaged the students so much. I like the signage with quotes about quilts. But what I liked the most were the audio clips, which add such a personal touch. I don't think I've seen anything like this at a county museum before. This is excellent!"

He continued, "I've taken up a chunk of your time here. When do you finish up work? Could I buy you supper to say thank you?"

I checked my watch, making sure my sweater covered my other wrist. "Sure, thanks. It's after five, so I'm done here. I need to get my things downstairs."

We walked down to my workroom, where half a dozen quilts for the new exhibit were on the back table. Thank goodness I'd taken the time to straighten up earlier. He looked around with genuine curiosity and asked me a few questions.

Then I grabbed my coat, purse, and messenger bag, and we walked back upstairs. David helped me with my coat in a kind, matter-of-fact way. I put my messenger bag in my car and locked it, and then we walked to Aunt Shirley's. Aunt Shirley raised her eyebrows when we came in together, but didn't embarrass me when she took our order.

We chatted over supper, and I thought, *Maybe I've found a new friend.* Not only did he enjoy teaching at the community college level, but he also loved exploring museums and traveling around the Midwest, researching, reading, and playing board games.

"I'm not used to being around a young woman who enjoys hanging around museums, appreciates history, and collects old quilts. Have you always been so strange?" he teased.

I told him about hanging out with Grandma and the aunts when my older brother went to kindergarten. They took me with them to quilt at church, and I learned how to drink "a cuppa tea" at age four. Then I told him about listening to Grandma's cassette tapes with Aunt Violet.

"The tapes got me thinking about the power of hearing someone's voice for the quilt exhibit. I realized Grandma totally sucked me into the story about these three young sisters going out to California and working on a Navy base and at an aircraft factory because she was narrating the story."

"It sounds like it inspired you, alright." David wore glasses, which made him seem more scholarly, but I admired his athletic build and curly brown hair. "Those tapes sound intriguing. What a terrific way to tell your family's story."

I told him more about the tapes and how they told the story of Grandma Grace—and the twins and their trip to California during World War II. David listened quietly.

"What a lot of family drama. Your grandma and aunt sound like resilient women." He looked at me. "Dare I add, just like you."

Our food came. As we ate our sandwiches, David told me about his fascination with the history of Jubilee Junction. I promised to help him.

His parents lived about a half-hour away in a nearby town and he moved back to help, when his mother suffered a serious health diagnosis last year—breast cancer.

"Mom is doing great now. I have no regrets about moving back. However, I ended a long-term relationship. Cynthia didn't understand why anyone would want to leave Chicago." He looked at me, and I nodded.

David lived in a suburb of Chicago, teaching at a community college there, before moving here. "I tried teaching online for a semester with just two classes face to face on Tuesdays and drove back and forth, which didn't work. Finally, I realized I needed to move here and find a new teaching job. My parents needed me."

He continued, "My little brother was in his first year of college, and I didn't want him to drop out. My sister and brother-in-law were juggling two small children and trying to help Dad at the store. My father lost twenty pounds from worry and stress and was trying to hold down his hardware store and drive my mother back and forth to chemo. She seemed more worried about him than her situation."

I understood. "I got my first job as a journalist out of grad school, and then Dad suffered a heart attack four years ago, and I knew I needed to be here. The move home complicated my relationship with Steve. I think we didn't know when to quit."

He looked serious, then nodded. "Gracie, if I've learned anything about relationships, you can't force them. When it's right, you know. I think the same thing happened to me and my ex."

We ordered pie and coffee for him, and pie and tea for me. Then we lingered over dessert, and he insisted on paying for my supper.

"Thanks. I enjoyed the conversation much more than eating by myself while watching *Wheel of Fortune.*" He grinned.

I laughed. "Yes, you're a much more interesting conversationalist than Agatha, my cat. Thanks, David."

Aunt Shirley smiled as she rang us up, and when he turned, she winked and nodded.

After we finished our meal, he helped me put on my coat, walked me to my Subaru in the museum's parking lot, opened my door, and thanked me for a great meal and conversation.

"See you on campus," he waved as he walked to his car. I noticed he waited for me to get into my car before he got inside his car.

The next Wednesday, I arrived at Aunt Violet's clutching the shoe-box with the tapes and tape recorder.

"How are you, Gracie? Ready for the big weekend?" She greeted me and hugged me.

I shook my head. "I think so, but a lot will depend on Vera's attitude. If she says anything mean about you or Grandma Grace, I'll have to restrain myself."

She chuckled and hugged me. "Thank you, honey. I don't think you'll have to slug Vera. There are too many people in line in front of you."

We sat down at her table, with a plate of spicy pumpkin cookies and a teapot with the fragrance of orange and spices from Constant Comment. She poured our tea into two cups and sat back. Her kitty woke up from a nap in a soft cat bed nearby and wandered over and sat at her feet.

Aunt Violet smiled and looked down. "No cookies for you, Trix. You can sit and listen if you're good."

I pressed play and sat back in anticipation. Aunt Violet half shut her eyes.

Tape #21, VE Day & Ed Comes Home
Grandma's voice was soft.

And just like that, the war in Europe finally ended.

German troops surrendered in Italy on May 2, and then all German forces surrendered to the Allies on May 7th. May 8 was declared VE or Victory in Europe day. However, we still needed to end the war with Japan. They sent the troops who fought so hard in Europe to the Pacific front.

The celebrations were amazing after VE Day. The aircraft factory announced the news over the loudspeaker. We laughed and cried as first Josie and I hugged, and then Joe hugged us both. Mac came out of the office, shouting and laughing. Reva ran over and hugged me, sobbing in relief. We weren't alone.

Violet told me the patients, doctors, and nurses shouted hooray as the news on the radio announced the end of the war in Europe. Some patients were overwhelmed, weeping, laughing, and thinking of their fellow soldiers and sailors. We knew there was still a long, challenging time ahead in the war in the Pacific.

When we returned to the boarding house, we celebrated with everyone there. Eddie wasn't sure what was happening, with so many of us in tears. At dinner, we raised glasses of iced tea or water. Those who lost loved ones or whose loved ones were in the Pacific front were more somber but wept, hugged, and celebrated with us. We'd defeated one enemy, standing with our allies. Surely, we would defeat the Japanese empire as well.

Unfortunately, it took many bloody battles, and the atomic bomb being dropped on Hiroshima and Nagasaki before the Japanese surrendered. This action saved the Allies a bloody landing on Japan's mainland. A week later, we celebrated VJ Day, for Victory over Japan, on August 14, 1945. The celebration of a world weary of war, resulted in a lot of dancing, shouting, whoops, and tears. But it took months to bring those soldiers all home.

When I saw Violet after work, we hugged and wept. Three of our brothers were alive, with minor injuries. We'd lost our big brother, Victor. We'd also lost cousins, classmates, and friends back in Iowa. Violet had lost Don.

Historians would later note that over 8,000 Iowans died during World War II.

Women left the boarding house after VJ day. Some women

returned home to prepare for reuniting with their soldiers, while others traveled home to mourn those they lost.

In mid-August, we received a telegram. "Donna Marie Anderson arrived August 20. Twenty inches, seven pounds, three ounces. Mother and baby doing fine."

Violet held the telegram. "A baby girl named Donna. Her daddy would have been so happy."

Mama wrote that a young Navy officer showed up at her house to give Vera two medals for Don's bravery. They awarded him the Navy Cross and a Purple Heart. Vera gave them to his parents.

In the fall of 1945, we were riveted to the news about the Nuremberg War Crimes tribunal, with many witnesses speaking about the order to murder Poles, Jews, and Russian prisoners of war. Survivors of the concentration camps testified, as did German officers. The trial lasted for a full year and passed sentences on many top officers.

Aunt Mae and Uncle Henry were overjoyed when their youngest son came home with injuries to his arm, where he'd been hit with flak during his last flight. Daniel had been the radio operator on a B-17 Flying Fortress. He joined us for dinner. I thought he looked tired, but his face lit up when he looked at his family—and the good food put before him.

Ed came home a few weeks later, limping from an injury on the ship, and thinner, but he looked good overall. He walked in the door with Uncle Henry just as Aunt Mae, Mary, and little Eddie came into the entry, and Eddie held out his arms and ran to his father. "Daddy's here!"

Ed dropped his duffle bag and swooped his little boy up into the air, then embraced him before Mary came to him.

Uncle Henry urged Ed and Mary to move onto the second floor and take a second room for Eddie while they made their next plans.

Uncle Henry told him gruffly, "I think you could use a few months with your wife and son before you worry about your next job. You can give me a hand around here with several projects."

Ed and Mary stayed until the spring of 1946, and Ed worked with Uncle Henry. They built a gazebo in the backyard and a firepit. They planted several trees and did some repairs around the boarding house. Then Ed got a letter from his father, and he and Mary packed up and drove home to Iowa to help with the spring planting. I watched Eddie while they packed. Their families couldn't wait to see Eddie, now a big boy of five. However, they would all miss Aunt Mae and Uncle Henry, and their children.

That's enough for now.

Forty-One

Grace meets Lily

"If you have to force it, it's not for you. Love should come with ease, freedom, and space to expand."

~Alex Elle

I looked at Aunt Violet.
"Let's listen to the next tape!"
She nodded in agreement as I swapped tapes.
I pressed play on the new tape.

Tape #22, The California Adventure ends
Grandma Grace's voice was reflective.

Gracie, I swear I'm not making this up! We started to run out of parts at the aircraft factory after the war ended in Europe. Every morning, we would do our regular work until we ran out of parts. After lunch Josie and I, with the rest of the girls, would gather around an enormous table and sort rivets. Then, every night, our foreman would dump out those rivets for the next shift! They didn't want to lay us off yet. By the summer of 1945, we were down to one shift and started retooling for commercial planes.

Mac introduced me to a friend, a flight instructor named Richard, and I took flying lessons, training on smaller planes. I also gained the mechanical skills to maintain a smaller airplane and its engine. My goal was to get a pilot's license, buy a surplus plane, and fly it home to Iowa.

It would take six to seven months to get my pilot's license, but I did it. I found a job at the plant, transitioning from war to peace.

Mac and Richard took me shopping for surplus planes. Finally, we found a two-seater, the Stearman Kaydet. The Army and Navy used it for training, and it could work for crop dusting.

Richard and I spent many hours together over the fall, winter, and spring. I liked him, and I liked how he treated me with respect and as his equal. He'd flown a variety of planes during the war and had been stationed in England, training crews for the B-17 Flying Fortress.

We ate dinner a few times, and I realized I'd developed feelings for him and tried to hide them. I didn't intend to stay in California forever. Lately, I'd been homesick for the rolling hills of North Central Iowa and our family farms in Jubilee Junction.

I dreamed about flying my plane over our family farms, crop dusting, delivering packages, or flying someone to the Mayo clinic. As much as I had enjoyed teaching, I wouldn't be going back to the country school classroom. California—and the war—had changed me, and I loved working with tools, building planes, troubleshooting engines, and best of all, flying!

It's time to talk about the end of our California adventures. I hope you have the photo album handy. You'll see pictures of Vera with Mama at the train station in San Diego, and pictures of Mama with me, Vera, and Violet at the boarding house and on the streets of Chula Vista. You should find pictures of me and Violet at the boarding house with Reva, Aunt Mae and Uncle Henry, and Ed and Mary and little Eddie. You will find pictures of us at church, as well as a dozen photos of Violet and Don. There should also be photos of me with Richard and my first plane.

Violet and I stayed at the boarding house after the war ended. She was caring for injured patients and liked California. She worked at the hospital until the fall of 1945. In late October, Violet and Bob took the train trip back east. His family lived in Omaha, Nebraska, so they stopped there first for a few days. His parents and sisters were friendly to Violet. They then took the train to Iowa so he could meet our family. Our parents and siblings liked Bob. A few months later, they got engaged. Bob and Violet married a year later, in 1946, after I returned home so I could be her maid of honor.

Reva stayed until August. She was excited on her last day of work. As we clocked out, she said, "I'd like to introduce you to someone. Would you like to grab a coffee and catch a later bus?"

I was curious. "Sure."

We walked out of the building and into the parking lot.

She looked for someone and waved, grabbing my hand. "She's here! Lily's here."

I turned and recognized Lily Namimoto, the lovely young Japanese American girl from the pictures. She waved back as she approached the entryway.

The girls hugged and squealed. Reva introduced us, and Lily held out her hand to shake mine. We found a small cafe across the street and drank coffee and talked.

"Lily is here to help me pack up," Reva explained. "We're going to get an apartment together and work at her uncle's greenhouse back in LA to save money for college."

"Wonderful." I turned to Lily. "I'm so sorry for what your family experienced, which was cruel. Reva told me all about you and your family, your friendship, piano lessons, and the internment camp."

Lily nodded. "Yes, she's a good friend. Her family has been so kind to us. Of course, we didn't like being sent off to the camp. Everyone was angry about Pearl Harbor. It was a tragedy. But my mother taught elementary students and my father ran a flower shop. How dangerous could we be?"

"Then Mother told us, 'We're stuck here. We may as well try to contribute something. The government will let us go.' So, we made life there more bearable. Then, Reva's father came to visit and brought us a box." She grinned. "It reminded us we weren't alone. Reva's family were our friends, and not everyone hated us."

"Toilet paper, chocolate bars, piano books, novels, and magazines," Reva recited.

The girls laughed and looked at each other.

The camp released Lily's family six months ago, and they returned to Los Angeles. Reva's father had collected rent on their two properties and saved it for them, which helped them start over. Mr. Namimoto set up a new floral shop, and they were working hard.

Lily also shared news about Harry coming home soon, and the look on Reva's face told me what I suspected—she loved Harry and he loved her—and Lily knew and accepted it.

We took a bus back to the boarding house and helped Reva pack up.

The next morning, I told Reva how much her friendship meant to me. "Please tell your grandma thank you for introducing me to avocados. I will always think of both of you when I eat one." I hugged her and thanked her for having been such a good friend.

Reva hugged me back. "Thank you for listening to me talk about Lily and Harry."

Lily chimed in, "Yes, thank you!"

We hugged, too, and I walked downstairs with them, carrying a bag.

Uncle Henry brought his car around, ready to take them to the train station.

We exchanged addresses and wrote to each other for years. Lily and Reva attended college together. Harry used the GI Bill for his college studies, and when he graduated, they married. Richard and I flew out for their wedding, and I stood up with her and Lily.

Harry became a successful lawyer, working for civil rights. Reva worked with him and became a photojournalist, chronicling the stories of oppressed people everywhere. Lily became an accomplished pianist and teacher who married a composer.

Our brothers came home to the farm during the spring and summer of 1946. Vincent seemed quieter than before; later we learned he helped liberate one of the concentration camps and saw terrible things. Many years later, we realized he struggled with memories of the war. He drank too much. He and Bob talked several times, and it seemed to help to talk to someone else who witnessed such inhumanity. But we didn't know about PTSD—we used terms like *shell shock*, *combat fatigue*, or *combat stress reaction*.

Virgil, who had spent time in the Philippines, seemed thinner but seemed eager to get back in the fields with my father. Vincent planned on going to Iowa State to study engineering on the new GI Bill, and Virgil planned to go with him to study veterinary medicine. They were glad to be home and called on girls in town. After they graduated, Virgil came back and started the veterinary clinic in town, while Vincent ended up in Des Moines, working for the state.

Our parents received a letter explaining Victor had been buried overseas in the Sicily-Rome American Cemetery in Anzio, Italy, along with 7,800 other American soldiers. We held a memorial service for him, and the military paid for a marker for him in the Founders Cemetery. Mama grieved his loss for the rest of her life and made us promise to look after *her boy's marker*, and we have. Later, my father received a check for $10,000 from Victor's Army life insurance policy, because he made our parents his beneficiaries. Daddy wept, took the check to the bank, and paid off the farm mortgage.

Vera did the accounts for the family farms and moved into a farmhouse with baby Donna. Twice a year she went to St. Paul to show off the baby to the other grandparents. When Donna turned five years old, Vera met Don's cousin, a war veteran named John. They married in 1953. He was a widower with two young boys.

She and Donna moved to his wheat farm south of St. Paul. Vera and John welcomed two boys together. However, during the 1980s farm crisis, John developed a deep depression and committed suicide. Vera came back to Jubilee Junction for a long visit after John's funeral, living in her old house for six months. Her children had all grown up. Finally, she put her things into storage and moved out of the farmhouse. It sat empty for many years until Mark and Kathy moved into it.

Vern came home with a war bride from England, Margaret Smith. We all called her Maggie. She fit into our family with her cheery smile and practical outlook on life. She and Violet and I became great friends. Maggie became an American citizen and then took courses at the college and became a licensed nurse, specializing in trauma.

I stayed in California for the longest time. I earned my flying license in the Spring of 1946 and talked my father into selling me several acres of land for a landing strip with a place for a large barn to work on housing and maintaining several planes.

The government wanted to sell off surplus planes, large and small.

I bought my two-seater Stearman Kaydet for $200, and Richard flew back to Iowa with me in early June 1946. We stopped to refuel and rest several times, and I was grateful for his company and expertise. We enjoyed the flight and agreed the plane flew well. I no longer wanted to deny my feelings for Richard. He met my family and stayed for a few days. Then I saw him off at the train station in Jubilee Junction, and he returned to California. We wrote to each other.

I started a career providing crop dusting and other transport services to farmers and small businesses. My father, uncles, and brothers helped me build an extra-large barn to store the plane and have a place to work on it. I helped Mama, Aunt Verdeen, and our other grandma and aunts finish the California quilt but could see it wouldn't heal what was wrong between Vera and Violet. By then, Mama couldn't stand to see it, so I hid it away.

Richard Walters showed up a few months later with his four-seater plane and proposed marriage and a partnership. I found out later he asked my father for permission to propose that summer. In the fall of 1946, we married. We lost our first child in 1948 but had a son and daughter—your uncle, Richard Junior, in 1950, and your mother, Rebecca or Becky, in 1953. We loved watching our children grow, right along with our business!

There should be a few photos of us with our first two planes out in the field, which became our second landing strip. Later, we built an even bigger barn to store the planes and a second landing strip. Many years down the road, this became the Jubilee Municipal airport, where private planes arrived and departed. We continued with our business, using the smaller runway.

That's all for now.

The kitten woke up and yawned. "Sorry, we bored you, Beatrix."

Aunt Violet smiled. "Your grandma was so happy with Richard. I could see he was the man for her. They loved to fly together. I hope you find such love, too, Gracie—someone who loves the same things you do."

I looked at her. "Yes, I hope so."
Later, she walked me to the door. We hugged.
"It should be an interesting week."

Forty-Two

Dinner with David

"I'm choosing happiness over suffering, I know I am. I'm making space for the unknown future to fill up my life with yet-to-come surprises."

~Elizabeth Gilbert

$\mathcal{I}$ walked into my house and put the shoeboxes down on my entryway table. Agatha ran up to me, so I walked out to the kitchen and put the cookies up on the counter. "I'll get your treats. These are for me," I told her and slipped off my long-sleeved cardigan sweater.

My cell phone rang. David asked, "How are you doing?"

"I'm all right. Hearing Grandma's voice in these tapes has been incredible. I'm going to miss her even more now."

"Want me to pick up Chinese? We talked about going to Aunt Shirley's, but something tells me you might want a quieter meal."

"Thanks, David. Please get me sweet and sour chicken, and could we split an order of crab Rangoon? I think you have my address."

"Yes, got it in a text message. See you soon."

He arrived half an hour later bearing Chinese takeout and a cheesecake.

David saw the baggie of cookies on my counter and grinned. "We're in good shape for dessert."

I'd set the table and poured some tea into small teacups, leaving the teapot on the table. We took the containers out of the paper sack and sat down to eat.

Agatha came up to David's chair and meowed, and he leaned

down to pet her. "Hey, Miss Agatha. How're you doing, little girl?" She purred and rubbed against his legs.

I thought, *He remembered her name.* "Don't let her fool you. She has food in the kitchen and doesn't need ours."

David laughed, then got up from the table, washed his hands at the kitchen sink, and called the kitty, who went to him. He pointed at her dish, and Agatha looked up at him, as if to say, *Oh, there's my food.* She nibbled at the Fancy Feast.

I sighed. She doesn't do that for me.

David came back to the table, opened his container of Mongolian beef, and dug in. His entrée smelled amazing.

I began eating my sweet and sour chicken. We split the crab Rangoons and cherry sauce.

"Thank you. This is just what I needed."

He smiled. "My pleasure. I love crab Rangoon, but there are too many for one person, so it's a great reason to share."

I turned my wrist to dunk the crab Rangoon in the cherry sauce just as David looked down, and I remembered too late that I'd taken off my long-sleeved sweater. The red marks on the inside of my wrist were fainter and a strange yellowish black color now. I dropped the food back on my plate nervously.

"Gracie?"

Our eyes met. His were solemn, the gold flecks in his brown eyes more intense.

"Did Steve do that to you?"

"Yes. He didn't want me to walk away."

I'd told him some details of that dinner, but not all.

He picked up my hand and tenderly examined the old bruising, leaned forward, and lightly kissed it. Then he looked up at me.

"My father taught me never to hit or hurt a woman." David paused. "Are you alright?"

I nodded, but tears trickled down my face. He cradled my hand. He let go, smiled, and gestured.

"I suppose you'll want your hand back to polish off that crab Rangoon before it gets too cold."

I exhaled, grateful for his kindness, but didn't want to be a victim.

He looked down at Agatha, who meowed up at him. I furtively dabbed at my eyes with the takeout napkin, realizing he was letting me compose myself.

I resumed eating, and he smiled gently at me as he dug back into his food as well.

We talked about the semester ending and what we needed to grade. We traded funny stories of kids coming to see us who haven't been to class in weeks, who wanted to *catch up* now when the semester was all but over.

David told me about a former office mate whose student asked if he could do extra credit to improve his grade. "The kid turned in the extra credit work but didn't complete his regular assignments. My office mate asked him why he didn't do the regular work, and the student told him he didn't have time because he was doing the extra credit."

We looked at each other and laughed.

Then, he commented on one of my recent columns about the way the quilt exhibit was drawing local families together, prompting the sharing of stories and a greater appreciation for their family history.

"You're a brilliant writer. You captured the impact of the exhibit."

"Thanks." I speared one of the last green peppers and some pineapple.

David leaned forward. "Have I told you how much I admire your work ethic, helping with your family newspaper while teaching and working at the museum?"

I sat up a little straighter. "You don't think I'm crazy to juggle three jobs? Really?"

"Do I have to ask if you're happy? I can tell. You won't be doing all these jobs forever, but for right now, I think you've found a balance that works for you. Teaching, writing, and creating exhibits takes a lot of the same organizational skills and creativity, but few people would take it all on."

"Steve kept telling me I needed to get out of Jubilee Junction and move to Des Moines. He thought I was wasting my time here and wasting my degrees. He sent me a job ad for a museum in Des

Moines and put in a good word for me with the HR person and then became angry when I didn't apply for it."

"Do you like Des Moines?"

"Yes, for a visit to the Capitol, the history museum, or the state fair. I can't see myself living there."

"Well then, there you go. I spent several years living close to Chicago and enjoyed going into the city to go to a play, museum, or to see friends, but I would never live there. I like small towns. You get to know people. I like Jubilee Junction. And if I need to do research, it isn't far from any of the major university libraries."

He saw my face. "Look, my ex-girlfriend wanted to change me, too. Cynthia had a lot of ideas and plans, but they were *her* ideas and *her* plans, not *ours*. She'd gotten promoted and wanted to live in a high-rise apartment in downtown Chicago and mix with the important people in publishing. I wanted to go to museums and battlefields, teach, and write. We sat down to talk and realized we wanted quite different things. We were together for several years but kept breaking up."

"I understand. Have you ever read a famous short story by Kate Chopin, "The Story of an Hour"? It's just two pages long?"

"Yes, that's the story about a young woman who thinks her husband died in a train wreck. And then he walks in, and she dies at the foot of the stairs?"

"Exactly. There's a line in there about trying to control others, bending them to their will. I use the story in my literature class, and my students always relate to the main character. Where's my textbook?"

I walked over to my desk, picked up the book, turned to the page, and read out loud.

"There would be no one to live for during those coming years; she would live for herself. There would be no powerful will bending hers in that blind persistence with which men and women believe they have a right to impose a private will upon a fellow-creature. A kind intention or a cruel intention made the act seem no less a crime as she looked upon it in that brief moment of illumination.

"And yet she had loved him—sometimes. Often she had not.

What did it matter! What could love, the unsolved mystery, count for in the face of this possession of self-assertion which she suddenly recognized as the strongest impulse of her being!

"Free! Body and soul free!" she kept whispering."

I repeated, "there would be no powerful will bending hers in that blind persistence with which men and women believe they have a right to impose a private will upon a fellow-creature." I walked back to the table and sat down.

David sighed and nodded. "Yes, that describes Cynthia, alright."

"And Steve."

"I love the phrase, *Love, the unsolved mystery.* Chopin was a remarkable writer. I read her novel, *The Awakening,* in grad school. She was ahead of her time and didn't get the respect she deserved."

"It's always shocked my students to see when the story was written, because *Vogue* published it in 1894. The story seems very modern somehow. People and human nature haven't changed."

"I didn't know *Vogue* existed in 1894. Now I've got to Google it to see the covers back then. Not many women get the significance of history like you do."

David's tone turned more serious. "The question is, can two intelligent adults have a healthy, romantic relationship and not focus on changing the other person?"

"I hope so," I told him, maybe too fervently. "When Chopin wrote the story, women were little more than the property of their husbands and not equal partners."

David looked at me and smiled. "I like you, Gracie." He stood up and held out a hand. I stood, too. He put his hands gently on my face, drawing me to him. "I'm going to kiss you. I hope that's okay?"

"I'm going to kiss you back, David."

David and I finally got around to eating our dessert and chatted about our plans for the holiday weekend.

"My father, brother-in-law Jared, and younger brother Alex are all Hawkeye football fans, but my mother and I would rather watch holiday movies or bake cookies with my sister Joanna and her kids, so it should be a noisy family weekend. How about you?"

I'd told him about the drama with my family and the tapes. "It looks like we're having two family gatherings. One on Thanksgiving and one on Saturday with Vera and her daughter's family."

"I can't wait to find out what happens." David's eyes were warm and concerned. "This could help heal some old wounds."

"I'm anxious," I admitted. "It could also blow up." I told him about Aunt Vera's phone call earlier in the fall and her reputation in the family.

"Want some support? I could be there. My family is having their Thanksgiving late, on Friday."

"Sure. I'd love to have you there. Things could be dramatic, but there should be lots of great food. Plus, you'd get to meet Uncle Vern and Aunt Maggie, Mark and Kathy, and my parents."

David grinned. "You hooked me with drama and then food. I'd like to meet your family."

I'd asked Aunt Violet if it would seem strange to have a family gathering in her old house.

She responded rather serenely, "I loved the house when Bob and our children were there. This place is easier to take care of, and Beatrix and I love our new home. I have a feeling the old farmhouse won't be vacant much longer, however."

Thanksgiving Day

Mom, Dad, and I got up early in the morning and met at Violet's old house to put the ham in the oven and the turkey in electric roaster on the counter. Mark and Kathy arrived next and then David. I made the introductions.

Mark and David set up the long tables and chairs in the dining room. Before long, they were chatting away like old friends.

Kathy and I helped in the kitchen. My parents brought Chinet disposable plates, forks, and cups, so there would be no dishes to wash. By the time our guests arrived, the house smelled heavenly, and we were all set. Dad brought along a CD boombox and holiday tunes, which he played softly during lunch.

I brought my tape recorder and an auxiliary speaker. Dad had copied all the tapes and pictures from the California trip to DVD and placed a basket full of the DVDs on the big oak sideboard. But I played Grandma's tapes for more of a dramatic effect.

My parents invited Aunt Violet, her oldest son Robert and his wife Elizabeth, Mark and Kathy, Uncle Vern and Aunt Maggie, Uncle Rich and Aunt Delores, their sons James and RJ and his wife Allie, and David.

Everyone brought side dishes and my parents bought four pies from Aunt Shirley's. We set the food on the dining room table, buffet style.

We did introductions, then Dad asked Uncle Vern to say the blessing. Everyone lined up, filled their plates, and sat down at the table.

David and I sat with Mark and Kathy and Uncle Rich and Aunt Delores. We chatted as we ate. As I watched David interacting with my family and saw how well he fit in. When I'd brought Steve to family gatherings, he seemed bored and wanted to leave early. In contrast, David talked to everyone, but didn't dominate the conversation. Kathy took me aside to say she liked him, and so did Dad, Mark, Aunt Violet, and Uncle Vern.

Later, we played the tapes regarding Don, Violet, and Vera, summarizing what had come before, and promising them all a copy of the complete set of tapes. When the tape where Grandma talked about the close of the California adventure ended, several women wiped tears, and the men looked emotional as well.

I stood. "There are just two more tapes. Do you want to hear them?"

"Yes!" Aunt Maggie responded, and Violet nodded.

"Let's get some coffee and dessert first," Mom suggested.

Fifteen minutes later, I popped in the new tape. David sat beside me, and as we listened, I realized I'd slipped my uninjured hand into his. I looked up, and he smiled at me. It felt so natural and right.

Forty-Three

Gracie's Family Listens to the Tapes

"The dynamic had changed. In past years, there might have been a yelling match. One of the grandfathers might have stepped in and offered to buy Vera a new car. Now Vera was intimidated by her sister, and Violet stayed very calm and controlled."

~*Grandma Grace*
Thanksgiving Day, Continued

Tape #23, "I wish you were my Mommy."
Grandma Grace's voice sounded cheerful.

Now, let me tell you about those two aprons. When we came back to Iowa, the whole country tried to put the war behind it in the transition from war to peace. Our VA hospitals were full, and they needed nurses and doctors. Maggie, Violet, and Dr. Bob kept busy at our local clinic.

After your grandpa Richard and I married, I kept working and flying. We built our business together with hopes and dreams. I wore the peach apron to entertain guests. Mama made the apron for me when we married. I loved the color and fabric. The old red and white checked apron belonged to your Great-Grandma Ginny, who used it to gather eggs, and we marveled she broke so few. I kept her apron to remember her, her love and devotion to her family and our farm.

I have so many happy memories of those years in the late 1940s and 1950s when your Aunt Violet and I were starting our families and building careers. After they married, Violet and Bob lived in Marshalltown for a year and worked at the Veterans' Home there. Then, the clinic here expanded, and they moved back in 1948.

They moved into Violet's farmhouse and started a family. Violet and Bob welcomed four children into their home. They were a lively and fun bunch. Robert, Jeannie, Bill, and Charlene grew up nearby, and when my children came along, they became friends as well as cousins. Rebecca and Richard Junior always wanted to find out what the others were up to.

Vera moved into a house on our other grandparents' big farm and divided her time between Iowa and Minnesota. But something had changed. When she tried to get her way after returning from California, Violet stood up to her. Her parents, grandparents, and aunts, and uncles stood up to her as well, and she could no longer sweet-talk her grandfathers into getting her way. She wanted to return to her job at the courthouse, but her parents pointed out she had responsibilities as a mother now, and they would support her if she helped with the books for the farm and focused on raising her little girl.

It all came to a head at a family dinner when Donna turned three. She woke up from her nap on Grandma Ginny's bed and came out to the living room and headed straight for her *Auntie Vi*, as she called her. Violet lifted her up onto her lap, along with her stuffed animal, and Dr. Bob put a blanket over her. They snuggled for half an hour or more.

Donna looked up at Violet. "I wish you were my Mommy."

Several of us sitting nearby heard her. Violet made eye contact with me and smiled sadly. Then she focused on the girl. "You have a mommy, Donna. But Uncle Bob and I love you lots." Then she pointed at us on the couch. "Who else loves you, Donna? Can you guess?"

Donna laughed and pointed, too. "Aunt Grace, Aunt Maggie, Unkie Richard and Unkie Vern." And she named everyone in the room. When she finished, we all clapped.

Aunt Violet told her, "Good job, Donna. See? Lots of people love you."

Donna sat up and looked around and smiled, while a couple of us had to avert our heads and dig for a hankie in a pocket or purse.

Meanwhile, around the corner, Vera complained loudly about how hard she worked, helping with the books, and how much she needed a new car. Mama told us all about it later.

Daddy told her, "Your car is perfectly fine. We keep it tuned up, and it gets good gas mileage. It's only three years old. Let's wait a year or two for a new vehicle."

Vera argued with him. "You don't care about me or your granddaughter."

"I care. But we've already spent a lot of money this year on clothes, painting your house, getting new furniture for Donna's room, and paying for three trips to Minnesota," he responded patiently.

"Violet got a new car," she pointed out defiantly.

"Violet's husband, Bob, bought the car. Their old car developed engine problems," Daddy retorted.

"It's not my fault my husband is dead!" Vera stood up and faced her father.

"Vera, show some respect to your father," Mama intervened. "Do you want to discuss your dead husband here? How long were you married? Two months?"

"You always stand up for Violet. Everyone loves Saint Violet." Vera's voice turned bitter, and she talked louder and louder. "It's been like this since you forced us to work on the California quilt. Everyone has turned against me. I should burn that quilt."

Vern walked around the corner and teased his sister, using his childhood nicknames for the twins. "Keep your voice down, Vera. Donna woke up, and she's sitting on Violet's lap. Guess even Donna likes Sweet more than Sour."

Vera, red-faced, marched around the corner and saw Donna on Violet's lap. She stared around the room, dramatically. Maggie, Richard, and I sat on the couch, talking. I saw Vera's face and prepared for another blow-up.

"So now you're all turning my daughter against me?" she snatched Donna from her sister's lap. Donna cried, but Vera ignored her.

"Want Auntie Vi, want Auntie Vi," Donna sobbed, holding out

her arms. Violet made eye contact with me, calm, but I saw my sister evaluating the best course of action. Vera wanted a fight, wanted confirmation we were all against her. Violet would not give it to her.

Maggie and I were ready to jump up when Mama rushed into the room and intervened. "What's the matter with my Donna baby? Vera, be gentle with her." She took the small girl from Vera and comforted Donna, who continued to sob.

Everyone stared at Vera. Violet stood up and looked at her sister calmly. "No one is saying things against you. You must be tired. I think it's time for you to go home and rest, Vera. Your little girl needs her Mama to be calm and rested. We'll bring her home later."

Vera started to say something, and Violet looked at her again, steadily. "Please apologize to our parents for being so rude." Mother sat down holding Donna, and Violet handed the small stuffed animal to her niece, who stopped sobbing.

"Thanks Auntie Vi. Luv bunny baby," Donna said and held the toy close.

Vera choked out a quick apology and ran for the door. We were stunned into silence. The dynamic had changed. In the past, there might have been a yelling match. Our Nelson grandfather might have offered to buy Vera a new car. Now Vera felt intimidated by her sister, and Violet stayed calm and controlled. Of course, Bob sat there beside her, supporting her, and meeting Vera's stare. And Richard, Maggie, and I sat on the couch, staring Vera down. But Violet dealt with the issue, and Vera fled. I was so proud of Violet!

Vera stayed away from our family gatherings and spent more time in Minnesota. She complained about the California quilt and insisted it should be burned. Violet and I finally hid it away in an upper bedroom at Mama's house, and made sure anytime Vera came to the house, someone watched her.

Vera avoided being around us, but Donna continued to dart for Violet whenever she saw her. By the time Donna turned five, her mother had remarried, after meeting one of Don's older cousins, a widower named John, also a World War II veteran. She moved to his farm south of St. Paul.

We missed seeing Donna but were relieved to not have to deal with Vera regularly. They came back every couple of months for a brief visit so the family could see Donna, but the visits started getting shorter, with longer periods in between.

Vera was gone, but all the secrets were still here, creating a barrier between the generations. None of the younger generation understood why Vera and Violet acted so differently. They all remembered many incidents where Vera was nasty, manipulative, or caused a fuss before the trip to California. Violet had always tried to appease her and intervene, but no longer. Only our parents' siblings and our grandparents knew the entire story, as well as Violet, Bob, and me.

Mama and Daddy hated scandal, hated the idea one of their daughters could have done such a terrible thing to her twin sister and could have become pregnant with her sister's fiancé. They asked us to stay silent, and the silence lasted long after the grandparents, aunts, and uncles, and our parents all died.

Our family made a big mistake by not talking about what happened in California. As the older generation died out, Violet and I talked about what to do. Like the children of Israel wandering in the desert for forty years until the older generation died, we were stuck.

The silence cost us all. Violet didn't tell her secret to Vern, and they'd always been close. After Bob died, Violet struggled with whether she should tell her children. She also struggled with watching Donna suffer from having never known her wonderful father.

Gracie, it's time to break the silence—it's time to tell the secrets.

The tape ended, and everyone tried to absorb everything. Several looked for a Kleenex. David held my hand gently.

"Powerful stuff," he whispered.

I nodded, grabbing for my Kleenex as well.

Uncle Vern looked at Violet, sadly. "I wish I'd known all this long ago. I'm so sorry, Violet, because I remember the family dinner when you held Donna. I teased Vera and didn't understand why she became so angry and then intimidated. It made little sense."

Aunt Maggie nodded.

Aunt Violet told him, "Mama could hardly stand to look at Vera for years, and Daddy was angry as well, which is why they sent her to live with my father's parents for the pregnancy. The only ones who knew the entire story were my aunts, uncles, and grandparents. They didn't tell any of the other boys, Vern."

Aunt Maggie spoke up. "Now I understand why Vera wanted to burn the California quilt. The quilt served as concrete evidence she'd betrayed her sister. Poor Donna. Doesn't she deserve to know? Oh, Violet. What a terrible experience." She stood up and hugged her sister-in-law.

Violet's son, Robert, looked upset. "I'm so sorry, Mom."

His wife, Elizabeth, nodded, with tears in her eyes. "Thank goodness you met Robert's father."

Aunt Violet nodded and put her hand on her son's. "It's all right, son. I hope you forgive us for not telling you when you were younger. Your father wasn't sure it was a good idea."

Mom asked, "When did you and your sister have the blow-up again?"

Violet thought. "Donna was three years old, so 1948."

Dad let out a deep sigh. "For the last sixty-four years, the family has been walking around on eggshells about Vera."

Mark exhaled. "Sixty-four years? No offense, Aunt Violet, but that's crazy."

No one spoke for several minutes, then I stood up. "Should we listen to the last tape?"

Dad looked around as people nodded. "Yes, let's listen to it."

I put the last tape in, pressed play, and sat back down between David and Kathy, sitting next to Mark. Kathy whispered, "Good job, Gracie," and Mark and David smiled. As I sat, David put his arm around me.

Forty-Four

Aunt Vera's Temper Tantrums

"Real love moves freely in both directions. Don't waste your time on anything else."

~Cheryl Strayed

Tape #24, Your Legacy
  Grandma Grace's voice became emotional.

For the past sixty years, I've thought about what happened in California. I didn't understand how God could let such a terrible thing happen to our family. Finally, I realized it all came down to choices. Vera chose to chase after Don, to talk him into thinking he could have her in place of her sister, and to deprive her sister of marrying him and having his child. She was too impulsive and too jealous of Violet to think through the consequences.

Sometimes you make choices, sometimes you make mistakes, and sometimes you suffer because of someone else's choices and mistakes. I grieved for Violet, my beloved younger sister, and best friend. When Vera tricked Don into marrying the wrong twin, I watched Violet suffer. I saw Vera harden her heart, and then pay for her sins by giving birth to a child she did not want, by a man she did not love, and then use the fake marriage and poor baby to win over a family of strangers—Don's family. Don died in the torpedo attack, but I cannot imagine how he would have endured being married to Vera. We already know he asked her for a divorce if he should survive the war.

John was a wonderful man and a loving stepdad to Donna. He paid attention to her and always had a hug or a kind word for her. Donna gained two stepbrothers—from John's first marriage. His wife died from cancer when the boys were young. We watched John and Vera together and saw she made more of an effort when around John, but Richard and I wondered how long it would last. They had two sons, twins. So, Donna became special to John, in a family of four boys and only one girl.

Donna became a beloved big sister to the twins, Thomas and Timothy. She also had a good relationship with his older boys. However, living with Vera for 38 years took a toll on John. The last time we saw him, he looked tired and stressed. The farm crisis provided the final straw. He'd gotten heavily mortgaged after buying some additional land and upgrading his tractor and other expensive equipment. He hoped his younger sons would farm with him. His older sons weren't interested, and Tom and Tim became engineers—one moved to Minneapolis and the other to Denver.

John became depressed and overwhelmed. Vera found him in the barn, hanging from the rafters, with a ladder and some tools. The official report claimed it was an accident, but most of us weren't convinced.

I tried to reach out to Vera several times, mostly because I felt sorry for Donna. She never knew her father and was raised by a stranger for a mother, but her family in Minnesota loved her dearly, as did her stepdad, John. Don would have been so proud of her.

Vera didn't want to talk about her stay in California because she wanted to forget it. She would have destroyed the California quilt if given the chance. Before she died, Mama cried and told me it'd been foolish to think she could mend the relationship between the twins with a quilt. I think the whole situation broke her heart—and my daddy's heart, too.

Please tell Vera I forgive her. I know her life didn't turn out the way she wanted it. I watched Violet's broken heart mend when she met Robert. They shared everything. He knew the truth about what happened in California, yet they enjoyed a wonderful life together. They loved each other and raised four wonderful children. Dr. Bob delivered several generations of children in Jubilee Junction, with Violet as his nurse by his side. They were a good team.

I didn't go to California to find a husband, but I loved your grandpa Richard because he knew my heart's desire—to fly! We built a business and a life together, and we raised your mother and uncle. We enjoyed watching them grow up and then watching all the grandchildren come along.

I thought my heart would break when I lost our first baby. Later, I thought I could not stand watching your Uncle Rich enlist in the Air Force to fly helicopters in Vietnam. Fortunately, I discovered how resilient we can be when we have the love of family and our faith. Violet has been my lifelong friend and someone I could always count on.

Your grandpa became my best friend, my sweetheart, and my partner, and when he died, part of me died too. I found a letter he wrote shortly before his death. He told me he felt he'd been the luckiest man in the world to have married his best girl and spent his life flying over our beautiful Iowa farmland. He had no regrets, and he hoped I didn't either.

I agree. I have no regrets. We shared everything. I hope you find this kind of love because you deserve it!

Gracie, you're not a little girl anymore. You have your hopes and dreams. You always liked to write stories, you always tried to help people, and you loved playing school when you were younger. Do you remember? You could read and write before you were in school. I think you will be a wonderful teacher or journalist someday.

Of course, I told all my grandchildren they were my favorite, and I love your brother Mark and your cousins RJ and James. But you're my only granddaughter, and I wanted to make sure you shared the story and kept the quilt in the family to remind future generations that secrets can destroy families.

I started making these tapes in 1998 but stopped when your grandfather became sick in 2004. Now it's 2008, and I've just finished the last three tapes. I dug through my journals and the small trunk of letters, photos, postcards, and mementos from the war years to refresh my memory. That includes my small California photo album and the scrapbook with articles about the war. Aunt Violet has my trunk—it is yours, Becky and Gracie. I haven't let anyone listen to the tapes yet, not even Violet, but she knows I'm making them. I hope it isn't too painful for Violet to listen to them, but she knows I'm right. We should've talked about these things decades ago.

Please apologize to your mother and your Uncle Rich if I am not there. Several long-lived aunts told me Mother didn't want the story told. But they're all gone now—may they rest in peace in the Founders cemetery—so it's time to tell the story.

Our generation is down to the three of us sisters, Vern and Maggie. We need to make peace. Vern, my baby brother and dear friend, please forgive me for not telling you all of this before now. I lost my nerve a dozen times. Maggie, you've been my other sister and my dear friend. I'm so sorry we didn't tell you everything.

Becky, you and Matthew have kept the family newspaper going, and I hope someone, maybe Gracie, will keep it going for another generation. Jubilee Junction needs *The Jubilee Times*.

Rich, I see your father's eyes when I look at you, and I'm full of gratitude that someone is still flying over our farmland, and I know you love it as much as we did. Delores, James, RJ, and Allie—I love you all. RJ and James, I trust you'll find the same sense of freedom we did in the air!

Mark, you found a good woman in Kathy, and I hope I'm there, listening to these tapes with you, and holding my great-grandchild. I'm so glad someone in your generation is still farming the soil my great-grandfather first planted. Vern, thank you for all you have done to keep the family farms going, and for helping Mark. I love seeing you walking out to the barn or into the fields, talking and planning. Keep working with your uncles and cousins, Mark. Share the equipment, work together, plant together, and harvest together. The thousand acres on our family farms is a treasure left for you all to manage.

However, you children and grandchildren are our greatest treasure—our legacy—and I hope you will cherish each other and the good Iowa soil as much as we did. I love you all.

Gracie, you've grown up and you're facing your own choices and making decisions. I hope you make the right ones for you. Just remember, God's grace is sufficient!

The tape clicked, startling me.

Mark spoke up first. "Grandma Grace spent hours making these tapes. I've learned a lot about our family, and now I want to listen to the entire set."

Several people nodded. Kathy softly responded, "You and Mark had a wonderful grandma. You can hear the love for you all in her voice."

Vern spoke then. "Grace was such a great big sister. It's good to hear her voice again." He found his handkerchief and wiped his eyes.

Maggie nodded and put her arm around her husband. "What a lovely lass. I wish you could have seen her when she was your age, Gracie. She put her hair up into a long blonde ponytail and changed into a pair of dungarees and tucked in a work shirt. She loved to work on engines, and she loved to fly."

A moment passed as we all composed ourselves.

Then, Mom looked around the room, stood up, and announced, "I've invited Donna, Harold, and Vera for Saturday brunch. I intend to play the tapes. Matthew has digitized them. Here, Mark and David, please pass out the DVDs."

Mark grinned at David, and they got up to pass out the DVDs.

Violet raised her eyebrows. "Oh, Becky. And Vera agreed to come?"

Mom nodded and then admitted, "Well, Donna told me yes."

Vern chuckled, "You're like your mother, Becky. Grace believed in forgiveness and redemption. When it comes to Vera, I'm not sure what to think. Good for you to open the door."

Maggie spoke up, "Who knows, Vern. She might surprise all of us."

Mom responded, "Yes, but really, I want Donna to hear the tapes. It's Vera's choice if she wants to make a fuss, but her daughter deserves to understand what happened."

Violet's son, Robert, spoke, his face flushed. "I don't know if I can forgive Vera for causing so much grief to my mother and this family." His wife put her arm around him, and Violet reached out for his hand.

Mom agreed. "Look at the ripples of hurt caused by her betrayal."

Aunt Violet nodded. "Yes, she broke my heart. I couldn't imagine anyone doing such a thing, much less to my own sister. Yet, I became weary of the weight of all the resentment and hurt. I found a new strength in letting go, and then I met your father, of course."

Mom's brother, Rich, spoke up, his voice husky with emotion, "I've heard a few stories about my parents meeting out in California, but knew nothing about what happened between you and Vera. I'm so sorry."

Aunt Delores nodded, her eyes brimming with tears.

I looked at David, who'd been quiet and respectful, listening to the family stories and watching it all unfold. He smiled and leaned over to whisper, "Lots of drama, but I think it's going well. This is a remarkable use of oral history. I wish I could have met your grandma. What an incredible life she lived, and what a gift these tapes are, Gracie."

I nodded and exhaled as I saw people processing what they'd heard and looking at Violet with admiration and love. She looked relieved to get the sixty-four-year-old secret out in the open, and I hoped it might bring healing. But I was genuinely nervous about seeing Aunt Vera. How would she respond to the tapes?

We met at the farmhouse again on Saturday. David helped Mark set up the tables and chairs. The rest of us were in the kitchen with the food. Family members arrived, bringing side dishes and dessert. About forty-five minutes later, Donna, her husband, Harold, and daughter Julie arrived.

Mom greeted them with hugs. I took their coats.

Donna looked behind her daughter. "Where's your grandma?"

Julie looked outside. "She's back in the car."

Harold walked toward the door. "I'll go get her."

Donna nodded and looked apologetically at Mom and Aunt Violet. "She raised a fuss on the drive down."

"I'm so glad you came." Aunt Violet gave Donna a big hug. Then she looked at Julie, now in her forties. "I haven't seen you since your wedding, but your Mama sends me a picture of you and your beautiful family from time to time. How are you?" They hugged and chatted.

Harold walked out and spoke to his mother-in-law. He walked back in, with Aunt Vera in front of him, looking like a stubborn child coming out of time-out.

Uncharacteristically subdued, Vera clutched her purse and cane and looked resentful. Uncle Vern and Aunt Maggie tried to say hello, but she did not respond.

Mom had prepared a lovely brunch with help from family members. We set it up as a buffet again, and people lined up to fill their plates with coffeecake, egg casserole, bacon or sausage, and fresh fruit.

Julie sat by her mother, Donna, with her father on the other side, and Vera sat next to Donna. My parents, Uncle Vern, and Aunt Maggie filled out the table. Vera poked at her food and didn't talk to anyone. Her family ignored her, except for Julie, who looked at her several times and tried to say something.

After we ate, Mom explained Grandma Grace left a series of tapes about the three girls going out to California, and she wanted to play them. She would send home a DVD with the complete set.

Mark, David, and Dad rearranged the chairs in a semi-circle.

I placed Mom's boombox on the dining room table and plugged in an auxiliary speaker. I inserted the tape.

Before I could press play, Vera stood up. "I will not sit here and listen to this nonsense. You tricked me into coming. You're going to humiliate me again. You might as well bring in the California quilt." Red-faced, she punched the air with one fist while the other held her purse and cane.

I sat down, trying to look calm, and David took my hand and kissed it to reassure me. We'd switched seats so he could hold my uninjured hand.

Uncle Vern stood up and gave her a look, but he spoke gently. "It's time, Vera. Please, sit down. We know what happened in

California—we've already listened to the tapes. Now Donna, Harold, and your granddaughter Julie deserve to know the truth, too."

Aunt Vera flinched. "You only think you know. Grace has poisoned you against me, and Violet, too. She wanted Don, but he married me. She's still angry. I want to leave!" She shouted, shaking with anger—and suddenly, I realized—fear.

I looked at Aunt Violet, who sat calmly, looking anything but upset.

Harold turned to look at Aunt Vera and spoke quietly in an even tone. "We've had enough of your temper tantrums, Vera. You've made my life miserable, and worse. You've made your daughter's life—my wife's life—difficult. I'm tired of seeing her cry because of your harsh words. So, please sit down!" He looked at her deliberately. Donna held his hand and looked straight ahead, not at her mother, and Julie looked embarrassed.

Vera seemed stunned, but stood still, defiant, but wobbling, her hand on her cane now.

Before Vera could say anything else, Donna stood up and put her arm around her mother. "I want to hear the tapes. I have a lot of questions you've never answered." She sat down.

Vera hesitated and then sat down in defeat. She seemed to shrink inside of herself and become smaller.

Her granddaughter, Julie, looked curious. Donna's husband, Harold, sat quietly now, holding Donna's hand. He looked calmer, and I think everyone mentally applauded him for standing up to the belligerent old woman.

We listened to the tapes about the three sisters in California, and I saw Aunt Vera get angry and then sad as the events unfolded. When she heard Grandma Grace's voice at the end of the tape, she sat up.

"I don't know if it's too late, but I would like you to try one more time. Tell Vera I forgive her. I know her life didn't turn out the way she wanted it."

Forty-Five

A Reluctant Confession

"The moving finger writes and having written moves on. Nor all thy piety nor all thy wit, can cancel half a line of it."
~Omar Khayyam

Grandma's voice continued.

*D*onna should know the truth. Her father died in the war, and her mother, a cold, calculating woman, always seemed more concerned about herself than her children. Donna's Minnesota family loved her, and she could turn to her stepdad, John, Aunt Violet, and Uncle Bob. But the three sisters are all getting older, and we need to make peace.

As we listened, Donna began to sob, while Aunt Vera lowered her head. But I saw her knee jiggling in agitation, and she clutched her cane.

Donna composed herself, took the Kleenex box Mom offered, and then turned to her mother. "I never felt wanted or loved by you, but now I understand. You married your sister's boyfriend, a stranger really, and didn't want a baby at all. I heard bits and pieces of gossip behind closed doors when they didn't think little girls were listening or would understand. I didn't understand why I didn't have a real father until you married John."

Her husband put his arm around her, and her daughter, Julie, turned to her mother, taking her hand.

Donna continued, "One of my earliest memories is crawling up on Aunt Violet's lap and telling her I wished she could be my Mama. She was always so kind and sweet to me. You didn't cuddle or kiss me at night. My stepdad, John, hugged me and so did my Minnesota aunts and grandparents. But I never felt you loved me, even when we took you into our home and cared for you."

Her daughter Julie cried and looked at her grandma. "Oh, Grandma Vera, did you do all of those terrible things in California?"

Vera seemed to search for answers, looking ashamed and angry. "I knew I was in trouble when we got here, and I noticed the tape recorder. Grace liked to send tapes instead of letters. I should have known she would leave her story behind, making me the villain. I won't stay here and put up with this." She stood up, trying to look self-righteous, but what we saw was an old woman whose past finally caught up with her.

Violet stood up, speaking in a calm voice. "Grace is dead, but I'm still here, sister, and her tapes tell the true story. Don proposed to me, insisting we get married the next day before his ship left. We'd only been dating for four months at that point. When I told Don I would be engaged, but I wouldn't marry him before he deployed, he got angry and took me back to the boarding house. Mary heard me crying out to Don and then saw you walk down the front steps. She followed you and saw you talk to Don after he left me at the boarding house. You married him the next day, according to the marriage license. Six weeks later, you realized you were pregnant with his child—Donna. Those are the facts, Vera. Time is running out. Didn't you hear Grace? It's time to make peace. It's time to tell Donna about her wonderful father and Julie about her grandfather. This is not about you and me." Then she sat down, gracefully.

Everyone stared at Vera, who faltered, and sat down, heavily.

Julie looked at her grandma. "Grandma Vera?"

After a long pause, Vera turned to her granddaughter. "Julie, you have to understand we were young—just twenty—when we traveled to California. I suppose I was jealous of Violet. Everyone liked her more, and I got sick and tired of it. I was tired of being a twin. I wanted someone to love me for *me*."

"Don was so handsome, and when I heard Violet tell Reva she'd turned him down, I thought, *Let's see if he picks me*, and he did. It was a terrible thing to do. The family never looked at me the same way after that. It started off as a joke, you know. I wasn't thinking about marrying him—I just wanted him to propose to me. But I let things go too far. I could see my parents wanted me gone, even if they were kind to you, Donna." Vera looked around, ashamed.

Then she turned to her daughter. "Donna, I was too young and selfish to be a mother. I never thought I could get pregnant so quickly. Looking back, I didn't think through my actions. I felt no attachment to your father. Don was a nice man, but my trick backfired. He only wanted me because I looked like Violet, and he thought he was going to die at sea.

"I was terrified that Violet and Grace would tell everyone what happened in California. I hated making the California quilt because all the aunts and grandmas treated me like a fallen woman, having stolen Violet's boyfriend. I was nauseated and furious. Everyone was thinking about poor Violet and didn't see that I was terrified of having the baby and figuring out how to survive in a family of strangers. My parents wouldn't even look at me. They sent me off to stay with my grandparents, who looked sad and reproachful."

"You were a cute baby, Donna, but so tiny. I was terrified of being a mother. I suppose if I were honest, every time I saw your sweet little face, I remembered what I'd done and felt ashamed."

"John came along, and I noticed right away how much he liked children. He told me he'd always wanted a daughter, and he loved you just like his own child. I don't think any apology can erase the pain you feel, but I'm terribly sorry. Can you forgive a foolish old woman? Donna, I do love you and appreciate all you've done."

Donna looked at her mother and aunt, at her daughter and husband. She took a big breath. "Mother, yes, I forgive you. You made mistakes, but I don't want to live the rest of my life feeling like something is wrong with me."

Aunt Vera broke down crying and so did Donna. They hugged for a long time. I noticed a few people passing around the Kleenex box.

Then Aunt Vera straightened up and looked at Harold. "Harold, you're right. I've been selfish and unkind to everyone. I'm sorry for causing problems between you and Donna."

She took a big breath and looked around, now regretful. "I wanted to talk to Grace before she died and make things right. Then she suffered that heart attack and died so suddenly. I was shocked. I didn't think she or Violet would ever forgive me, but I wanted to talk to her." Her voice wavered again.

Violet looked up. "Sister, I forgive you."

We looked at each other. The room became quiet.

Aunt Vera looked astonished, ashamed, and wary.

We all waited for an explosion. I felt anxious and thankful to have David there. He kept his hand on mine and murmured, "It's going to be fine."

A moment passed. Then Aunt Violet patted the empty folding chair next to her. "Let's look at the photo album from Gracie's basket, sister, and show your daughter some pictures of her father."

I exhaled as I watched what happened next.

Vera hesitated. Then she stood up with her cane and sat by Violet, with Donna on the other side. Donna's daughter Julie crowded in beside them, and Robert's wife, Elizabeth, did as well. They looked at the photo album and soon a crowd stood behind them.

Donna looked at the pictures, one by one. "He's handsome, isn't he? Grandma Anderson only has a couple of pictures of him in uniform, so I'm glad to see these, Aunt Violet."

Violet smiled at her. "Yes, he looks so handsome in these pictures. But his personality was even finer. Don had that wonderful laugh—everyone wanted to laugh with him. See his beautiful smile? You have his smile, Donna, and his eyes—and so does Julie."

Donna, Vera, Violet, and Julie flipped back through the photo album, enjoying the pictures of Don and Violet. The snapshots were all taken by Grace. She captured them on a picnic in the park near the waterfront, walking outside the hospital on base, and posing outside the boarding house. Other pictures showed them at church, at lunch with Ed, Mary, and Eddie, and on the streets of Chula Vista. There were no pictures of Donna's father with Vera.

Don and Violet were young, beautiful, and very much in love. It radiated from the photos, even after sixty years.

I could hardly breathe, watching them. Then Mom tapped my shoulder for help. Aunt Delores cut up two chocolate angel food cakes, and Kathy sliced up two apple pies. Aunt Maggie added some whipped cream. We passed around slices of warm apple pie or chocolate angel food cake, with forks and napkins, to everyone. Mark, David, and Dad walked around and offered refills of coffee and tea. We busied ourselves with eating and chatting quietly among ourselves.

The sisters remained seated side by side, and Vera looked humbled and saddened. Her granddaughter held her hand. A look passed from Donna to Violet and back to Vera.

Vera looked remorseful. "I've wasted the last sixty years, haven't I, with my pride and stubbornness? I thought if I were difficult, no one would get too close and no one would find out my secrets. What I did was foolish and wrong. I've been lonely, and I don't know how to apologize for causing so much grief. I can't make up for it, and I certainly can't apologize to Grace." Her voice broke.

Then she looked around and found me. I felt frozen in place.

"Gracie? Please come here," she asked, softly.

I remembered why we were here and walked over to her side. "Aunt Vera?" I asked.

"I'm sorry I called you up and yelled at you about the quilt and basket. I made some nasty remarks about my sisters, and I know I was wrong. Can you forgive me?" she asked.

I took a breath. "Yes. When I heard Grandma Grace talk about forgiving you, I knew we all needed to make things right."

She reached out for me, and I knelt to hug her, and then Aunt Vera looked for Mom. "Becky?" she asked, and Mom came over and joined in the family hug. Kathy passed around the Kleenex, and Aunt Vera hugged her too.

Vera called Vern and Maggie to come over, and apologized to them, too, and there were more tears, laughter, and hugging.

When we'd calmed down, Dad told everyone, "I scanned all those photos, and they're on the DVD along with the two dozen tapes. We made copies for everyone, and there are extras, so take several for the family back in Minnesota."

Later, as we cleaned up, Violet and Vera were still sitting and murmuring, and occasionally laughing, catching up on sixty years or more.

Uncle Vern looked at Mom. "I wish your Mama could be here to see this, Becky. I can't believe it. Vera has never apologized for anything. I think she's sincere. I just wish Grace were here."

Mom looked at her aunts. "I have a feeling she's looking down from Heaven and smiling, Uncle Vern."

Mark and David walked around with garbage bags, collecting paper plates and forks and foam coffee cups. Then they talked with cousins and uncles about football, the family, the crops, and the weather. The women started wrapping up leftovers. Uncle Vern, Dad, Harold, Robert, and Rich were talking in a circle, and I saw Dad pat Harold on the back, and several men shook his hand.

Harold, Donna, Aunt Vera, and Julie were spending the night with Uncle Vern and Aunt Maggie. Mom put together a few leftovers to send home with them. The sisters were still sitting side by side talking.

I walked by David, who reached out for my hand, and asked me, "How are you holding up? I think you have a great family."

I smiled. "Thanks for being here, David. My family is never boring."

He hugged me and rubbed my back for just a minute. "I'm going to help Mark with cleaning up and wiping down the tables and chairs. Your Mom told us to leave them upstairs for Christmas. Then, let's go back to your house and process all this family drama."

I nodded, and he gave me a sweet kiss.

When I turned around, Mom and Kathy were looking on with total approval, and I blushed. Aunt Delores came over as soon as David left to help Mark. "That's the man for you, Gracie. We all like him, and I promise not to tell any embarrassing stories about you having a crush on Cary Grant when you were younger."

I'd confided my hot crush to her as a preteen when I found out she and Uncle Rich owned a copy of *North by Northwest* on VHS.

I'd watched it on the TV/VCR setup at *The Jubilee Times* over and over until I had the dialogue memorized.

I laughed. "I almost wore out your tape of that movie. But guess what? I already confessed, and David likes the movie too."

Aunt Delores gave me a thumbs up. "It's a sign, Gracie!" She walked into the kitchen.

Kathy walked up and hugged me. "You and Becky brought the sisters together. Your grandma would be so happy."

"Thanks, Kathy. Grandma Grace did it. All I did was play the tapes. Hearing her big sister's voice saying she forgave her—and her twin sister too—melted Aunt Vera's heart. I think she was tired and scared. Can you imagine keeping a secret for sixty years?" I looked at Aunt Vera, who was talking to Maggie and Vern now, as Donna and Violet talked.

Kathy smiled. "Yes, and the whole family likes David."

"I like him, too. He likes cats! He treats me like an equal, but he's affectionate too. And he knows the value of literature and history." I rattled off my eccentric list of requirements, and Kathy laughed.

We helped clean up and walked around to talk to relatives. An hour later, my parents thanked David for his help. Dad shook his hand and motioned David aside. "Thank you for coming, David. You were a big help."

David nodded. "You're welcome, sir."

Dad told him, "Oh, call me Matthew. I'm probably not supposed to say anything, but I like how you treat my daughter. Gracie deserves a good man."

Kathy and Mark took the last containers of food from the fridge to my parents' car.

Mom thanked us, too. "OK, kids, now go relax. I'm taking the last two pieces of pie, but there's a plate of Angel food cake in our car for you, Gracie, and one for Mark and Kathy."

As we walked out, Mark asked, "Hey, David—do you play board games?"

David nodded. "Yeah. I haven't played since I moved here, but I have a couple of new games I can't wait to play."

Kathy and I smiled because his answer meant we were a four-some for games.

We followed Mom to get the cake and then drove back to my house.

David played with Agatha while I prepared the tea and grabbed plates and forks. We sat at my table, talking while we drank tea and ate cake. We ended up on the couch with Agatha on his lap and his arm around me, watching an old holiday movie. Agatha looked adoringly up at him as he petted her.

David laughed. "Did I ever tell you my grandma had two cats? Agatha reminds me of one of them, a cute little calico named Clementine."

I smiled. "Looks like we're a package deal."

"I see."

He kissed me, and Agatha meowed.

Epilogue

*"To be fully seen by somebody, then, and be loved anyhow—
this is a human offering that can border on miraculous."*
~Elizabeth Gilbert

Monday morning, I showered and dressed, then grabbed tea and a granola bar, packed my messenger bags, filled Agatha's water dish, and gave her one last pat before walking out the door and heading off to college.

I felt at peace. I couldn't wait to tell Shelly and Tiara about our family meetings. After my second class, we were all back in the office.

"I've been waiting to hear about your weekend. What happened?" Tiara asked as I walked into the adjunct office.

Shelly appeared at the door. "I thought I saw you walk by."

I told them about playing the tapes, Aunt Vera's resistance, how she finally broke down, Donna talking about how she felt like a little girl—all of it.

"Sounds like a happy ending if the sisters reconciled." Shelly exhaled. She'd heard a few Aunt Vera horror stories over the years.

Tiara looked at me. "And how are you doing? The tapes are over."

I nodded. "It's bittersweet. But I'm okay."

"And David? Any news?" Shelly asked.

I smiled. "He likes me. He likes Agatha. My family likes him. I'm crazy about him."

Tiara smiled. "We can see."

Wednesday, I headed to Aunt Violet's apartment. She greeted me at the door, her kitty at her heels.

"Let's listen to the last tape again, please?"

"I know you're busy with finals. I wasn't sure you'd have time today."

A pot of tea with two teacups and a plate of cookies were already in place.

I put the tape into the cassette player and pressed play. She poured the tea. I took a cookie, and we both sat back and listened to the last tape while Beatrix slept in her bed nearby.

As the tape ended, I exhaled. "Thank you for saving Grandma's gifts for me and helping me process all these stories and secrets. I understand what happened to the family now. Like Mark said, sixty-four years is a long time to fuss about something. How are you doing after listening to all these personal stories about you and Vera?"

"I'm fine, Gracie. I expected your grandma would explain what happened in California. I miss her, but we have her voice on those tapes, and we have her truth. My parents, grandparents, and aunts decided we shouldn't talk about it, but our family fractured around the secrets about what happened in California."

"When your Great-Grandma Ginny was alive, we hosted enormous family gatherings with her siblings and their families. We'd do a cookout, and everyone brought blankets and picnic baskets. Those get-togethers stopped after World War II. But now, there are no secrets. I hope you'll learn from our mistakes. Besides that, I've enjoyed our Wednesdays together."

"Me too. So, what happened with Vera?" I nibbled a cookie. "We tried to give you some privacy as we cleaned up."

"Hearing Grace's voice grabbed Vera's attention and hearing both of us say we forgave her knocked down her defenses. She's called me every day. She's been lonely. At first, she lived in fear her Minnesota family would figure out she was an imposter who didn't know their son and was raising a baby she didn't want. She and Harold are getting along better. Vera and Donna are talking a lot more, too."

Her kitty yawned, licked her paws delicately, and repositioned herself on the cat bed.

"I'm glad she's opening up to Donna."

"I know. She's my twin sister, and she's had the last sixty-four years to think about it all. She has regrets. I heard her apologize to you."

"She seemed sincere."

"Donna called yesterday and asked if she could see the California quilt next time they come. She told me to say her mother promised not to burn it, so it's time to get it out."

I smiled, remembering my conversation with Aunt Vera, and my crazy dream. "Yes, I agree."

I opened the second shoebox on the table. "Here's your packet of love letters from Don, still wrapped up in ribbon, and then the packet of letters you got from him before he died. Here's a letter you wrote to Grandma Grace about Bob after you left California. You tell her you're in love with him." I handed her the letter, and she beamed as she held it.

We found a stack of photos from when the three girls returned from California at the bottom of the box. Dr. Bob with his arm around Violet. Grandma Grace with Grandpa Richard and the first two-seater airplane they flew back to Iowa. Vera with a toddler-aged Donna and, much later, Vera with John, his sons, and Donna. Family gatherings with Great-Grandma Ginny, Vern and Maggie, and Vance wearing farmer's overalls, standing by the tractor. The other two brothers, in their military uniforms. Grandparents, aunts, and uncles.

"You know, Dad would scan in all these photos for you, and then we could make DVDs for your children, or copy them to flash drives, or even post them on a website," I told her.

"You and your father are so good with technology. Yes, please take them to your father."

After we finished looking at the pictures, making notes, and recording comments, I talked to her about Don and Dr. Bob—and David.

"How did you trust again after Don hurt you? Was it hard to trust Bob?"

"No. As I look back, I remember Bob's kindness, sense of humor, and wonderful smile. He was a skilled doctor, and I watched him with patients. He listened, he asked questions, and he showed empathy. They trusted him, and soon I did, too. We shared common goals and values and shared interests. The more time we spent together, he made me laugh, and he made my heart sing. It just felt right."

I nodded. "Yes, when I look back now, dating Steve was exhausting. He wanted me to be someone else. Maybe I wanted him to be someone else, too. I kept thinking, *If he would just move to Jubilee Junction, we would be happy*, while he was thinking, *If she just moved to Des Moines, we would be happy*. I wouldn't be surprised if his new girlfriend gets the ring I turned down at Christmas. David is different. I'm myself around him. He makes me laugh, and we share a lot of common interests."

Violet smiled. "I'm happy for you, Gracie. I can't wait to get to know him better."

"You will, over the holidays, after the semester's over," I promised her.

We looked at the letters for another half hour, with Aunt Violet turning them over in her hands, making comments, and sighing. "Would you like me to leave them here?"

"Yes, I'll take the one I wrote mentioning Bob. I might show the love letters from Don to my daughter and then add them to my scrapbook. I'd like to show them to my children."

"I've enjoyed our Wednesdays too, and I don't plan to stop visiting you. I could help you identify people in the old photos, so we know who all those people are."

"What a good idea."

Then we talked about the tapes and the gift again.

"She almost gave you the basket when you graduated with your master's degree. But your dad suffered his heart attack not long afterward, so she waited. Grace passed away two years later, and it was so sudden. We didn't see that coming, did we? We always think we have more time. So, I took the basket and hid it upstairs and waited."

"I hope Grandma Grace knew how much I loved her."

"Oh yes, never doubt it. She knew. Speaking of love, David was a wonderful guest. He's a kind man, and very attentive to you."

"David is great, isn't he? He's been so supportive. He's easy to talk to, and I enjoy spending time with him." Impulsively, I told her about David seeing my wrist and kissing it.

She smiled, remembering another man's sweet kisses. "He's right. Men shouldn't hit or hurt women. I watched him, and he cares for you."

"I really like him."

We walked to the door.

"See you next Wednesday?"

"I'm counting on it." She hugged me.

The next two weeks were a blur of grading, finals, and deadlines. Wrapping up the semester always seemed like a stressful marathon. I enjoyed seeing how my students progressed over the semester, but reading and evaluating the final papers, tests, and presentations took a great deal of time.

David and I enjoyed several quick dinner dates, going to Aunt Shirley's or dining on her takeout salads and sandwiches. Thank goodness, I only had two classes—as a full-time teacher, he taught five classes.

With the continuing success of the quilt exhibit, Carl and I were reviewing options for a second quilt exhibit. I'd done a series of columns on the various quilts for the newspaper, including a Christmas quilt we unwrapped a few weeks ago. Dad didn't need me to do the ads anymore, but I still wrote a column and other articles as needed and went to the newspaper on Tuesday and Thursday mornings.

I was ready for the holiday break and hoped to have a couple of days to relax. David and I made plans to see a movie with Mark and Kathy. We planned to drive to his hometown, so I could meet his family.

David enjoyed meeting Uncle Vern and Aunt Maggie at the Thanksgiving meal and wanted to sit down and interview both about their World War II experiences over the holidays. Vern told David several of his neighbors used German POWs on their farms.

We talked every day. I realized my family already liked him much more than Steve, and I liked the way he treated me.

Shelly, Tiara, and I sat in the adjunct office, having a final chat before leaving for the holidays. I sat at my desk and began packing up my messenger bags.

"What are you and David going to do next?" Tiara asked as she stood up and started straightening her desk.

"Grandma Molly O'Connor came to see the quilt exhibit a few weeks ago and loved it. Grandma Molly found an antique red and green quilt hidden away in her mother-in-law's closet forty years ago. No one else wanted it, so she took it home. She was told it goes back to the Civil War era and wants to know for sure, so David and I are going to visit her and get the quilt over the Christmas holidays. We plan to take it to the Grout Museum in January. They have an expert there."

Shelly stood up, her messenger bag filled. "Has David met your Grandma Molly yet?"

"No, but so far he's charmed all the women in my family," I admitted. "We also want to see if the Underground Railroad came anywhere near Jubilee Junction, and if not, why do we have so many quilts with those patterns? Tiara, we're going to need your help. And yes, you'll both meet David. I'll need your help too, Shelly."

Tiara grinned. "Girl, you know I'm in."

"Me too," Shelly grinned. "Another quilt mystery? Another adventure in the past? Sounds about right, and David is your perfect sleuthing partner."

Cast of Characters

The Contempory Cast

Grandma Grace Nelson Walters—The narrator of the twenty-four cassette tapes, who died two years ago, in 2010. She's Gracie's grandma, and mother to Becky and Rich.

Richard Walters—Grace's deceased husband, who helped her get her pilot's license after WWII. He trained pilots during the war.

Dr. Robert Johnson (Dr. Bob)—Violet's husband, deceased in 2005. He deployed to Europe. They had four children, but only two live in Iowa: Jeanne and Robert, Junior.

Gracie O'Connor—Grace's namesake and granddaughter. She's Grandma Grace's only granddaughter, and the main character of the story set in 2012.

Rebecca (Becky) Walters O'Connor—Gracie's mother.

Matthew O'Connor—Gracie's father, editor of the *Jubilee Times*.

Mark O'Connor—Gracie's brother, a veteran of the Iraq war, a farmer.

Kathy O'Connor—Gracie's sister in-law, a high school teacher.

Aunt Violet Johnson—Grandma Grace's youngest sister, one of the twins. She's also a major character in both timelines and Grace's best friend.

Uncle Vern Nelson—WWII vet, farmer, younger brother of the three sisters.

Maggie Nelson—Vern's wife, a British war bride.

David MacNeill—A new full time history teacher at Jubilee Community College.

Shelly Kellogg—An adjunct in the Communications Department at Jubilee Community College. She is Gracie's best friend since childhood.

Tiara Butler—An adjunct in the Communications Department at Jubilee Community College. She's African American and teaches Oral Communications: she also has a radio show.

Aunt Vera Anderson—Violet's twin sister. She has been married twice, with both of her spouses deceased. She lives in Minnesota.

Richard (Rich) Walters—Grandma Grace's son and Becky's brother, runs the family business, N & W Air, a crop dusting, and delivery service with his son RJ (married to Allie) and James.

Delores Walters—Rich's wife, works PT at *The Jubilee Times*.

Donna Anderson Jenkins—Vera's daughter, a farmer's spouse, lives outside St. Paul, Minnesota. Never knew her father, Don, who died at sea during WW3 before she was born.

Harold Jenkins—Donna's husband.

Julie Jenkins—Donna's daughter and Vera's granddaughter.

Aunt Shirley Carlson—Becky's cousin, runs the Jubilee Café in Jubilee Junction with her family.

Carl Patten—Director at the county museum.

Steven Smith—Gracie's long-time boyfriend. Live in Des Moines, and works for a state senator.

Stephanie Smith—Steven Smith's younger sister; a friend of Gracie.

Mr. and Ms. Smith—Steven Smith's parents.

The Historical Cast

Cousin Ed Nelson—A California relative who joins the Navy.

Mary Nelson—Ed Nelson's wife.

Little Eddie—son of Ed and Mary Nelson.

Mr. and Ms. Henry Hamilton (Aunt Mae and Uncle Henry)—Landlords at the boarding house. They have two teenaged children, Helen and Hank.

Reva Cooper—A sweet girl at the boarding house who becomes close friends with Grace and Violet.

Don Anderson—A young sailor, about to deploy. Vera's first husband.

Dr. Bob Johnson—A doctor at the navy base, recently returned from Europe.

Richard Walters—A pilot who teaches Grace to fly and helped her get her pilot's license after the war ends.

Mama and Papa—Virginia (Ginny) Carlson Nelson and William (Will) Nelson. They have five sons; Vincent, Victor, Virgil, Vance, and Vern Nelson.

The Nelsons and the Carlsons—Grandparents on both sides.

The Namimoto Family—A Japanese American family sent to an internment camp. They have two children, Lily and Harry. Harry enlists and serves in the famous Nisei unit, the 442nd.

Mr. McCabe (Mac)—A manager at the aircraft factory who befriends Grace.

Acknowledgements

*W*riting a book requires research, imagination, and feedback—Thank you to everyone who helped me!

Thanks to Anne Fleck, Editor at Novel Spirits Books, for helping shape the story. www.novelspiritsbooks.com

Thanks to Gail Kittleson for her editing prowess, humor, and encouragement. You have become my WordCrafts Press mentor, and you've gone above and beyond supporting me. www.gailkittleson.com

Thanks also to 'my tribe' of writer friends and role models in the Cedar Falls Christian Writers Workshop, www.facebook.com/groups/419247374817756

Jolene, Anne, Jocelyn, Mary, and Gail—you read excerpts of the first drafts, gave critiques & encouraged me along the way. Shelly, Wanda, Joy, Lyn, Sheri, Dave, Jean, Bonnie, Vicki Jolene, and Sue. Thanks for your friendship and support.

Special Thanks to Barbara Lounsberry, my friend, mentor & literary partner in all things Ruth Suckow (www.ruthsuckow.org) and the Cedar Falls Authors Festival (www.cfauthorsfestival.org) who gave me feedback and encouragement on several drafts of this book, and book two, *The Legacy*.

Thank you to my publisher, Mike Parker, and the staff at WordCrafts Press for helping me bring this story to life.

Thank you to my husband, Mike Dargan, a retired Reference Librarian, for all his expertise with farming, WWII planes and military "hardware," factory work, and fact-checking—for his love and support, and thoughtful critiques.

Thank you to my beta readers, especially childhood friend bestie Beth Lyman, who read several drafts of this book, and then read all the drafts for the other books in the series and continues to cheer me on.

Thank you also to my other beta readers: Aunt Jeanne Egger, Mikki McGrath, Laurie Diemer Kroon, Ed Egger, and Lavonne Vichlach.

Author's Note

*T*he *Grandmother's Treasures* series, set in the fictional town of Jubilee Junction, Iowa, is women's fiction with a twist of history, mystery, faith, and love. Every family has secrets and stories to be discovered. When we learn about our family history, it strengthens our resolve and faith. Those of us with deep Midwestern roots understand the cycles of sowing and planting, of generations farming the same land, and learning our family stories while visiting country cemeteries.

Each book in the series focuses on a quilt, a time in American history, and has dual timelines and narrators, starting with *The Gift*. In the present day, Gracie O'Connor learns about her family history, while her Grandmother Grace tells the story of three Iowa farm girls who went to California during WWII.

If you would like to learn more about the research I used for different aspects of the *Grandmother's Treasures* series, I invite you to visit my website: www.cheriedargan.com.

Thank you, dear reader, for giving your time to read this book. Stories need an audience. It means a lot that you trusted me to entertain, and hopefully inspire, you with this story.

Finally—and this is a big request—if you liked this novel, would you please consider leaving a review on your favorite online bookstore, social media platform, or blog? I love this story and want as many readers as possible to discover it; your voice can reach people I cannot. The best compliment you can give an author is to recommend their book to your friends and family. Leave a review and tell a friend.

Cherie Dargan

About the Author

$\mathscr{C}$herie Dargan is a retired Community College teacher who reinvented herself in retirement as an active volunteer, a writer, blogger, and family historian. She's also a geek, who loves to play with and write about technology

She earned her B.A. from Buena Vista University, an M.A. from Iowa State University, and another M.A. from the University of Northern Iowa. She's a member of the Cedar Falls Supper Club, a member and webmaster for the Ruth Suckow Memorial Association, as well as the Cedar Falls Authors Festival.

Cherie writes from her home in Iowa where she lives with her husband Mike, a retired librarian.

Connect with Cherie online at:

www.cheriedargan.com

or

www.facebook.com/CherieDarganAuthor

and now a Sneak Peek at:

The Legacy

We heard the back door open. Grandfather Patrick O'Connor came into the room, dressed in a pair of old jeans, denim work shirt, heavy sweater, and boots. His hair, once dark, was now streaked with gray, but his green eyes twinkled when he saw me.

"Gracie, is this the young history professor you keep talking about?" he asked.

Then Grandpa saw the red and green quilts laid out on the table and stopped smiling. David stood up and held out his hand. "Hello, Mr. O'Connor. My name is David."

The older man shook David's hand absently, staring at his wife reproachfully. "Ah, Molly, what are you doing with this old Civil War quilt again? Can't you let it go?"

Before she answered, he turned abruptly and left the room. We heard the basement door creak open and shut, and then footsteps thumped as he retreated to his office downstairs.

I glanced at Grandma, who'd lost her sparkle, and seemed on the verge of tears. She sat heavily in a chair. I couldn't remember seeing her so distraught.

"Grandma Molly, what's going on? Are you alright?" I asked, rushing to my grandma's side.

David opened and closed his mouth, confused. We sat back down at the dining room table. I found Kleenex and brought it over to her.

"It's all right, Gracie. I'm sorry, David. What an awkward introduction. Patrick's been after me to get rid of this old quilt. He says I'm obsessed with it. Forty years ago, my life revolved around our children and volunteer work with the League of Women Voters and other community organizations. Patrick was the editor at *The Jubilee Times*, and I'd help." Grandma Molly sighed. "I was busy, so I put the quilt in my closet and promised myself to investigate it later.

"The family had a big argument about the quilt years ago. His older sister Catharine mentioned the quilt—and the mysterious envelope—to an aunt who called me up. She urged me to get rid of the quilt and forget I'd ever found it because she overheard her mother and grandmother arguing about it when she was a teenager.

"Her grandmother asked her mother, 'Do you want to have *those people* in your family tree? Get rid of it.' About that time, the envelope disappeared after a big family gathering here, and I always thought his aunt snuck upstairs and took it."